# Don't Bite the Director

## By T. M. Kirk

**For Meggan.**

Wherever you are, I hope you still love vampires.

# Also by T. M. Kirk

## The Don't Bite Me Series

Don't Bite the Director

Don't Bite the Botanist

## The Onyx Palace Series

The Diamond Palace

The Golden Palace

## The Magical Mishaps Series

A Fragile Spell

# Author's Note

First off, I would like to thank you for picking up my book and giving these characters a chance to find a place in your heart!

I would like to note that while this is a humorous romantic comedy meant to be lighthearted and fun, it is still intended for readers 18+ as it does contain sexual scenes, adult language, violence, dealing with terminal illness, and a brief, non-graphic threat of assault (nothing actually results from the threat).

Reading should be a pleasant experience, and I hope you will take these themes into consideration.

Enjoy!
T. M. Kirk

# Chapter One

## Saiden

He'd only been awake for an hour and already had a chunk of vampire flesh in his mouth. Bits of gore and bright red blood were splattered across the white shirt he should have known better than to wear.

It was going to be a good day.

Two. He had gotten two in one go. Baylin's intel had only confirmed one rogue vampire nesting in the old Seattle bread factory, but to get a second at the same time? Fucking progress.

Saiden spat the rancid flesh from his mouth and pulled a bottle of water from the pack he'd dropped by the door upon entering the warehouse. Rinsing the coppery taste from his mouth, he looked around the decrepit space. He'd been busier than usual the past few years with the population of rogues on the rise, but he knew neither of the decapitated bodies at his feet were responsible. They were so young they had barely put up a fight. And living in this fetid squalor? Definitely babies who'd never been taught how to survive among humans.

He tipped the bottle over his head and let the water wash away the worst of the remnants that lingered in his hair. It helped, but he would need a proper shower sooner rather than later. Nothing stank worse than rotting vampire flesh.

Personal hygiene would have to wait though. As the prime enforcer for the West Coast, finding any information in this awful place about who made these rogues or where they came from had to take priority.

Saiden ripped off his ruined shirt and tossed it onto the pile of body parts he would burn before leaving, then made his way deeper into the warehouse.

His nose warned him what he would find in the back room before he even opened the door, but despite hundreds of missions, he was still never prepared for the sight. He kept reminding himself that was a good thing. If he ever became so numb to the carnage of his job that a pile of mangled, desecrated corpses didn't make him feel sick to his stomach... Well, that would be the day he would ask the cadre to add his own body to the pile.

The acid churning in his gut told him today would not be that day. He didn't feel an overwhelming urge to count the multitude of body parts, but there had to be at least five or six victims. All ripped to pieces.

He shook his head. The violence was just so unnecessary, and it was a huge reason why rogues were increasingly dangerous for their kind. They were usually abandoned right after their turn with no concept of what was happening, forced to resort to their primal instincts.

Hunt. Kill. Feed.

That level of predatory behavior hadn't been required for almost a hundred years now, and even before the invention of blood banks, it was never necessary to kill the humans. All you needed was enough restraint to take a few sips and send them on their way. No harm, no foul.

But these rogues were all about harm, and the acrid scent of decay assaulting his nose was definitely foul.

Saiden sighed as he splashed gasoline over the corpses. The ones who committed these heinous crimes weren't the true monsters. Not by a long shot. The one that deserved the full force of his wrath was the vampire who made them.

Made them and *left* them.

Saiden and his cadre still hadn't been able to figure out if this increase in rogues was intentional or accidental. Either they had one very dangerous vampire that had become lost to their madness and didn't even realize the chaos they were unleashing, or they had one who knew exactly what they were doing and didn't care about the fallout for humans and vampires alike. Neither was fun to deal with, but Saiden much preferred the former as opposed to the latter. He would take insane over evil any day of the week.

Not that he enjoyed killing at all, but someone had to do it. And every now and then, Saiden would find one that he could save. It was how he was able to sleep at night. For over three hundred years, he'd been hunting his own kind. Carrying that burden would have been too much if it weren't for the fact that every other enforcer operated under Kill On Sight protocols. Saiden was the only one who opted for talk first, murder later. He needed to know they were beyond saving before taking their undead life.

He often wondered what kind of man he would be if it weren't for the fact that his own sire, Marquin, had almost become a rogue. Turned and abandoned, Marquin nearly went insane fighting his urge to kill. It was only by the grace of Lilith that he met his mate, Eliana, who was able to pull him back from the brink. One could only survive alone for so long before the pressure of eternity became unbearable, and you surrendered all pretenses of humanity.

Something Saiden felt more and more with each passing year.

A thorough search of the factory turned up little more than the ID's of the deceased and a few personal effects that gave no clue as to who actually created the rogues. The victims were all locals—students from Seattle University and what appeared to be a couple of addicts based on the track marks he'd seen.

Poor souls. Probably just partying in the wrong warehouse at the wrong time.

The rogues gave him even less information. No ID, no wallets, no phones. Nothing to indicate if they even came from this area.

Saiden drenched the remaining scattered limbs with the last of his gasoline and lit the match. He hated desecrating the bodies even further, but he also couldn't let the authorities find them. A mass of mutilated corpses would only lead to the press using words like 'serial killer' or 'monster.' The last thing they needed was another Montrose incident.

Part of him wanted to grab the ID's from the victims and leave them somewhere to be found so their families could have closure, but that would appear too suspicious. This needed to seem like a wild party gone horribly wrong.

He could see the headline now; *Drug Addled Maniac Murders College Students Then Lights Himself on Fire.*

It was extremely unrealistic, but Tressa would handle the details with the police. She always did. She had a knack for blending fact and fiction when she wove compulsions that left only absolute certainty in her targets' minds, regardless of the absurdity of the situation.

On the opposite side of the spectrum, Saiden's compulsions had always been shit. Not that he couldn't compel, it was just that he never practiced, and it tended to be a 'use it or lose it' kind of deal.

Tressa was essentially a master painter, while he was a kid with a box of broken crayons—he could usually get his point across, but no one would call it art.

Thankfully, he was rarely sent on the kinds of missions that involved interacting with humans.

Saiden would take slicing and dicing rogues over talking to people any day of the week.

# Chapter Two

## Cora

She'd only been awake for an hour and already had a chunk of vampire flesh in her mouth. Bits of gore and bright red blood were splattered across the white shirt she should have known better than to wear.

It was going to be a shit day.

"Cut!" Cora screamed, then grabbed a towel off the table next to her.

"I am so sorry," Rick cried, rushing over to her. "I swear it wasn't supposed to explode like that. If he yanked the heart out properly, then it should have just been a little spray."

Wiping streaks of red corn syrup off her face, Cora reminded herself that she didn't have the funds to alienate her crew. If Rick wasn't the cheapest special effects guy around, she never would have hired him to begin with. And by cheapest, she actually meant free and desperate for credits to put on his resume. Though, in all fairness, his shoddy construction was only half the reason she currently looked like an extra in a Tarantino film.

Ignoring the bits of fake blood and flesh still coating her long auburn hair, Cora strode over to the mess that used to be the prop dummy.

"Dammit," she muttered under her breath when she saw just how ruined it was. They simply didn't have the budget for another one.

"What happened?" she barked, whirling on the group of nervous people standing behind her.

"It was my fault," Jake offered, stepping forward. "I was just so into my character that I felt like I should grab my victim and hold her. You know, romance her a little before the big death scene. I think I just hugged a little too hard and triggered the mechanism."

*Do not murder the actors*, Cora thought, rubbing her forehead. *Murder is bad. Murder will not help get this film made.*

She gave Jake a death glare in lieu of her preferred response that came with a prison sentence. "Please tell me you took some time and read all the way through the script before we started filming," she fumed. "Because this is only day two, and I'm getting a disturbing feeling that you have no idea who your character is supposed to be."

Jake shifted awkwardly, giving Cora an ashamed look. "I mean, I mostly read it. I skimmed the important bits."

Anger colored her cheeks, and she fought to hold back the scream that tried to claw up her throat. "The. Important. Bits?" she seethed through gritted teeth. "And what exactly did you determine were the important bits?"

Jake ran a hand through his dark wavy hair. "You know, the character stuff. I felt like I was really understanding the role of Drake. Tortured vampire, looking for the love of his life, forced to kill the only girl he ever wanted. You know, the important bits."

"You have *got* to be kidding me," Cora raged at the dipshit in front of her. The only reason she had cast him was because the number of muscular, attractive men willing to commit to a two-week film shoot for free was depressingly low. He had initially seemed semi-competent, but now she was starting to realize that had been an overly generous assessment.

"It's a horror film!" Cora screamed. "Key word being 'horror.' This isn't some damn sparkly vampire romance story. The vampire is the bad guy. He kills people. He enjoys it. He doesn't fall in love with them for fuck's sake!"

Cora collapsed into her director's chair and massaged the back of her neck where she carried far too much tension lately. She made a huge mistake casting Jake, and now it was going to cost her hundreds of dollars that she didn't have. She debated shouting at the pretty idiot to get the hell off her set, but re-casting the role of Drake would set them back days.

"Everybody take ten," she called out. "I need a second. And somebody tell Jinx I want to see her ASAP."

An assortment of hushed murmurs reached her ears, and she knew at least a few of them were comments on her mood swings. They'd increased in frequency and intensity over the past year which was not a good sign. Not that dwelling on them would help. Thinking about how they'd gotten worse only made her more anxious about getting the film wrapped. She didn't know how much time she had left.

At twenty-five, Cora should have felt like the rest of her generation—like she was immortal and had all the time in the world. Sadly, she'd long since accepted that was not the case.

A pert nose and vibrant green eyes framed by an untamed mess of blonde waves suddenly popped up in her field of view, startling her to the point that she nearly rocketed up and smacked into said pert nose.

"Dammit, Jinx, you know it's not a good idea to surprise me. I almost head-butted you."

Jinnifer, or Jinx as everyone called her because she was quite possibly the unluckiest person to ever live, just laughed.

"Wouldn't be the first time, won't be the last time," she replied, pulling up a chair to face Cora head on. Plucking a chunk of bloody rubber off Cora's shoulder, Jinx gave it a squeeze only for it to squirt from her fingers and fall into her shirt. Fishing the gross bit out of her bra, she gave Cora a curious look. "What happened here? I thought the victim's heart was just supposed to spurt a little when Drake ripped it from her chest?"

Cora lifted her heavy head so Jinx could see her mouth when she responded. Contrary to popular belief, lip-reading was far from accurate, but the little device nestled in her best friend's left ear could usually fill in most of the blanks. "That's what was *supposed* to happen," she replied. "But our leading man decided my film should be a love story, and he wanted to cuddle the victim first. It triggered the explosion that Rick apparently calibrated incorrectly and destroyed the dummy. I'm not exactly surrounded by geniuses on this set."

"Well, you are now," Jinx said, leaning in to give Cora a hug.

Cora tried to pull away before the fake blood got all over her pseudo sister slash assistant director, but it was impossible to fight off a Jinx hug. She made up for being a walking disaster by also being the most empathetic person you'd ever met.

Allowing herself to simply be held for a moment, Cora considered her lack of options. "I don't know what to do," she confessed once Jinx released her from the tight grip. "Can you help?"

Jinx put her hands on either side of Cora's face, squishing her cheeks just a little. "Do you even have to ask?"

No, she didn't. Ever since making decisions had become more and more difficult for Cora, Jinx was always there to walk her through the possibilities until they reached a logical conclusion.

"Okay," Cora said, straightening in her chair, her foul mood easing a bit in the glow of Jinx's eternal optimism. "So, what do we do?"

"Well," Jinx mused, tapping her chin with her finger. "The way I see it, you have three options. Option one: Bag the film."

Cora winced. "Obviously that's not going to happen."

"Obviously," Jinx agreed. "Option two: Start over from scratch. Cast a new lead vampire, preferably one who knows how to read a script."

Groaning, Cora slid out of the chair and walked over to the remains of the fake body. Scanning it from top to bottom, she highly doubted it could be saved in any way. She kicked the useless prop, then turned back to Jinx. "It was hard enough to find Jake. Half the actors who auditioned used awful fake Transylvanian accents and said shit like 'bleh bleh bleh, I vant to suck your blood.' Frankly, I was embarrassed for most of them."

"Okay, okay," Jinx replied, throwing up her hands. "Then you have option three: Keep Jake, but go talk to your dad and ask for financial help to hire an acting coach for him. And maybe buy some extra prop dummies while you're at it."

Cora picked up a chunk of the destroyed prop heart and looked over at Jinx. "I would rather eat this entire thing than speak to my father."

Hopping out of her chair, Jinx snatched the hunk of corn-syrup coated silicone and tossed it on the floor. Per Jinx's usual luck, it promptly bounced back up and nailed her in the crotch, leaving a blood stain in a rather unfortunate area.

Completely oblivious, or possibly past the point of caring, Jinx ignored it and said, "I'm sorry, Cor. I wish I had better options for you, but that's it. I know this film means everything to you, so if you won't talk to your dad, then you need to find a new Drake and start over."

"With what money?" Cora wailed, her dreams slipping through her fingers.

"Hmm…" Jinx grabbed a Red Vine from the bucket on their snack table and chewed on it for a second. "I got it! What if you try casting for an actor who is also an investor? See if you can find someone who is willing to basically become a partner in the film?"

Cora gave her self-proclaimed sister a rather dubious look. "I had the slimmest of pickings when I was casting for a free role. You think I'll do better if I ask *them* to pay *me*?"

Jinx shoved the rest of the sticky red treat in her mouth and shrugged. "Worth a shot. Maybe someone will see it as a decent investment opportunity."

Cora chewed on her lower lip for a long moment, running the idea through her head. Her gut told her it was implausible that anyone would volunteer, let alone anyone with money, but… stranger things *had* happened in Hollywood. And Jinx was right. She was out of options.

"Okay," she huffed out, resigned. "Place the ad for Tuesday afternoon at that old factory we used before. I think I still have the keys. It's likely nobody will show up, but I guess it's worth a shot. Who knows, maybe the perfect vampire will come walking through my door."

# Chapter Three

## Saiden

"You've got to be joking," Saiden argued, glaring at Marquin. Like himself, Marquin looked no older than late twenties, but his youthful appearance made it difficult to take him seriously at times. Perhaps it was the long blond hair and pale blue eyes that made him such a successful vampire. No one thought you might be a demon when you looked like an angel.

Marquin leaned back in his leather chair and laced his fingers behind his head. The casual gesture was at odds with the old-world feel of his office. Mahogany bookcases lined the walls, and a wet bar took up most of the right side, complete with some of the most expensive bottles of scotch that ever existed. Even Marquin's three-piece, navy Hugo Boss suit screamed sophistication. Yet the look on his face was pure childlike amusement.

"Now, Saiden, you know I never joke. Unless it's about your hair, but never about work."

Saiden ran a hand through his chin-length black hair that was currently shaved on the right side. He tried to maintain a modern hairstyle but often found himself somehow missing the mark. Something

Marquin and the rest of the cadre never let him forget.

Saiden glowered at his sire and crossed his arms indignantly. "We have a dangerous and potentially crazed vampire actively pumping rogues into our territory. I can't leave now. Send Tressa if you think it's that important."

"Tressa has not yet returned from Seattle where she is busy handling the fallout from yesterday's incident," Marquin replied, unfazed by Saiden's attitude.

Right. *His* incident. Not that he'd had any choice but to burn down the building. He couldn't exactly take body parts to the city landfill, and he didn't have time to wait for Tressa to arrive and 'handle it.'

"Send Derrick then," Saiden offered. "You mentioned the target is a female. He'll be perfect."

"Not an option," Marquin dismissed with a wave of his hand. "Derrick left this morning to spend a few days in the mountains. And before you continue to go through the roster, I should tell you..." He leaned forward, all semblance of relaxation fading as his features settled into a level of resolve that left no room for argument. "...Eliana said you would be the best choice."

*Fuck.*

Saiden collapsed into the chair in front of Marquin's desk. If Eliana recommended him, there was no avoiding it. Marquin would never take sides against his mate.

"Did she say why?" he asked, resignation filling his voice.

Marquin cocked his head. "Does she ever?"

*Good point*, Saiden thought. Eliana was a seer, among other things. She never caught more than glimpses, but what she saw was always important in the end. Most of the time even she couldn't see how it would play out, which was more than a little frustrating at times. If she saw him on this mission, then it had to be necessary for some reason.

Maybe it was related to the surge of new rogues. Eliana knew how hard he'd been working to hunt down the one siring them. If this trip somehow gave him insight...

"Fine," he conceded, standing up and placing his hands on Marquin's desk. "I'll do it. Tell me what I need to know."

Marquin flashed his patented smile. The one that said he would allow Saiden to pretend like there was ever a choice in the matter.

"Thank you, Saiden." Marquin pulled out a manilla folder and slid it across his desk.

Saiden briefly flipped through the papers, then looked back up at Marquin. "A filmmaker? You're sending me to Los Angeles to look into a filmmaker? Sorry, but I'm going to have to revisit whether or not this is a huge joke."

Marquin poured a glass of scotch from the decanter on his desk. "I'm afraid this is no joking matter. Check out the summary at the end."

Saiden flipped to the last page and started reading. Before he was halfway done, he slumped back into the chair again. So that's why it wasn't a joke. If this filmmaker knew one of the best kept secrets of his kind, then it warranted investigating just how she came about that information.

He looked up at Marquin. "How did Baylin even find this?"

Marquin took a sip of his drink and turned his attention back to his laptop. "How he finds everything else, I imagine. With as many computers as he has, I'm sure one of his algorithms stumbled across it."

Saiden frowned and attempted one last chance to extricate himself. "And this has been verified?" he asked.

Marquin didn't even bother to look up as he crushed Saiden's hope. "I would not send you on a ten-hour road trip without verifying the intel."

"Ten hours? Why can't I take the... Oh. Derrick is in the mountains."

Fuck. His cousin's timing couldn't be worse. Sooner or later, Saiden would really need to learn how to fly a plane. Being reliant on Derrick, who tended to use his aviation skills to wine and dine ladies, had caused more than one hiccup in a mission.

Tucking the folder under his arm, he stood up and strode toward the door.

"Saiden?" Marquin called from behind him, and Saiden glanced over his shoulder.

"Do take some care with this one. You've spent too many years dealing with rogues. Try to remember what it's like to actually speak with a human, won't you?"

"Yeah, yeah," Saiden muttered, shutting the door behind him and heading straight toward his room to pack. The file told him exactly where his target would be that afternoon, and he would need to haul ass to get there in time. Not a huge challenge with the way he drove but annoying nonetheless.

Once he stuffed a spare change of clothing into his duffel bag, he made his way to the massive garage to pick out the fastest car available. The cadre's compound covered more than fifteen acres, and there was never a shortage of vehicular options in the ten-car garage.

He tossed his bag into the passenger side of his favorite option, a black McLaren GTS, then clicked the button to open the garage and took off down the driveway. After pausing only long enough for the main gate to swing open, he slammed his foot on the gas pedal and pushed the car to it's limit as he flew down the dirt road that would lead to Fall River Mills and Highway 299.

# Chapter Four

## Cora

"Sorry! Sorry!" Jinx shouted, racing into the abandoned factory past a row of guys sitting in cheap, plastic folding chairs.

Cora eyed her frazzled best friend but forced down the irritation that sparked in the pit of her stomach. She firmly believed that Jinx really did try her best in life, but a higher power was clearly out to get her.

Jinx plopped into the seat beside Cora and dropped her messenger bag on the floor. "Some bitch parked her POS behind my car, blocking me in," Jinx ranted. "I had to knock on five doors to find the woman and convince her to move it before I called a tow truck."

Cora nodded sympathetically. Something similar happened almost every other month.

"So, who do we have?" Jinx asked, digging a pen and paper out of her messenger bag.

Cora handed over the stack of headshots and tried to hide the depressed look on her face. Tapping Jinx's wrist to get her attention, she said, "We have four guys who have never acted before but are willing to contribute money, and six guys who are trained actors that believe their 'superior skills' will make up for their inability to contribute funds." Then, knowing Jinx would be able to pick up the majority of it, she mouthed, "There is also one guy with no money and no acting experience who seems to think this is a porn shoot."

Jinx giggled and scanned the waiting men before turning back to Cora, her eyes sparkling with curiosity. "Ooh, which one is he?"

"Second from the end," Cora replied silently, then suppressed a laugh at Jinx's shudder once her friend located the guy in question. "Yeah, that was my thought too."

Taking a second to sift through the headshots again, she compared them with the men seated in front of her. Most didn't look even remotely close to their picture. Not that she was surprised since it was fairly common in Hollywood, but she was pretty sure at least one guy's photo was over ten years old based on the thinning hair and deep crows feet he was now sporting.

Pasting on her professional director persona, she decided to get the pain and suffering over with. "Max Castor?" she called out, and the first guy, a stocky ginger with a face full of freckles, stood up.

"That's me," he announced eagerly as he hurried forward.

Cora gestured to the blue X on the ground and flipped the switch on her camera. "Whenever you're ready."

Two hours later, Cora was contemplating throwing herself in the L.A. River. Granted there was no water in the L.A. River, and all she would likely do is end up with two broken legs and a head injury, but at least a few days in a coma might scrub the memory of eleven guys butchering her screenplay. She cringed when she remembered the porn star wannabe. He'd made it three seconds in before he started taking off his pants. There wasn't enough bleach in the world to scrub away the image that had been seared into her brain.

Cora packed up her camera and turned to Jinx. "Well, I don't know about you, but I'm in desperate need of a drink. Tiny's Hi-Dive?"

"You know I'm down," Jinx replied, her eyes twinkling.

Jinx was nowhere near becoming an alcoholic, but at the same time, she was also never *not* down for a drink. Cora handed over the stack of headshots and waited for her friend to make eye contact. "I need to clean up first," she said. "I'll meet you there. Do me a favor and burn these, will you?"

Jinx nodded but took another second to shuffle through the pile. "I don't know. The one with the British accent was kind of cute. His acting career might be limited to Grey Poupon commercials, but you gotta admit something about the way he said 'dahling' was enticing." She waggled her eyebrows suggestively.

"He's all yours," Cora dismissed. She agreed the British guy was attractive, and the accent was a plus, but every part of him screamed romantic vampire. The kind that begged to be saved from their own darkness if only they could find their one true love.

Cora tried not to vomit in her mouth. Maybe she was asking for the impossible—a guy that radiated menace and danger. The kind that looked like he would brutally murder you and then go home and watch TV like it was just another day at work. Her vampire wasn't a bad boy. He was a bad *man*. A villain in the truest sense.

Where the hell was she supposed to find someone like that?

# Chapter Five

## Saiden

Saiden whipped his car into the parking lot of the warehouse. An icy chill ran down his spine, his senses alerting him to danger. It was enough notice that he was able to narrowly avoid the old, blue Ford Focus trying to exit through the entrance lane. He thought he vaguely heard a 'sorry' come from the other driver, but they were halfway down the street in seconds.

Pulling in next to the dinged-up red Mazda Miata that his file told him belonged to his target, he sent a quick thanks to Lilith that he wasn't too late. He'd done nearly 100 mph the entire trip to L.A. and had to compel three different police officers along the way. Tedious and annoying, but these so-called auditions were a perfect excuse to get this girl talking.

Sliding out of the McLaren, he snapped his head over to the door of the factory when it opened. A woman carrying a large camera bag stepped out, and he halted halfway out of his car, his hand lingering on the door handle. He had memorized the photo of Cora Lee in the file Marquin gave him, so he was certain the slender, awkward creature mumbling profanities as she fought with a set of keys was the person he needed to speak with. Her long auburn hair was twisted into a braid that fell most of the way down her back, almost hitting the shapely ass that was partially hidden beneath a baggy, long-sleeve purple sweater.

He stood there for a second, watching her struggle to lock up the factory, and found himself mildly entertained by the creativity of her cursing. He'd never before heard a person threaten a doorknob with being melted into ball bearings that would be shoved up the ass of a constipated rhino. He absently wondered what the rhino did in her little scenario to deserve such a fate.

It wasn't until her head popped up and she took notice of him that he realized he had completely forgotten his cover story.

*Lilith take me*, he thought. Her eyes were incredible. The way the bright amber color practically glowed in the fading sunlight. His vampire sight allowed him to see each and every speck of brown that drifted in her honey-colored irises, and he wanted to get closer, wanted to look even deeper.

"Hello?" Cora called out to him, and the sound of her lilting voice tore him from his blatant staring.

She approached him cautiously.

*Smart girl.* On her own in a secluded location with a stranger and no witnesses? She had every right to be wary. Saiden knew what he looked like, and even a grown man would be nervous if they were alone together in a parking lot.

Remembering his mission, he cleared his throat and finally shut his car door. He didn't miss the way her eyes widened slightly as she took in the $200,000 vehicle. *Investor*, he recalled from her ad. She had been looking for an actor as well as someone to help with financing. Glancing down at his Linkin Park t-shirt and faded jeans, he wished he'd dressed a bit more appropriately, but time had not been on his side.

"Hi there," he said, smoothly striding toward her. "I'm looking for Cora Lee. Am I too late for the auditions?"

He could barely hide his grin as he realized he wouldn't have to deal with any deceit from this adorable creature. Every thought that went through her head played out across her face, and he watched as her expression morphed from worried, to curious, back to worried and then, after another long glance at his car, ended on curious with a hint of hopefulness.

She looked up at him and smiled.

His pulse thrummed a little faster, and Saiden couldn't remember the last time it had done that. He was an enforcer, the very definition of unflappable, yet the curve of her full pink lips reminded him of hope, joy, and a million other things he had long since given up on.

Things that would ultimately just be a distraction if he didn't focus on his goal. It was supposed to be a quick mission. Get in, get the info, deal with any liabilities as needed, and get out. He'd told Marquin he would be back at the compound by tomorrow morning, which meant he really didn't have time to stick around just because his target had a pretty smile.

A really, *really,* pretty smile.

"You're here for the auditions?" she asked, tossing her braid behind her once more and smoothing down the loose strands atop her head.

A nervous tick, he noted, committing it to memory. "I am. My name is Saiden Massaro. I'm sorry that I don't have a headshot, but I saw your posting at the last minute." He gave her his best imitation of a Hollywood grin and hoped it didn't come off too much like an axe murderer. He didn't have a lot of experience with charming ladies these days. Not that he ever did, if he was being honest. Like most vampires, he would only truly care about one person in his undead lifetime, and the fates would let him know when they finally arrived.

If they ever did. Lately, he was beginning to question what he'd done to piss Lilith off.

"Do you mind if we go inside?" he asked. "It's a little warm out here."

It wasn't actually that warm. In fact, most Angelenos would probably consider it closer to the chilly side with the coast nearby. The longer he spent in the sun, though, the sooner he would need to feed, and he'd stupidly forgotten to pack a blood bag. If the McLaren didn't have custom tinted windows, he could only imagine what kind of hangry state he would be in.

He should have fed before he left, but in all the chaos, it had slipped his mind. Not exactly an ideal situation when spending time around humans, but he considered himself more disciplined than most, so he could keep his fangs to himself like a true gentleman. It just sucked.

He watched the debate play out on Cora's face as she tugged at her thick sweater. Watched her eyes flash back to his expensive car and then down to his decidedly inexpensive clothing. He guessed it was his face that ultimately made her decision because she analyzed his features for considerably longer than a person should in polite society. Whatever she saw must have intrigued her because she turned and unlocked the door to the warehouse.

"Come on in," she said pleasantly. "I can make time for one more." She walked briskly into the room, stumbling as she crossed the threshold.

Without thinking, he dove forward and caught her arm before she could crack her pretty face on the concrete.

She steadied herself and gave him a curious look. "Thanks. Those are some quick reflexes you have there."

"Can't have my future director getting injured," he replied with a wink.

She let out a self-deprecating laugh as she passed through the open space. "Wouldn't be the first time." She set her things down on a table in the middle of the room and began unpacking her equipment.

Saiden lingered just inside the doorway, watching her curiously. He could hear her heart pounding against her ribs, so he decided to hang back until she calmed down a bit. It wouldn't pay off to scare her away too soon.

As she set up her camera, her heart rate slowed back to normal, and the slight tremble to her fingers disappeared.

She sat down and pointed to an X made out of blue tape on the concrete floor. "You can stand there." Cora scanned a piece of paper in her hand, then set it aside. "I'm guessing you didn't have a chance to memorize the audition script if you came here last minute, huh?"

He shook his head as he prowled closer, moving at a slow and steady pace so as not to frighten his prey.

"That's fine," she said. "We can improv it then." Cora reached up and flicked a switch on her camera. "If you're ready, let's get started. Tell me, Saiden, why do you think you would make a good vampire?"

He couldn't help it. The question was just too perfect. And if he was going to be forced to deal with humans, he might as well have some fun and give the girl a little thrill before he wiped her memories.

He grinned.

"Because I am one."

# Chapter Six

## Cora

Cora hesitated for a second at the guy's response to her question. She wasn't opposed to method actors, and this guy looked exactly like what she imagined for her film—like, *exactly*—but if there was even the slightest chance that he genuinely believed he was a vampire, then she needed to get somewhere safe ASAP. She'd watched a movie a few years back about the cult in Florida that killed a girl's parents because they believed themselves to be real vamps. You just couldn't be too careful these days.

She let her eyes wander up and down his body again. She couldn't have painted a better picture in her mind for the villain of her movie. His hair cut was a little modern, but everything else about him screamed violence. And not the leather jacket wearing, motorcycle riding, '*look at me, I'm such a bad boy*' kind of violence. No, this was '*if you mess with me your body parts will be washing up in the harbor for days*' kind of violence. It was in his deep-set scowl that lurked on the corner of his mouth even when he tried to smile. His defined muscles that spoke of hours in the gym, likely with a personal trainer. The firm set of his square jaw and those eyes, so dark and piercing she almost thought they were black. She wouldn't even need contacts for him.

Not to mention his smooth olive skin that made her think his heritage was Italian or Spanish. She was so over the whole pale creature of the night thing. This guy was the perfect dark vampire she envisioned. The kind that lured you into his bed with promises of pleasure you knew he could deliver on, wringing out every ounce of ecstasy from your soul just before biting and draining you dry in the end.

Oh yeah, she would cast this guy in a heartbeat.

Provided he wasn't planning to bite her with plastic fangs then drag her into a coffin in his mom's basement.

She let out a soft, placating chuckle. "Right, of course you're a vampire. Which is what makes you perfect for the role. But how about you tell me a little bit about what you're like when you aren't a vampire. Do you have any other hobbies beyond acting?"

The smug grin dropped from his face, replaced by something that almost looked a little like sadness.

"I mostly hunt down and kill rogue vampires," he stated plainly, as if discussing his job as an accountant for a mid-level dental firm. "I'm the prime enforcer for my cadre, and there's been an increase in rogue activity lately that keeps me occupied most days. I do get to travel, though, so that's nice."

Cora sighed and leaned back in her chair. Fucking actors.

"Look, Saiden, I really appreciate the dedication to your craft, but can we just talk person to person for a second? Obviously you have the acting chops. If I didn't know better, I would swear you were being serious. But we also need to talk about the financial side of things. Did you see in my ad that I'm looking for an investor as well?"

"I did," he answered nonchalantly, grabbing a chair from the back of the room and sitting in front of her. "And I can assure you that money is not an issue."

Her heart skipped a beat hearing that dream phrase, and she fought back a blush when he raised an eyebrow. She'd thought she kept her features neutral since it wouldn't help negotiations if he knew she was practically drooling at this opportunity.

"That's good to know," she replied, keeping her voice steady as she reached up to switch the camera off. "Let's go over some details then. This film is basically my life's work, and I've spent nearly five years perfecting the script. More than anything I want to see it completed and get it submitted to festivals, but I'm running out of time to do that."

Saiden narrowed his eyes on her. "Why exactly are you running out of time?"

Cora focused on unscrewing the camera from its tripod, not wanting to meet his gaze. There was something about his eyes that made her want to spill all her secrets, but she wasn't about to go there with this stranger, no matter how devilishly handsome he was.

"That's personal," she asserted, carefully setting her camera back into the case and securing it. "All you need to know is that I am fully committed. I have a crew, a script, and most of the shooting locations locked down. However, thanks to a recent incident with a former cast member, I now find myself in need of a new villain. That's where you come in."

Saiden leaned back in the chair, balancing it easily on two legs. "And you think I would make a good villain?"

Cora snorted. "Yeah, I mean look at you." She gestured idly at his chiseled physique that was obvious underneath even the baggiest of t-shirts. "You're like the epitome of tall, dark, and viciously handsome."

The corners of his mouth curled up into a feline grin, and he leaned forward, resting the chair on all four legs again. "You think I'm handsome?"

"Oh, please," she groaned, shaking her head at him. "Don't tell me you're one of those actors that needs constant validation? I really don't have the energy for that right now. So do you want to discuss the film or not?"

"Yes, I would love to in fact. That's why I came here." Saiden drew his tall frame out of the plastic chair that looked tiny by comparison and moved over to Cora's side. Perching on the edge of the table, he locked eyes with hers. "Tell me more about this script of yours. How did you come up with the plot?"

Cora leaned back slightly. Hotness level aside, he was a little too close for comfort. "Um, I don't know. Ideas just come to me randomly. It's gone through four or five different revisions at this point, but I didn't steal the story if that's what you're asking."

Saiden inched forward, closing the gap between them until his thigh rested against her hand, and she had to crane her neck to look up at him.

"And did anyone help you with the story or the plot points? Anyone suggest little details for you to incorporate?"

"No..." she answered, confusion beginning to outweigh her attraction. "I never even let anyone see my rough drafts. Nobody saw the script until a week ago when we started production. So I don't know what you're accusing me of, but it's my script. Completely one hundred percent mine."

"Interesting," Saiden commented as he stood up and paced in front of the table.

She watched him move back and forth like a trapped jaguar evaluating the quickest method for escape.

He paused after a second, fixing his intense stare on her. "One last question. Has there been anyone new in your life recently? A boyfriend perhaps, or a close friend?"

Oh, for fuck's sake. This conversation had gotten a little too bizarre for her tastes. She had limits on how much she would endure just because a guy had money, and she was done letting him test those boundaries.

"No," she snapped, grabbing her camera case and jumping to her feet. Whatever this guy wanted, she didn't think it was to finance her movie. "As weird as this has been, I think I'm going to go now."

Hitching the bag over her shoulder, she started for the door, but between one blink and the next, Saiden went from standing on the other side of the table to blocking her escape.

"How did you...?" She looked back to where she was certain he stood a second ago.

"My deepest apologies, Cora," he offered. "I didn't mean to startle you or make you feel uncomfortable. The strange questions are just part of my job."

She wrinkled her brow. "Your job?"

"Yes, my job. I told you I am the prime enforcer for my cadre. Typically that involves hunting down rogue vampires, but on occasion I do assist with other tasks as needed. One of them being following up anytime a human gets a little too close to the truth about us. Tressa is the one who would normally handle these kinds of visits since she has, well, let's just say she has more of a gentle touch than I do. She was occupied, though, so you get me."

Cora could have sworn that he looked a little embarrassed.

"After speaking with you, it does seem like everything in your script was merely a coincidence," he continued as if discussing something no more exciting than the weather. "I had thought perhaps a rogue was feeding you information, but apparently this has been little more than a waste of time."

Saiden reached out to place a hand on Cora's shoulder, and she jerked away like it was a snake that might bite her. Easing herself away from the nut job, she did her best not to let it show that she was seconds away from running for dear life. She was such an idiot to let herself get trapped in a warehouse with a stranger. Especially when she had literally just been thinking that he looked like the type of guy who would lure a girl to her death.

"Um, I think I need to go check some things in the upstairs office," she stammered, wishing she was an actor instead of a director. "How about you let yourself out, and I'll be in touch after I make a decision." She tried to give him a reassuring smile, but it probably came across more like a manic clown.

"I'm afraid I can't leave you just yet, Cora," Saiden declared, re-claiming the small amount of distance she had put between them. "Regardless of how our secrets got into your script, I can't let them stay there. If you will just calm down, this can all be over soon."

# Chapter Seven

## Saiden

*This is why I don't go on these kinds of missions,* Saiden thought, trying to squash his annoyance with himself.

It was more than obvious that he had handled the entire situation poorly, as was evident by the girl's racing pulse and twitching facial muscles. He trusted that Eliana knew what she was doing most of the time, but nobody could always get it right, and sending him here was clearly a mistake. Maim and murder were his specialties. Covertly retrieving information and wiping memories? Not his bag.

His original plan was to compel her into destroying every copy of the script she had shared then forget about meeting him entirely. He figured he could leave a memory behind that the auditions were so awful she decided to make a different movie instead and wanted no reminders of her failed attempt.

That ship seemed to have sailed, though. His weak compulsion skills would barely take hold if she was this scared, and the slightest reference to vampires in the future might trigger something.

He sighed. Nothing he did at this point was going to end well.

Unless... He could always try seducing her to see if that got her to calm down enough. He was pretty sure that women found him relatively attractive, and while seduction would never be listed under the skills section of his resume, he could always give it a shot. He couldn't be that rusty, right?

He took a step closer to Cora. Her eyes widened, and he fought the twinge of guilt that look of fear sparked in him.

"I think we got off on the wrong foot," he said, dropping his voice low and aiming for a husky, sensual tone. "Perhaps we could try again. I'm very interested in getting to know you, Cora."

To his pleasant surprise, her tight lips relaxed into a smile, and she eased up close to him, her face hovering mere inches from his. A familiar scent wafted over him, and he had to force himself not to be distracted into analyzing it. He needed to keep all his focus on charming this meek little mouse.

When she placed a hand on either of his shoulders, he knew he had her.

"You're interested in getting to know me?" she asked, gazing up at him with enchantment in her eyes.

"I am," he purred, his voice deep and sultry.

Leaning in even closer, her breath dancing over the shell of his ear, she whispered, "Well I'm not."

Then she kneed him squarely in the balls.

Saiden crumpled to the cold floor, clutching his sac. Lilith save him from modern day women. This would never have happened in the 1700's.

Massaging his abused genitals, he lifted his head to see her dashing across the warehouse toward the front door. So much for seduction. And so much for that adorably awkward and innocent little creature he'd first assumed her to be. She had fight and fire in her. Normally those were qualities he'd admire in a woman, but not when his nuts were aching and he still needed to get the job done.

Since seducing her was clearly out, he had exactly one option left to keep her from fighting him. He didn't love using it, as annoying and time-consuming as it was, but this little hellcat left him no choice. He would just have to convince her that he was a legitimate vampire, then wait for her to calm down after the truth settled in. Eventually she would accept her fate, they always did, and compelling her would be smooth sailing. Or as smooth as one could get when traversing the Atlantic in a rowboat.

Giving his balls one last soothing rub, Saiden climbed to his feet and raced over to block the front door. To her mortal eyes, his vampiric speed probably appeared as if he teleported, but he needed to shock her into hearing him out.

She came skidding to a halt and tried to veer around him, but lost her balance and made a nosedive toward the floor. His hand shot out, snagging the back of her sweater and preventing yet another fall. He wrapped his hands around her waist to steady her but dropped them the moment she started to struggle.

Cora reared back and gawked at him while he merely watched her, waiting patiently. It was always the same. She looked to where she left him and then back to where he stood now.

*Yes*, he thought, *keep going. You'll put it together.*

"You..." she stuttered. "You were..."

"I was over there. And now I am over here," he confirmed. "Excellent deduction, Sherlock."

Okay, now he was just being snarky, but he was exhausted after spending his entire day in a car just to deal with this mess. The trip had yielded nothing but a coincidence, and he just wanted to get back home to resume his hunt. One-track mind, Marquin always said about him, and the assessment was accurate if also somewhat depressing.

When Saiden was younger he had spent some time walking amongst the mortals, trying to get to know them, but in the end it was always pointless. They were too breakable, too easily scared, and it always hurt when he had to wipe their minds. Humans simply couldn't be trusted with the truth of his kind.

"No one moves that quickly," Cora declared, shaking her head in denial.

Saiden let out a heavy exhale. This part was so tedious that it bordered on painful. It was like taking a cat to the vet. You knew you'd get there eventually, but damn it was annoying to deal with their scratching and yowling the entire way.

He crossed his arms and leaned against the door frame. "I believe I told you earlier, Cora Lee. I am a vampire. You of all people should have some idea of what that means. If you promise not to scream or hit me, then I'll be happy to give you another demonstration."

"Look," she said, backing away slowly. "I'm happy for you that you're committed to your LARPing or cosplay or whatever, but just because you can sprint faster than the average guy doesn't mean I'm going to believe that you're a vampire. If you could please just let me leave, then we can both go about our day like this never happened."

Saiden glanced back at the distance from where he started to where he currently stood. "Now you're hurting my feelings. I'd say that was more than just sprinting fast."

Cora's eyes darted side to side, and he could sense that she was about to bolt again. "Okay," he began with as much calm as he could muster. "What will it take for you to believe that I am a real vampire? Ask for any display of my abilities, and I will oblige."

She bit her lip for a second, eyebrows knitted together in deep thought, then tossed her braid behind her shoulder. "*Any* display, huh? How about you step aside and let me leave?"

Saiden didn't even recognize the bark of laughter that escaped his throat. He was pretty sure he hadn't laughed in decades. She was a clever one, though, he had to give her that.

"Well played," he remarked, shifting closer to inhale her scent again. She smelled like some kind of fruit, but it was smothered beneath something else he couldn't identify. Something medicinal. He didn't like the acrid tang that reminded him of death, but his sense of smell was strong enough that he could mostly sort through it to find the sweet pheromones that were distinctly Cora. Damn, she would be delicious if it weren't for the chemical taint that burned his nose. How many medications was this human taking?

Ignoring the faint tickling at the back of his brain that told him he was missing something, he smiled wanly at her and said, "Ask me for anything that doesn't involve letting you go. I have no intentions of hurting you, Cora. I really don't. I can hear your racing pulse, so I know that I've frightened you, but I need you to settle down enough that we can conclude our business. So again I ask, what can I do that would prove to you that I'm actually a vampire?"

Cora eyed him warily, the visible stiffness in her muscles not fading in the slightest bit. "Okay," she said, waving her hand toward the upper balcony of the four-story warehouse. "Fly up there."

Saiden rolled his eyes at the lack of originality. "I can jump pretty high, but I'm not a bat, Cora. I can't fly."

Folding her arms, she cocked a hip and gave him a dubious look. "Fine, then turn into fog."

He pinched the bridge of his nose. Saiden didn't think vampires could get migraines, but she was strongly testing that theory. "You know, based on the accuracy of your film script I would have thought your requests would be more realistic. The entire reason I am here is because your movie contained a few key secrets of our kind, but if you honestly believe that I can fly or turn into fog, I'm seriously doubting the validity we gave to this concern."

Cora threw up her hands. "I don't know. Show me your fangs, I guess."

Now that he could do.

Saiden gave her a wide, wolfish grin, allowing her to see the second set of teeth that emerged from behind his incisors. He touched the tip of his tongue to one, offering up the ruby red drop as evidence before sucking it down and retracting the fangs. The damn things were too sharp to be left out unless he was feeding.

Cora's eyes widened slightly at the display, but after a second her features hardened again in disbelief. "You can do that with special effects teeth."

*Then why did she even ask to see them?*

Okay, this was taking far too long. Perhaps the bulldozer approach would be more effective. Saiden cracked his neck from side to side then unleashed his power in a blast of abilities, one after the other. Using his vamp speed, he raced up the stairs to the balcony and leapt off, slamming down in what this new generation called a 'superhero landing' before springing back to his feet. He grabbed the heavy table in the middle of the room with one hand and balanced it on two fingers, spinning it like a basketball. Dropping the table, he grabbed one of the plastic chairs and chucked it across the room. While it flew, he snagged two daggers from their hidden sheaths at the small of his back and hurled them at the flying object. The knives slid perfectly through the slats of the chair, nailing it to the wall.

*There. That should do it*, he thought, plucking a splinter from the table out of his pointer finger.

He strolled back toward Cora, trying to keep his expression as non-threatening as possible. Baylin would tell him he wasn't capable of that, but he at least attempted to soften his perma-scowl. It wasn't even his fault that he unintentionally terrified people. If males had the equivalent of resting bitch face, then that would describe him perfectly. It was just how he looked. Regardless, he still made an effort to tone down his murderous vibes.

"Well?" he asked the female who stood perfectly still, watching him as a scientist might evaluate a new snake they just discovered but hadn't yet determined if it was venomous. Cautious intrigue was what he could see glittering in her eyes. "Was that enough, or do you require further proof?"

She shook her head robotically, her wide eyes still a bit glassy from the shock.

"You believe me now?" he prodded, hoping they could finally move on.

She lifted and dropped her chin in a subtle nod.

"Any chance you'll relax sometime soon, or do you have questions?"

Cora's throat bobbed, her rough swallow audible, and her eyes dropped to his mouth, to the exact spot he knew his fangs would emerge when feeding. "Just one," she croaked out.

He gave her a pitying look, confident he knew exactly what she would ask. It was what they all asked. "And what would that one question be?"

Cora lifted her face, and something bright twinkled in her eyes now. All traces of fear were replaced with a dancing excitement.

It was going to hurt him to crush her little heart.

Patiently, he waited for her to ask the age-old question that every vampire had to deal with.

"Will you be in my movie?"

# Chapter Eight

## Cora

*Holy shit.*

*Holy. Fucking. Shit.*

Cora had always suspected that vampires were real. It only made sense. There were simply too many stories, too many mythologies across nearly every culture for them to be completely fabricated. Of course, the real thing wouldn't be at all like the books and movies. It was why she had written her film differently, the way she imagined vampires might be if they did exist in some form or another. But to have this definitive confirmation standing before her? There was a decent chance she could die happy now.

At least, she could if he would agree to be in her movie.

"So will you?" she asked again when Saiden just gaped open-mouthed at her. "I'm sure you have all kinds of important vampire duties, and there's probably some kind of rule about exposing your kind, but we can work around that."

The possibilities started racing through her mind, and she bounced on her toes from excitement.

"We'll give you a fake name and a wig. Something more old-world looking. And I'm sure we could find you a prosthetic nose. Not an ugly one, just something different enough to alter the shape of your face. Maybe we'll give you a scar. I think most girls are into that, and it works with your character. Whatever we go with, I promise no one will recognize you. And I'll keep the rest of the crew in the dark, too. Except Jinx, she's my bestie and AD. But don't worry, she'll totally keep your secret. You have no idea how perfect this is."

Cora let out a squeal and whirled around to look at Saiden. She frowned when she realized his jaw still hung open slightly. "What?" she asked, raising her eyebrows.

Saiden blinked, shook his head, then closed his mouth before approaching her. "You believe that I'm a vampire?"

"Of course," Cora replied, giving him a confused look. Why was he surprised that she believed him when that was his entire goal? She wasn't an idiot. He had fangs and obvious supernatural powers. Not to mention an allure that was proving to be more than a bit challenging to fight off now that she knew he wasn't insane. What else would he be?

"And your response is to ask me to be in your film?" He enunciated his words as if that might change her question.

"Well, yeah. What else would I ask you?"

He threw up his hands. "I was expecting you to ask me if you could become a vampire. It is what literally every person asks when they find out the truth."

Cora wrinkled her nose. That was the last thing she wanted from him. Sure, other people in her situation would probably jump at the chance. Saiden was beyond gorgeous when he wasn't scowling, and even when he was, if she was being honest. Most straight women, and probably a significant number of men, would kill to spend eternity with a guy that hot. Cora, on the other hand, had no intention of living forever, and certainly not as a vampire.

"Yeah, that's a hard pass from me," she insisted. "Like the hardest of passes. No amount of money in the world would have me hopping on the vamp train."

She couldn't quite read the expression on his face, but he seemed almost upset by her declaration. Was it a vampire pride thing? Did she insult him in some way by not begging to spend forever by his side? It was always sad to witness a fragile male ego in action.

Saiden slumped back against the wall, and she walked over to pat him on the shoulder. "I'm sorry if I hurt your feelings. It's nothing personal. I'm sure you're a wonderful vampire, and there are plenty of girls out there who would love to be with you for all time. I'm just not one of them. Becoming immortal is... Well, let's just say it's so far off the table that it's on the floor in the next room over. But it would mean the world to me if you acted in my film." She paused, remembering the McLaren he arrived in. "And maybe kicked in a little of that vamp money to help fund things."

Saiden gawked at her. "It's not... That's not..." He scrubbed his face then blurted out, "I'm not trying to spend an eternity with you."

"Good," Cora said. "We're on the same page. So, what's with the fluster?"

"Most mortals do ask me to turn them into a vampire."

And we were back to that; it *was* a fragile male ego thing.

She stuffed her hands in her pockets and rocked back on her heels. "Well, I guess I'm not like most mortals."

"No, you are not," he agreed, and she fidgeted under the intensity of his stare.

"Soooo... Getting back to my movie," she began.

"And people say I have a one-track mind," he muttered, standing up straight. "I'm afraid that is never going to happen for a multitude of reasons."

"Damn," Cora exhaled, her entire body going slack with defeat. She knew it was a long shot, but a girl could dream. "I guess this is the part where you wipe my mind, and I forget all about you? Any chance you can just erase your face but leave the rest? That whole knife and chair thing was a whole new level of badass. I want to put it in my script."

Saiden scratched the back of his neck awkwardly. "While I do appreciate the compliment, that's not going to be possible either. I need to make you forget about more than just my visit here, but don't worry. Everything will be fine."

Cora did *not* like the sound of that. He needed to work on his soothing voice because she was pretty sure he was lying through his very pointy teeth. Not to mention she refused to believe it whenever someone said 'everything will be fine.' Life had taught her that was rarely the case.

A thought crashed into her brain, and she recalled the litany of questions he asked earlier.

"Wait... This doesn't have anything to do with my script, does it?" Horror spread through Cora when she saw his subtle flinch. "No," she cried, backing away from this man who suddenly posed a very different threat to her. "You can't. My film is everything to me."

"I am so sorry," Saiden said, and the look of pain in his eyes told her that he really did regret it. "There are some things in your film that we can't have getting out to the public. We've stayed hidden by playing it safe and containing certain aspects of our existence. I'm going to have to compel you to destroy your script and any notes."

Anger gripped her in a chokehold. Who the hell did he think he was to show up here and ruin her entire life?

"Why can't you just compel me to change whatever it is that you don't like about my story?" she argued.

The pitying look he gave her was almost too much. She didn't want pity. She wanted to keep her damned movie and possibly knee him in the groin again for tormenting her.

"Because," he began slowly, as if speaking to a toddler who just got told they can't have ice cream before dinner. "The constant exposure to the modified script would eventually trigger a memory. Having you destroy the entire thing and move on is the only way to be sure. I really am sorry, Cora."

Anger faded to despair, and her eyes ached from the pressure of holding back tears as the reality of the situation hit her. He was a vampire, and there was literally nothing she could do to stop him.

"Please," she begged him softly. "Anything but that. I won't tell anyone about you, I swear. Just please don't do this."

"I have to," Saiden replied gently, stepping back into her space. He lifted a hand, and for a second she thought he might caress her cheek. He must have changed his mind because he dropped his hand to her shoulder instead, the other one following suit to lock her in his grasp. Claiming the entirety of her focus with nothing but his presence, he captured her amber eyes with his and whispered a single word.

"Forget."

# *Chapter Nine*

## **Saiden**

Saiden would have rather she regained a bit more composure first, but he was officially done waiting. Every time she started breathing easier, he stupidly said something to ramp her back up. He just wasn't any good at being calming and never would be. Her current state of depressed acceptance was about the best he could hope for at that point.

Saiden watched her for any evidence that his compulsion had taken root. As soon as he saw her eyes go cloudy, he would know he had her under his control and could compel her to forget everything.

It really did break his heart a little. There had been so much pain in her eyes when she begged him to let her keep the film. He didn't quite understand it. Why did she care so much about a single horror movie? He'd read the script, or more specifically his text-to-speech app had read it to him while he sped down I-5. He wasn't much of a movie buff but could tell it was decent. She had talent as a writer, so why couldn't she just come up with something else? Make a different movie. Why was this one so important?

Whatever the reason, there was nothing he could do about it. Protocol was protocol, and no traces could be left behind. Tapping his foot impatiently, he waited for the fog to roll across her eyes.

And waited.

And waited.

They both blinked a few times.

Well, this was getting embarrassing.

Cora cleared her throat. "While I do enjoy staring deeply into your eyes, which are quite gorgeous b-t-dubs, is something supposed to be happening?"

Saiden dropped his hands and stepped back, staring at her in awe. He knew she was still somewhat upset, and compulsion was not his strongest gift, but still... He hadn't been able to latch onto her mind at all. Not even a hint of a connection.

"Fuck," he grumbled and shook himself like a wet dog. He was just tired, that was all. And perhaps part of his subconscious felt guilty about killing Cora's dreams. He couldn't deny that she was incredibly attractive, and he hadn't been with a woman in far too long. Under different circumstances he might have even asked her out despite her human status. That was probably why he was struggling so much.

He slapped himself a couple times to dislodge his own hang-ups and reached for her again, settling his hands on her shoulders.

*She's just another mortal*, he told himself. *She might be cute, but they're a dime a dozen with lifespans like mayflies. Do your job and move on.*

He leaned in even closer this time, practically touching her nose with his own. Ensnaring her gaze once more, he whispered, "Forget."

A second of silence passed, and he held his breath in anticipation.

"Why do you keep saying 'forget'?" Cora asked, her eyes as clear as a placid spring lake.

*Son of a bitch*, he cursed internally.

Frowning, he dropped his hands. "It's a framing word. Once I capture your psyche with my own, I am able to form the compulsion around all the things I need you to forget. If I used a different framing word, it would go in a different direction."

Cora tapped her finger to her chin, seemingly intrigued by his statement. "So, if you said 'laugh' then you could start listing all the things I would laugh at from then on?"

"Something like that," he deflected and began stalking around the room. His mind sifted through all the things he knew about compulsion. There was usually only one reason a vampire couldn't compel a human, but that was simply impossible. He would have known if *that* was the case.

Just to be certain, he took another deep inhale of her scent. Delicious, no doubt, but not quite the perfect complement to his own. Too much of that medicinal stink. And he had felt nothing when he touched her skin.

He had touched her skin, hadn't he? He was pretty sure he had to have grazed it at some point with all the times he grabbed her. She did have that bulky sweater on, though...

A scuffling noise pulled his attention back to the present, and he whirled around to see Cora edging slowly toward the back door. He couldn't help but smile at her attempt to escape. He had to give the girl props. She had moxie.

"You can't outrun me, if that's what you're thinking," he insisted, crossing the space between them in the blink of an eye.

She lifted her chin defiantly. "I wasn't trying to. I just... wanted some fresh air."

He almost laughed at her pathetic attempt to deceive him, but she did have a point. The factory was damp and musty, and he suspected its original purpose had been the manufacturing of petrochemicals based on the lingering odor. Perhaps some fresh air would help him figure out a plan. The sun should be close to fully set by now, so it wouldn't tax him much, if at all, to be outside.

"Fine," he said, stepping aside and gesturing to the door. "After you. Just don't bother running. We both know you'll never get anywhere, and it's a tad insulting at this point."

They emerged from the building, and the soft glow of sunset settled over them. He took in a deep inhale, gagged, then debated heading back into the factory. He forgot how badly Los Angeles stank when you could smell all the layers of filth beneath the fresh ocean breeze the humans raved about.

Striding over to Cora's Mazda, he settled onto the vehicle's partially dented hood.

Cora crossed her arms and glared at him. "You're going to scratch the paint. Go lean on your own car."

He raised an eyebrow at her, then flicked his eyes over to the pristine McLaren GTS.

"Fine," she conceded with an exaggerated huff, sliding up next to him on the hood of her beat up sedan. "What now? You can't compel me?"

"Seems like," he grumbled, racking his brain for possible options.

"If you're having performance issues, we can always try again later," she offered pleasantly. "Or never. Never is good for me."

He shot her a scathing look that might have wilted a lesser woman. "There are no issues with my performance."

She rolled her eyes, and he almost volunteered to prove right then and there just how good his 'performance' could be. But he was getting sidetracked. She had that effect on him, and it was becoming increasingly aggravating.

Beside him, Cora jolted upright. "You aren't going to kill me now, are you? I know how these things work. You can't leave any witnesses, can you?"

Before he could say a word to assuage her fears, Cora leapt from the hood of the car and took off down the dirt road leading back toward the main street. The fact that she held her auditions in such a secluded place really made him question her self-preservation instincts. Although, she was pumping her little legs faster than he would have thought her capable of, so maybe she had some semblance of a will to survive.

He took a deep breath despite the unpleasant odor and counted to ten to calm his swirling thoughts. Then he stood, dashed over to where she had made it perhaps two hundred feet away, and snatched her up. Slinging her over his shoulder like a sack of rice, he marched back to the parking lot. Her little fists pounding against his ass felt a bit like a massage, and he had to suppress a chuckle that she was even trying to fight him. She didn't have moxie, he decided. She had reckless determination.

Cora didn't cease her kicking and screaming until he deposited her roughly onto the hood of the Miata. He winced a bit at the new dent he'd just added, but given the state of her car, he doubted it harmed the value that much.

"Stop," he growled as she scrambled to get down. "What did I say about running?" When she just glared back at him, he added, "I don't kill humans. I told you I wasn't going to harm you, and I meant it. Now would you just give me a second to think?"

Cora scooted away from him but thankfully didn't attempt another pointless escape. "Sorry, but I can't exactly be all chill about this when you said earlier that you're some kind of enforcer," she pointed out. "You told me your job is to hunt down and kill people."

"Vampires," he bit out, annoyed. "I hunt down and kill rogue *vampires*. I'm not a monster, Cora."

She scoffed. "You're joking, right? They literally make monster movies about you people."

"You people?" he repeated, glaring at her. "For someone who was so excited to meet a real vampire minutes ago you turned racist pretty fast."

"What?" Cora sputtered. "I'm not racist, you rude jerk. Besides, vampire isn't even a race, it's a species." She gave him a derisive little huff then slumped onto the hood, all the fight draining from her body. "So what are you going to do if you can't compel me?"

"I'm still trying to figure that out and your prattling isn't super helpful, so can I get a little quiet please?" Even though he was initially enchanted by it, her lilting songbird voice tended to take on a screechy tone when she was scared or upset.

To his immense relief, she listened to him for once and kept quiet.

For about thirty seconds.

Her ring and pinky fingers drummed rapidly on the car's hood, and the sound grated against his last nerve like nails on a chalkboard.

"Do you mind?"

"Not at all," she snapped defensively.

His head swiveled to look at her. "Well, I mind. So could you stop that?"

"No."

"No?"

Cora tilted her head. "I'm sorry, was there confusion the first time? I thought I was clear when I said no."

"And why in Lilith's name not?" Anger overtook him, and his words came out harsher than he intended.

She flinched away, and he forced his breathing to slow. He couldn't do anything about his resting murder face, but he could at least control his posture and tone.

"I don't always have control over my muscles," she muttered. Her cheeks reddened in embarrassment, and a sense of uneasiness dropped into his stomach.

As if on cue, the evening breeze wafted that medicinal smell to him once more, reminding him of her unknown illness. He hadn't encountered many sick humans before, but maybe...

"What's wrong with you?" he asked, far more bluntly than he should have.

She straightened up, her body going rigid as she tucked her hands behind herself. "None of your business."

He glowered at her. He couldn't tell if she was being antagonistic on principle, or if she genuinely didn't want to talk about it. Either way, he didn't care about her personal preferences at that point. "I was just trying to help the situation, so would you please tell me what's wrong with you?"

The scathing look she gave him might have been worrisome if he wasn't an immortal vampire. "Nothing is wrong with me, you asshole!" she shouted. "And if I happen to have a medical condition, then it's none of your goddamned business!"

Clenching his fists, he slid off the car and let out a frustrated roar. Why did females have to be so problematic? He swore she was acting like a petulant child just to annoy him.

*Maybe you need to simmer down*, he told himself. *See things from her point of view.* What was it Tressa always said? Teddy bears have more friends than grizzly bears? Okay, he could try that approach.

"I apologize," he said, reducing his voice to a more subdued tone. "I phrased my words poorly. Of course there is nothing *wrong* with you, and it is your right to keep your medical situation private. I should not have intruded."

The wary look Cora gave him spoke volumes about his lack of achieving teddy bear status, but it was an improvement at least. She now looked at him as something more like a Koala with a butter knife. Not entirely dangerous but not exactly adorably innocent either.

He could work with that.

"The only reason I asked," he continued, "is that perhaps your condition is something that is impacting my abilities. You don't need to divulge more than you feel comfortable with, but can you tell me if I might be on the right track?"

Cora picked at a stray thread on the hem of her oversized sweater. "I guess it's possible," she mumbled. "The nerve cells in my brain..." she trailed off, and he decided pushing her for more details was a bad idea.

He sat back down beside her and patted her thigh in his best attempt at being reassuring. "This is great news."

She looked up at him aghast, and he quickly clarified. "Not that you're sick, but that it might just be a matter of my compulsion skills being too weak for your... unique situation."

"How is that a good thing?" she asked, edging away from him again.

"Because all I need to do is take you to someone more skilled than I. Marquin has the strongest compulsion I've ever encountered. He can take care of this."

Cora sighed. "And there's no way I can convince you to just let me go? Let me keep my script?"

Saiden knew it was a bad idea before the words came out, but he couldn't help himself. A compliant passenger would be much easier to handle than someone who was constantly trying to escape.

"You can always ask Marquin," he suggested. "He is the leader of my cadre, so he ultimately makes the decisions. You are welcome to plead your case to him."

The light that sparked in her eyes made him feel like tiny needles were stabbing at his insides. Even though nothing he said was a lie, he was still a bastard for giving her hope. In the nearly three hundred years he'd known Marquin, the vampire had never once budged on protocol when it came to secrecy from humans. Saiden didn't relish the idea of sleeping with one eye open, though, so he'd let her hold onto the dream for a little longer.

"That's great," Cora gushed, jumping up. "Let's go see Marquin. I know he'll see reason. Does he live nearby?"

Saiden puffed out an annoyed breath, cursing Derrick once again for his unreliability.

"Not exactly."

# Chapter Ten

## Cora

Cora crossed her arms and glared at Saiden. "It's non-negotiable."

They'd been arguing for nearly ten minutes, but she wasn't about to give in. Sure, Saiden could just throw her in the trunk of his car, but something about the way he looked at her said he wouldn't. He'd been hurt when she called him a monster, and for some reason he didn't want people to see him that way. Which made little to no sense given that he was a vampire who apparently murdered other vampires on the regular. Whatever the reason, her opinion of him mattered to some degree, and she wasn't going to budge. If he wanted this road trip to be even remotely pleasant, he would grant her this one thing.

"And what do you think you're going to say, hmm?" Saiden asked, holding the passenger door to the McLaren open for her.

Now that was something she'd agreed to in a heartbeat. Ten hours in her Mazda with the broken heater that gave off a moldy smell was no competition for his swanky sports car with a leather interior.

"I'll tell her that you're an investor interested in my movie, and I'm going to meet with some of your friends to discuss funding."

Saiden snorted. "Now tell me, Cora, if the roles were reversed and this Jinx fed you that same line of horseshit, would you let her go gallivanting off with a random stranger she just met?"

"Well no, of course not. I'd tell her she was about to be sex trafficked, and I'd chain her to the radiator so she couldn't leave."

He wrinkled his forehead. "You actually live in a place with a radiator?"

"Well excuse me, Richie Rich, but we don't all have treasury bonds that have been maturing for a thousand years."

Saiden dug his fingers into his temples. "There are so many things wrong with that statement I don't even know where to begin. But we are getting off track. Again. If you wouldn't believe your own story, then why would your friend? I'm sorry, but you can't go home, and you can't talk to anyone. You'll be back tomorrow, so there's no point in arguing and that's that."

Cora stamped her foot in the dirt, hoping the action came off as more unyielding and less temper tantrum. "I'm going home first and *that's* that."

"No, you're not."

"Yes, I am."

"No, you're not," Saiden gritted out and stomped over to her.

He reached out to grab her around the waist, but before his hands made contact she screeched, "I don't have my medication, okay?"

Saiden went still for a second then slowly backed off.

She swallowed roughly and forced the excuse out. "I don't keep my meds with me, and I can't function without them."

It was a total lie, of course. She always had an emergency stash in her purse. She also despised using her condition to manipulate people. When she'd been diagnosed years ago, she told herself she wouldn't let it rule her life. Wouldn't let it change how she acted around others. But desperate times needed desperate measures or whatever that saying was. She simply had to get home. Had to get a moment of privacy to leave herself a note just in case this Marquin refused her request.

Saiden mentioned that triggers could undo compulsion, so she just needed to leave a shitload of triggers for herself. Maybe she could go full Memento and slap up some sticky notes in her bedroom or scrawl reminders all over her inner thigh. Somewhere Saiden would never see.

His eyes flicked back and forth between hers, and Cora could practically see his internal debate. He hadn't said anything about mind reading, so he couldn't know for sure that she was lying, could he?

Whatever he saw in her must have passed his inspection, because he finally shook his head and grumbled, "Fine. Get in the damn car. I'll take you home first."

The tiny apartment Cora shared with Jinx was only twenty minutes away from the warehouse, but at the rate the speed demon was piloting the sports car they would make the drive in less than ten.

"You're going to get a ticket," she pointed out as the speedometer passed 85 mph.

"Unlikely," he replied, thankfully keeping his eyes on the road. "But if I did, let's just say I know how to handle those."

*Right, compulsion*, she thought. *Damn, no wonder he gets away with murder on a regular basis.*

As the glowing speedometer inched closer to 90 mph, she gripped the leather armrest tighter. "Not all of us are immortal, you know. If you crash this thing, you might walk away, but I won't."

"That *would* solve my problem," he muttered, downshifting and taking a tight corner on two wheels.

"Please tell me you're not serious," she squeaked through clenched teeth as beads of sweat rolled down her neck.

He must have heard the fearful quiver in her voice, because he turned to look at her. "I don't crash," he snapped, locking his dark eyes on hers.

"Watch the road!" she screamed when he left his focus on her face and not the oncoming traffic.

He smirked for a second longer, then faced forward just in time to avoid a head-on collision with a semi-truck.

"Are you insane?" she demanded, suddenly very afraid that she might be locked in a car with a deranged vampire harboring a death wish.

"Depends who you ask," was his only response.

She didn't say anything the rest of the trip, hoping her silence would keep his attention on the road. By some miracle, they made it to her apartment in Silverlake in one piece.

She yelped when he slammed his foot on the brakes and cranked the wheel, spinning the car 360 degrees to slide perfectly inside the lines of the visitor space.

She gaped at him for a long moment. "Who even are you?" she asked incredulously.

"I believe we have covered that already, but for the purposes of your question, let's just say you get really good at a lot of things when you have unlimited time to practice."

*He's not wrong about that*, she thought, peeling herself out of the leather seat and crawling from the low riding car. She wasn't sure she would survive a ten-hour trip if he drove up I-5 like it was the Indy 500.

Her chances of dying from a heart attack were already higher than the statistical average, and she really didn't need to push it.

Saiden's hand settled on her low back as he stepped up behind her, and she jumped at the unexpected contact. "I'll be right back," she stated, hurrying toward the door of her crappy two-bedroom apartment. The last thing she wanted to see was his judgmental face if he took in how she and Jinx lived. "You should probably stay here anyway. A car like that in this neighborhood will be gone in minutes."

"I'm not worried," he replied, following close behind her. "I'll hear if anyone approaches."

"From inside my apartment?"

When he didn't even bother with a response, she wondered just how good his hearing was.

Fiddling with the key in the lock, she struggled to think of an excuse to get some time away from him. She'd been planning on Jinx acting as a distraction until she noticed her friend's car missing from the parking lot.

*Shit!*

Jinx was still waiting at Tiny's for her to show up. Cora mentally berated herself for forgetting about drinks with her bestie. It wasn't the first time she'd screwed up plans, nor did she think it would it be the last. She knew Jinx might be annoyed, but would ultimately understand. Still... the more frequent memory lapses were becoming increasingly frustrating.

Pushing the door open, Cora stepped inside and pulled her cellphone out of her purse. She'd put it on mute for the auditions, and sure enough she had a string of worried text messages from Jinx.

"I forgot that I was supposed to meet my friend at a bar, so I need to message her," she said to Saiden. "I'm just going to pop into the bathroom real quick, okay?"

Cora glanced up at him when he didn't reply and stifled a giggle at the horror on his face. She'd known the condition of her apartment would be a drastic change from his usual, but she didn't think he'd look quite so traumatized.

"You live like this?" he asked in a tone that suggested he viewed her living situation as little better than a refrigerator box under a freeway overpass.

Okay, so maybe her home was a bit messy. The dining room had been converted into Rick's workshop for building the special effects devices, and fake blood was splattered across the walls, but getting the spurting action just right took trial and error. And sure, the living room was covered in costume pieces, black cases containing film equipment, and five tubs of Red Vines—which more or less made up the entirety of their craft services—but that was nothing. He should have seen her place when it was clean. The mess on the floor was doing a solid job of hiding the stained carpet, and the assorted movie posters decorating the walls were blocking the peeling paint that had to contain more lead than was legally allowed.

It wasn't fancy or posh like he was probably used to, but it was hers. And she didn't feel the need to explain to him that, thanks to the cost of her medications, it was the nicest place she could afford. The last thing she wanted was judgment from a grouchy vampire determined to ruin her life's work.

She waved her hand in front of his face until his eyes focused on hers. "Did you hear me? Bathroom? Gotta text Jinx. I'll be right back. And don't worry, there's no window in there so it's not like I can sneak out."

"I would hear if you did," he replied, not taking his eyes off the chaos before him.

"Of course you would," she muttered and shuffled her way through the mess toward the bathroom at the back of the apartment.

Plopping down on the cold linoleum floor, she sent a quick message to Jinx's number before opening a blank email on her phone. With Saiden monitoring her every movement, the chances of leaving herself a physical note had pretty much vanished, so email reminder it was.

Now she just had to figure out what to say that a skeptical future Cora might believe.

She didn't think '*you've been brain wiped by a vampire so go dig the old version of your script out of the trash*' would quite cut it.

Triggers, Saiden had mentioned. She needed lots and lots of triggers.

She stared at the phone for a minute until an incoming text from Jinx pulled her attention away from the email that was still blank. The message was long but ultimately understanding. Jinx was always understanding, and Cora felt awful about lying to the most important person in her life. Her friend deserved better than a half-assed excuse about how she was feeling overwhelmed lately, but it was all Cora could give right then. The bulk of her focus had to be on composing an email that she could schedule to be sent to herself every hour starting tomorrow.

Now if only she could figure out what to say.

# Chapter Eleven

## Saiden

Saiden nudged a severed limb to the side to clear a path to the couch. He grimaced when the prop left a streak of blood on the laces of his steel toe Harley Davidson boots. He rarely cared much about material possessions, and if he needed something, he just chose the most durable and practical. For the most part, he never bought anything he didn't need save for his boots. They weren't the most tactical or the highest quality, but they were his one vanity. They also never went out on rogue hunts with him primarily because he didn't want to end up with them covered in blood.

Finding a spot on the sofa that looked relatively safe, he sat down and waited. His eyes scanned over the assortment of movie posters, and it didn't take long for him to realize a theme. Nosferatu, 30 Days of Night, Salem's Lot, Fright Night. She obviously had a thing for vampire films, and he was pretty sure that these were the ones that depicted his kind as nothing but vicious, evil blood suckers.

Ouch.

Leaning back against the threadbare couch, he closed his eyes and listened to Cora move about in her bedroom. She'd let him know that she messaged her friend saying she was going to spend a few days with her father, and they could leave once she packed up some clothes, but there had been a somber tone to the way she said 'father' that pricked up his ears.

Not dad or papa. Father.

Apparently Cora's relationship with him fell under potentially lengthy backstory, and he would have to ask her about the history there later.

Crossing his legs at the ankles, he folded his arms and mentally berated himself. No, he didn't need to ask her a thing. The less he knew about this human the better. Get her to Marquin, get her wiped, and send her packing. Her life story was not his concern.

He listened to her throw some clothes into a backpack along with what sounded like an absurd number of pill bottles, then she was striding back into the living room.

"Okay," she proclaimed, reminding him of a determined little pit bull. "Let's do this."

She really believed she was going to convince Marquin to let her keep the memory of her script. It was almost adorable. Most humans he encountered lacked this level of conviction for anything in their life.

"Great," he said, getting up from the couch and carefully picking his way through the junk on the floor. "Let's get this over with as quick as possible."

Content to wade straight through her mess, Cora beat him to the door and held it open. "My thoughts exactly. I'm already behind schedule and unless you've changed your mind, I still need to find a new lead actor. If I miss the deadline for Screamfest, I'm going to stake you."

*Not likely*, he thought, but refrained from voicing the obvious.

When she wasn't being annoyingly obstinate, he found her little vicious streak somewhat entertaining.

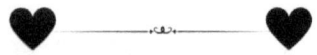

Saiden tossed Cora's bag into the trunk of the McLaren and peeled out toward the highway. He expected Cora to grab her cell to do whatever it was humans did all day on their phones, but the device stayed tucked away in her purse.

"You're not going to play on your phone?" he asked casually, pulling onto I-5 North.

"I'm not really big into social media," she said, hitting the button to recline the seat back a little and resting her hands behind her head. "Plus I figured you wouldn't let me use it anymore. Afraid I'll leak vamp secrets or something."

She was right, he had been prepared to take the device from her. The internet was hell on their kind. So much so that Baylin spent nearly all his time on his computer tracking any potential rumors that might hit too close to home. On the flip side, modern tech had made hunting rogues considerably more efficient, so he couldn't fault the humans too much for their technological addictions.

Still, he'd been expecting a fight from her.

He shook his head. This was better. They'd both keep quiet and make the drive in peace.

But if that was what he truly wanted, then why did the need to fill the silence weigh so heavily on him?

"So…" He cleared his throat and glanced over at her. With her eyes closed and her face relaxed, she looked even more beautiful. Like a sleeping angel. Her pulse told him she wasn't sleeping, though. In fact, it was beating a bit faster than when he'd first met her. Was she still nervous about being around him?

"You know I'm not going to hurt you, right?" he asked, needing something to pull her from her faux reverie.

An inch at a time, her head rolled over so she could look at him. "Yes, you've made that abundantly clear."

"And you believe me?"

"I do."

"Then why is your heart beating quick enough to rival a humming-bird's?"

She sat up and gave him her full attention. "I don't know, maybe because it's almost pitch black outside, and you're pushing a hundred miles per hour?"

This again. She really had no faith in his abilities.

"I would have thought you'd want to get this over with faster," he remarked as he darted around a slow-moving truck.

"Yeah, but faster doesn't mean dick if we die in a fiery crash. What's that saying on the billboards? Slow down and arrive alive?" She bit her lip and sank back into her seat. "Or unalive in your case. You are dead, right?"

He resisted the urge to bang his head on the steering wheel, mostly because he didn't think it would help with her increasing discomfort. He really had no desire to spend the next few hours answering a slew of questions about his kind when she wouldn't even remember it twenty-four hours from now. Although, if it took her mind off his impeccable driving skills, then perhaps he could indulge her curiosity a little bit.

He just wouldn't think too hard about why he cared so much about her comfort level.

"Here's the deal," he started. "I recognize that this is a lot for you, and you've probably got a million questions. If it'll help you relax and accept that we are not going to crash at any point during this trip, then I'll answer... Let's say three. You get three questions. Choose wisely."

He flicked the cruise control switch and settled back, preparing himself for what would no doubt be a painful conversation.

# Chapter Twelve

## Cora

Three questions? That was it? She had a legit freaking vampire sitting next to her, and she only got three questions?

To be fair, she was genuinely surprised he was willing to answer anything at all. He seemed pretty certain she was going to get mind wiped. Little did he know her persuasion skills were legendary. How else had she convinced an entire crew of film students to work for free? Maybe it was her cherubic smile or her glowing red hair. Or, more likely, it was that they could sense her increasing fragility. Either way, people loved to say yes to her, and this Marquin would be no different.

In fact, Saiden had been the only one so far that seemed oddly immune to her charms. He'd fought her on just about everything. Annoying, but a nice change of pace. She hadn't encountered such resistance since her father, but that was an entirely different set of circumstances.

Okay, three questions.

"How are you so sure that we won't get in a crash?" she blurted out without thinking. It probably wasn't the best use of one of her questions, but it was the most likely to have a shot at reducing her current level of anxiety.

Saiden turned to face her fully, and her heart leapt into her throat. She wanted to tell herself that it was because he wasn't looking at the road, but she couldn't deny how the harsh red glow of taillights across his face really accentuated his strong features. She knew there was no chance in hell he'd agree to be in her movie, but damn... She would promise him just about anything to make it happen.

"It's my Gift from Lilith," Saiden answered calmly before turning back to the road.

Six seconds. He'd stared at her for six full seconds. Any other time six seconds would feel like nothing, but when you were doing a hundred on the freeway without looking, it was an eternity.

Cora gulped, then relaxed when she realized she had a death grip on her seatbelt. "Care to expand on that? Because I don't really consider that an answer. An answer needs to make at least some kind of sense."

Saiden let out an annoyed chuff as if giving her an actual explanation was more than he signed up for. "You know the story of Lilith, right?"

Cora racked her brain but only came up with characters from horror movies. "Wasn't she a succubus or something?"

"Close, but not quite," he corrected. "She was Adam's first wife, originally created to be his equal. Problem was, Adam didn't really want an equal. He wanted obedience and compliance. Since Lilith refused to be his little submissive pet, she was cast out of paradise, and Adam got a new wife, Eve. Needless to say, Lilith was pissed."

"I can imagine," Cora said, sinking back into her seat. The soft rumble of Saiden's voice was practically hypnotizing. It was the first time he wasn't tense or annoyed, and she could listen to him talk like this for hours.

"Consumed with rage," Saiden continued, "she turned to the fallen angel, Samael, to help her get revenge. She wanted Adam and all his children to suffer for the rest of eternity for what he did to her. Since Samael had no love for the new human creatures walking the earth, he agreed. Bestowing some of his power unto Lilith, he helped her conceive the first vampire.

"Lilith gave birth to a daughter, Sura, who became a creature that would live forever, feeding on the blood of Adam's kind. And because she wanted her daughter to be protected from any harm, Lilith used the power granted to her by Samael to gift her daughter the ability to see the future. Sura saw how vicious and hateful the humans would become, so she begged her mother to give any offspring she would have their own special abilities, ensuring they could always remain superior to Adam's kin. Now, every new vampire is reborn with an ability that is unique to them. Something they need or crave to be successful in their new life as a vampire. We call it Lilith's Gift."

The muscles in Cora's hand started spasming, and she drummed her fingers on the window to hide the small twitches while she mulled over the story. She quickly stopped when she remembered how Saiden reacted to her seemingly idle gesture earlier and just tucked the misbehaving appendage under her thigh.

The tale of Lilith was fascinating, regardless of whether or not she believed it. There was probably an inkling of truth in there somewhere, but few origin stories were completely accurate. It was a little fantastical for her tastes, but then again, so was the concept of real vampires. She'd always assumed that if vampires existed, then it was probably the result of a genetic mutation, not a biblical rivalry.

Cora gave him an appraising look, her brain attempting to wrap itself around the one thing in his story that didn't make any sense. "So every vamp gets a super cool ability, and your Gift was precision driving?" she asked. "I gotta say, if other vampires were getting things like the ability to see the future, then it kind of sounds like you got screwed."

"My Gift is not precision driving," Saiden bit out, his hands tightening on the wheel. "My Gift is threat awareness. I get a feeling when something potentially fatal is about to happen. It lets me direct all my attention to my surroundings so I can discern the extent of the danger before it happens. It's what makes me such a skilled rogue hunter."

"Oh! You have spidey sense," Cora blurted out.

Saiden cringed, and his eyes squeezed shut for a second. "I'd rather you didn't compare my Gift to that of an insect-obsessed comic book human."

Cora scoffed. "I mean, I thought it was a compliment. Spiderman's a literal superhero. He saves lives."

Saiden didn't say anything for so long Cora thought he wasn't going to respond.

Then he replied, so quietly that she almost missed it, "That's not who I am."

They both said nothing for a long moment, and Cora stared out the window, watching the freeway exits pass by in a blur. She didn't mean to offend him. His Gift was fascinating, and she couldn't deny that it did calm her fears about his driving.

"Thank you for letting me know," she said, needing to break up the awkward silence. "I guess if I got a heads up about any potential crash with enough time to prevent it, then yeah, I'd also drive like a bat out of Hell."

Realizing what she just said, Cora slapped her hand over her mouth and whipped her head to look at Saiden. She rushed to formulate an apology, but to her surprise he... laughed.

Saiden threw his head back and let out a full blown belly laugh. "You should see your face," he choked out through guffaws.

She frowned. So much for apologizing. She thought her words had been insulting, but apparently not.

"In that case, for my second question I want to know about all the vampire mythologies that aren't real. I'm guessing by your amusement that you don't turn into a bat nor were you born in the bowels of Hell."

"The bowels of Hell?" he repeated, giving her a patronizing look. "Where do you humans come up with this shit?"

"Movies and books, mostly. But spill. What else is made up?"

Saiden ran a hand through his messy dark hair, then absently rubbed at the shaved side. She wondered if that short bit of hair was soft or prickly. Not that she would be running her hands over his scalp anytime soon, but she could still imagine.

"Let's see," he said thoughtfully. "You already know about the no flying thing. Garlic is also not an issue. I happen to really like it on pizza. And yes, we do eat food. It doesn't keep us alive in the way that blood does, and oftentimes I will go days without it if I'm busy. We enjoy the taste and the experience of dining with others, though."

"So, you do drink blood then?"

"We do," he confirmed, his voice lacking any evidence as to his thoughts about that. She must have visually tensed because he quickly added, "from blood bags, not people. If it can be avoided. Our bodies would not function without it, and we are incapable of making our own blood cells."

"What happens if you go without?" she asked, realizing she hadn't seen any blood bags in the McLaren.

"I think we are moving past your original question. Would you like that to be your third and final one?"

Cora bit her lip. She wanted a second to analyze her thoughts. If she only got one more question, she wanted it to be good. "No," she replied finally. "I haven't decided on the third one yet. So that's all the vamp stuff that's not real? Everything else is true?"

Waving a hand dismissively, Saiden changed lanes without so much as a glance behind him. "No, there are other inaccuracies. We do not sleep in coffins, and we can and do go out during the day. Though we tend to be more sensitive to the sun than humans, so you won't usually find us on the beach." He paused for a second, then added, "And to harken back to your original question, no, I am not dead. Well, not anymore. I died as a human and was reborn as a vampire, but any medical examination would classify me as alive. So long as I consume blood, my heart beats just like yours. I breathe just like you. And I am not cold and clammy as the stories love to portray."

She should have resisted. It would have been the smart thing to do. But damn if she wasn't a slave to her impulses.

Cora reached out and ran her hand down his bare arm.

He wasn't cold and clammy, that was for sure.

Not even close.

# Chapter Thirteen

## Saiden

It was such an innocuous thing—the light brush of her skin against his own—yet it changed his entire world. The second her fingers grazed his arm, he felt it.

The Spark.

In the warehouse he thought he'd touched her skin at some point, but now he realized her sweater must have always been in the way. How could he be so smart and so fucking stupid at the same time? His honed senses kept him alive for three hundred years but failed him the second his mate showed up.

He should have embraced the one thing he craved more than life itself, but instead he fell into firm denial mode. He couldn't compel her, but that could have been her illness. And yeah, she smelled delicious, but only after you worked past that acerbic medicinal tang.

He'd lived for so long that he'd just given up and dismissed everything as coincidence.

He couldn't deny the Spark though. It was like a bolt of lightning to the soul. A connection snapping into place. The universe screaming at him, 'She is the one.'

His mate.

She was his mate.

The one thing he wanted his entire life and assumed he simply wasn't worthy of having. She existed. He found her. And she was...

A messy, quarrelsome human who only cared about making movies and didn't even want to be turned.

Damn, Lilith could be a real bitch sometimes.

Cora yanked her hand back as if she'd been bitten, and the action only cemented things further. She'd felt the Spark too. Only she had no idea what it meant.

*Shit. Shit. Shit.*

What the hell was he supposed to say now? He'd been nothing but a dick to her. How was he supposed to convince her that they were meant to spend the rest of their lives together? He didn't know much about human women, but he'd seen enough movies to know they tended to freak out if a guy went too fast. There was no way she would understand that even though they just met, the universe knew they would be a perfect match, and she was the only one he would be able to love for an eternity.

A concept that would probably go over the heads of the Tinder and TikTok generation. Though, she had said she didn't care for social media, so maybe she wasn't like the others.

Play it cool. That's what he'd do. He'd play it casual, like nothing had changed.

Even if the truth was that *everything* had changed. He felt even more awful now that she'd never get to make her movie. Once she became one of them, making any kind of vampire flick was out of the question.

*Shit. Shit. Shit.*

There was also the tiny, insignificant fact that she didn't want to be turned. Well, that was going to have to change and fast. He'd given up on ever finding his mate over a hundred years ago. Convinced himself that hunting rogues was all his existence would ever entail. And he was fine with that. He had a purpose in protecting the people he cared about. He didn't need a mate.

It was easy to pretend you didn't want something when you thought you'd never have it, but now that she was sitting next to him... he'd just have to convince her. There was no other option. Vampires only ever got one mate. If Lilith finally got off her ass and brought them together, he couldn't go back to his previous lonely existence. Not when he saw how Marquin and Eliana were together. The level of happiness that a mate could bring was not to be dismissed.

He glanced at her out of the corner of his eye and saw her rubbing her hand absently. Probably blaming the Spark on static electricity.

"So," he began, suddenly unsure how to even speak to her. "Why don't you want to live forever? Just curious because in the warehouse you made it seem like a bad thing."

He hadn't meant to sound quite so awkward, but he really needed to know what kind of opposition he was up against.

"I just don't want to," she answered quietly. "It's not really something I can explain to you, so just accept that some people don't see your immortality as a gift. Some see it as a curse."

Okay, so he was up against a mountain of opposition. He thought the religious zealots that viewed vampires as 'cursed beings' died out ages ago. She didn't seem overly devout, what with making horror films for a living, but anything was possible.

He needed to know more about her, which meant he needed to keep her talking.

"Have you thought of your third question yet?"

Hell, he'd answer a thousand questions if that's what it took to convince her that becoming a vampire was not the tragedy she viewed it as.

Cora brushed her braid over her shoulder, and he tried not to smile at the nervous action. He liked that the question was important to her. Liked that learning about his kind seemed to matter so much to her that she put value on asking the right thing.

"I'm not sure yet," she replied, sounding considerably more tired than she had a moment ago. "Give me some time to think."

He nodded and focused his eyes back on the road. If she didn't want to talk then he wouldn't push. For now, anyway.

Glancing at the speedometer, he pulled his foot off the pedal and let his speed drop to something more reasonable. Her pulse had slowed when she heard about his Gift, and he would gladly drive like a near-sighted grandma if it increased her comfort level even the slightest bit.

Something had changed in the last few minutes and not just for him. She'd been so excited to learn about vampires just moments ago, but now? Her shoulders drooped, and she stared listlessly out the window.

He didn't know what caused this new sadness in her, and it was making him depressed by proxy. He racked his brain, but the only thing that happened was her touching him. Had he jerked away? He didn't think he did. Maybe she had seen the look of shock on his face and misinterpreted it?

*Shit. Shit. Shit.*

He'd know about his mate for less than five minutes, and he'd already upset her. His teeth clenched as he struggled with his urge to say something that might fix the situation.

Before his brain could provide anything insightful, he registered the soft rise and fall of Cora's breath that told him she had drifted off to sleep. As much as he wanted to talk to her, she looked so peaceful that he would bite off his own tongue before he would wake her up.

It was probably for the best since he needed time to figure out a game plan. He would have to break out the kid gloves that were so foreign to him and handle the next few days very carefully. Whatever he'd done just now to upset her was nothing compared to how pissed she would be when she found out she wasn't ever going home.

He didn't care what it took; he was never letting her go.

# Chapter Fourteen

## Cora

The thunk of a door shutting pulled Cora from sleep. Groggy, she lifted her head and looked around. Were they there already? She didn't know how long she had stared out the window feeling sorry for herself before she drifted off, but she doubted it was long enough that they'd already be up in Northern California.

She still couldn't believe she'd fallen asleep at all. Most nights it took enough pills to choke a horse to get any shut eye. And yet one second she was pissed off that she couldn't even touch a hot guy without her body betraying her, and the next she was wiping crusties from the corner of her eyes while squinting at the neon lights of the roadside motor lodge in front of her.

A quick glance at her watch told her it was close to midnight. She'd only been out for a couple hours, yet the disorientation was similar to coming out of an Ambien nap.

She leaned back in the seat and watched as Saiden strolled into the motel's office. She didn't know how anybody could look at him and not realize that he was something other than human. The way he walked with the confidence of someone who had nothing to fear, like a lion who knew he was the top predator in the jungle, was not a vibe human guys could pull off. And she would know because she spent over a week trying to find someone who could. It was the only reason she'd hired that dumbass, Jake, in the first place. He wasn't on the same level as Saiden, but he'd come a lot closer than most of the actors who'd auditioned.

Every aspect of Saiden, from the darkness present in his eyes to the rich gravelly texture of his voice, just screamed death incarnate. He was the kind of guy you knew would break more than just your heart, but if he crooked a single finger, you'd leap into his arms and wrap your legs around his hips all the same.

Well, other girls would anyway. Even if she didn't know that he was a vampire, she still had a rule about men. She'd had a few flings shortly after she was diagnosed, but it all just felt too hollow. Because really, what was the point? Instead, she'd simply bought an assortment of impressive vibrators and called it a day on their whole gender.

She had to admit, though, the vampire walking back out of the lodge was almost tempting enough for her to make some insane decisions. If he hadn't essentially kidnapped her, she might have tossed her rule out the window and climbed into his lap the second they weren't doing ninety on the freeway.

Or maybe *while* they were doing ninety if his awareness Gift was really that good.

"What's going on?" she asked, shaking the visual from her head and stepping out of the car as he approached.

Saiden held up a keycard in answer.

She blinked at him. "Are you serious? Why are we stopping? Aren't you a creature of the night? Let's just drive right through."

Saiden gave her a look she couldn't quite decipher, then walked around back to pull her bag from the trunk. Slinging it over one shoulder, he said, "It seems I missed another misconception about vampires. While we do enjoy the night, we aren't completely nocturnal. And since I woke up rather early this morning to make the ten-hour drive down to L.A., I don't really fancy doing the entire return trip without a break." He paused, then softly added, "If it's okay with you."

That was a first. He actually cared about what she wanted? Did he hit his head at some point while she was asleep?

"Uh, yeah. That's fine."

Cora cracked her neck, grimaced, and decided it was more than fine. Her muscles didn't like her on a good day, so nodding off while leaning against a car window had them essentially staging a coup. She could use a comfy place to relax for a bit.

As soon as Saiden fell asleep she would have time to sort through headshots on Casting Networks. It was a stretch, but maybe she could find another lead actor that came somewhat close to her vision. With her dwindling timeline, she had to operate under the assumption that Marquin would let her hold onto her script. It was the only thing that was keeping her going.

She held out a hand for her bag, but he just beeped the car and took off toward the right side of the lodge. She glared at his back for a second then ran to catch up.

"Hey, I can carry my own—Shit!"

The muscles in her legs revolted, and pavement raced up to meet her face. She threw out her arms on instinct, but the impact never came.

A strong arm circled her waist and swung her up into a firm chest. She looked up at Saiden, and she would bet the last five bucks in her bank account that she saw genuine concern on his face.

"Are you okay?" he asked, his brow wrinkling.

"Uh, yeah," she exhaled, struggling to form a coherent thought when she was this close to his face. At first glance in the dim warehouse, she'd considered his eyes to be almost black, but she couldn't have been more wrong. Up close, she saw that they were a deep shade of rich chocolate, and the lamplight overhead caused the tiny flecks of honey gold scattered throughout to twinkle like stars in a dark sky. They weren't human, those eyes—the way they expanded and contracted like a cat's to adapt to the light.

Saiden dropped her bag and brushed a stray hair behind her ear with one hand while the other remained firmly wrapped around her waist. She couldn't be certain, but it felt like his arm tightened, as if he refused to let her go. His eyes flicked back and forth between hers, searching for something. "You do that a lot," he murmured.

When she spoke, the voice that came out was distant and detached, as if filtering through a thick fog. "Do what a lot?"

"Fall."

"Clumsy," she replied, her mouth on autopilot since the rest of her was still mesmerized by his eyes.

He smiled, and it lit up his whole face, changing him into a completely different person. The hard edges of his face softened, and his entire demeanor changed from murderous to magnificent.

She swallowed roughly and noted how his eyes were drawn to the movement at her throat. Something flared hot in his expression, and it was enough to kickstart her brain back into rational thinking. She'd seen enough movies to recognize *that* look. He was a hungry vampire, and she had no intention of putting herself on the menu.

"So, you mentioned that you only feed from blood bags, right? No humans?" She took a step back now that the spell was broken, and he looked somewhat disappointed by the movement.

"Mostly, yes. Though emergency situations have called for a natural feeding."

"I see." She glanced around nervously. The lodge was the only building around aside from a closed-up gas station, and there wasn't another living soul in sight. "And is this an 'emergency situation?' Because honestly, I don't care how much control you supposedly have. I know how this ends. 'It's just a little nip,' you'll say, and then the next thing you know my body is buried in a shallow grave out behind Ray's Motor Lodge."

Moving faster than she could track, Saiden captured her face in his hands. "Cora, I am going to say this one last time, and I beg of you please listen carefully to my words: There is no safer place for you to be than in my presence. I swear that no harm will come to you so long as I breathe."

Then he scooped up her bag and headed toward the stairs to the second story rooms, leaving her staring after him and wondering why she was beginning to believe him.

# Chapter Fifteen

## Saiden

"There's only one bed," were the first words out of Cora's mouth when she caught up to him and entered their room.

"I'm aware," he replied, dropping her bag in a chair next to the king-sized mattress. "They didn't have any double beds left."

He couldn't even bring himself to feel guilty about the lie. The lodge had plenty of options available, many of them with two beds, but the words 'single, please' were out of his mouth before he could stop himself. Some part of him simply wouldn't let her sleep in a different bed. His body screamed at him that they belonged together.

It was the curse of new mates. The constant tug to keep them nearby. He'd written the feeling off earlier as nothing more than his hunter instincts needing to keep close tabs on his quarry, but now that he knew what it really was, he was completely and utterly fucked. He might be able to keep her in his bed tonight, but when they arrived at the compound tomorrow, he doubted she would sign up for moving into his room straight away.

He still had no idea how he was going to explain things to her, but maybe his cousins could help. Tressa, Raven, and Liessa were much better with words than he was.

Well, maybe he wouldn't ask Liessa. She was still relatively young, having only been turned less than fifty years ago, and was currently convinced that she would never want a mate. His carefree cousin always said an eternity of freedom was the best gift she'd been given. Not exactly a ringing endorsement for Cora becoming a vampire and staying with him forever, but he was pretty sure Liessa was still freeliving in the Bahamas anyway.

Tressa and Raven, though, that could work. They were two of the biggest romantics he'd ever met. They would convince Cora. Even if it took years, they would eventually wear her down, and he'd wait decades if he had to. However long it took for her to realize they were meant to be.

Cora took a seat at a little desk, the only other furniture in the tiny room save for an old dresser with more than a few scratches. He should have held out for a nicer place, but she just looked so uncomfortable with her face squashed against the glass and her neck cricked at that unnatural angle. Her relief was far more important than five-star accommodations, so Ray's Motor Lodge it was.

"This is fine," she said, waving a hand at the room. "I wasn't planning on sleeping anyway."

He frowned at her. "You were passed out in the car. You're exhausted, Cora. Get some rest."

"I'm good," she said, hefting her bag onto the desk. "That was honestly rare for me. I don't usually fall asleep in strange places. Hell, I don't usually fall asleep in familiar places. I'm used to it, though, so you can take the bed."

He cocked a head at her. She had trouble sleeping? Maybe that explained her medicinal smell. If she took sleeping medication on a regular basis it might affect her scent over time.

He smiled. She wouldn't need those pills anymore. Cora didn't know it yet, but her days of having trouble falling asleep were over.

Not that sleep was the top thing on his mind at present. Being alone with her in a room with a bed was presenting all kinds of scenarios that were getting harder and harder to ignore. If she was going to fight him about resting, maybe he could use the time to try a little teaser and see how she reacted to him.

"Whatever you say," he replied as he strolled toward the bathroom, pulling his shirt off as he went. He knew it was a shameless move, but he wasn't about to play fair when it came to his mate.

"What are you doing?" she squawked behind him.

He smothered his grin and assumed his best bored expression. Turning back to her, he dropped his shirt on the floor and started unbuckling his belt. "Taking a shower. Unless you want first dibs?"

"Stop!" she screeched as he started to lower his jeans.

He froze and raised a single eyebrow at her. "You can go first if you want, I don't mind. No need to get loud."

Jumping up, she stalked over to him and snatched his shirt off the floor. She thrust it at him, but he didn't even acknowledge the fabric in her hand. Her heart was pounding, and he was pretty sure it wasn't from fear this time.

"I don't need a shower," she argued, a blush creeping over her face, "but I do need you to put your clothes back on."

He gave her a mock look of indignation. "Cora, I'm not going to shower fully dressed."

"That's not what I meant," she sputtered, and it took everything in him not to grin. She was even prettier when she was flustered, the hint of pink on her cheeks highlighting her rich auburn hair. He wanted to reach out and loosen the braid so he could run his fingers through her thick tresses.

This was going to be a long night.

"Then what did you mean?" he asked, continuing to play dumb as he watched her cheeks deepen in color to a beautiful shade of strawberry.

Strawberries! That's what she smelled like. Damn, he was an idiot for not realizing she was his mate right off the bat. If he hadn't been so hung up on the medicine smell, he would have identified the fruity scent easily and known the truth.

"I just meant, keep your clothes on until you get into the bathroom." She jabbed his shirt into his chest, but he continued to ignore it.

Holding her gaze, he slid his jeans off his hips and let them drop to the floor. "Sorry, Mary Shelley, vampires don't care about nudity." Keeping his black boxer briefs on, he turned and strode into the bathroom. He'd pushed her enough for one night.

It took all his willpower, but he shut the door behind him without turning around to see her reaction. Was she intrigued or disgusted?

*Kid gloves*, he reminded himself. *Play it casual.*

Fighting the urge to go back out to her, he turned on the shower instead.

"Mary Shelley was Frankenstein, you idiot."

He laughed under his breath, wondering if she was aware that he heard every single muttered curse she sent his way.

Moving the faucet all the way over to cold, he stepped in and let the freezing water rush over his burning skin.

# Chapter Sixteen

## Cora

Cora nearly collapsed onto the bed, and it had nothing to do with her medical condition and everything to do with the naked guy in the shower. His tight boxer briefs had left little to the imagination, and her brain was having no trouble filling in the blanks as she listened to the water turn on.

She cursed him again under her breath, not caring if his vamp hearing could pick it up.

It was driving her nuts, trying to figure him out. Had he intentionally been trying to get a rise out of her, or did vamps just not see anything wrong with stripping in front of humans?

If it was the former, then what kind of game was he playing? It felt like seduction, but why would he be interested in her? She needed to figure things out fast because if it was a game, she was pretty sure she was losing.

It dawned on her then that he never really answered her question about his needing to feed. He said she was safe with him, but safe was a very subjective word, and one that they might not agree on. Was that his game? Was he trying to seduce her so he could bite her?

Fucking undead asshole. He was trying to turn her into dinner. Just because he was convinced that he could control how much he took, didn't mean she would offer her neck up as a midnight snack.

Or maybe she should. Maybe if he got a sample of how disgusting she tasted, then he would give her a wide berth. It'd be like eating a burger and realizing the cow had Ebola.

Okay, that was an exaggeration, but there was no way she could taste good. Not with all the medication coursing through her diseased blood.

She'd spent a good chunk of time debating if she should bring up her condition. If he heard about her situation, he might take pity on her and let her make her film. It's not like she was freaking Spielberg and the entire world would see her movie. He could show a little damned compassion.

Ultimately, she decided to save that ploy for her chat with Marquin. She would not use her illness to invoke pity unless she had to.

Well, at least not a second time. The first one barely counted, though. He should have been willing to let her swing by her apartment just as a basic human decency. It wasn't her fault he wasn't human, and she had to employ a little manipulation to stay on his level.

She heard the faucet turn off and leapt from the bed. Grabbing his pants and shirt, she deposited them right outside the bathroom door and then slid into the desk chair, pointing it noticeably in the opposite direction. Her willpower was only so much, and if he walked out naked and dripping wet, even a hoard of catholic nuns wouldn't be able to resist the allure of his seductive darkness.

Reaching into her bag, she pulled out her phone and scrolled through her messages. There were a few texts from her crew letting her know they were fine pausing the film for a few days while she dealt with family business. Mentally she thanked Jinx for handling all of that. There were also a couple emails from actors who had missed her open call but would like to be considered. She dug out her laptop so she could watch the videos they sent over.

She was halfway through a rather painful demo reel from an acne-riddled adolescent when the door to the bathroom opened.

*Don't look. Don't look. Don't look.*

She forced herself to continue watching this kid butcher Shakespeare in his garage. It was beyond painful, but she was caught between a rock and a very, *very*, hard place. She had known Saiden was in good shape but hadn't realized he was hiding that many muscles under his baggy t-shirt. He was the complete opposite of those lean, emaciated vamps she typically saw in horror films. Which was precisely why she'd been drawn to him. She wanted her villain to radiate strength and virility. There was just something decidedly un-intimidating about Bram Stoker's pallid and sickly kind of vampire. How were you supposed to be scared when they looked like a strong wind might knock them over?

Saiden, on the other hand, looked like he could stroll through a damned tornado with less concern than a lamb frolicking in a field.

Hot breath tickled her neck as Saiden leaned down behind her.

*Don't look. Don't look. Don't look.*

She looked.

And found herself with a washboard stomach inches from her face. A bead of water rolled down his olive skin. She watched that single drop slide down the valleys and ridges of his six—eight?—pack abdominals until it reached the band of his jeans and wicked away.

"My eyes are up here, Cora."

His words were all sinfully smooth, but she could have sworn she heard a tiny waver, as if he was almost worried about how she might react.

Slowly, she slid her eyes up to meet his and gulped at how intensely he was drinking her in.

He tracked the subtle bob of her throat and gave her a lascivious grin. "You know," he purred, all hesitancy fading as he dropped his already sultry voice into a deeper octave. "I still owe you a third question from the car ride. So, if you've seen anything that you want to ask me about, and I do mean anything, I'm all yours."

The implications behind that statement almost broke her, but irritation kicked the door shut on her lust. Instead of breaking, she snapped.

Slamming the laptop shut she burst out of the chair, forcing him to back up quickly.

"Okay, I'm not doing this," she blurted out. Perhaps this was one of those times Jinx kept mentioning when she lacked the social awareness to keep her mouth shut, but she lost all ability to care about stupid shit like that when she found out vampires existed.

"Yes, you are hot," she declared, gesturing animatedly toward his chiseled torso. "You are extremely attractive. You look like the kind of guy that women imagine in their heads when they read romance novels. You look like the kind of guy who would awaken a number of sexual kinks both disturbing and oddly fulfilling. You look like the kind of guy who could walk into a bar and suddenly there would be so many wet pairs of panties that the owner would need to open a window."

Saiden's eyebrow quirked up at that last one, and she didn't miss the slight curl to his lip as he fought off a grin.

"And you have the kind of seductive smile that would require zero words to get a girl into bed. But if you think I'm going to throw my panties or my jugular at you, then you are seriously mistaken. Now, if you don't mind, how about you take your third question and shove it up your obscenely tight ass because all I'm planning to do is sit at this desk and watch a hundred demo reels from guys whose acting is so bad they couldn't even be in a Marvel movie. All in the hopes that I will find someone who has even a fraction of your innate menace. And I don't need your shirtless body and sexy grins distracting me. Okay?"

Her chest heaved up and down from the exertion of her rant, but it needed to be said. Despite Jinx's many attempts to reign her in, she was always the first to address any elephant in the room, and Saiden was one big ass pachyderm.

Crossing her arms, she stared at him and waited for a response.

His lip twitched. It must have taken a solid minute before he quietly walked over to the bathroom, picked up his shirt, and slid it on over his still damp torso.

"Is that better?" he asked, amusement coloring his voice, that damn lip still trying to curl up into a full grin.

"It's a start," Cora mumbled, turning back to her laptop.

She started to open it, but a muscular hand slid over the top of hers, keeping it shut. Sighing, because obviously her speech had resulted in little more than him putting a shirt on, she turned to face him.

She was surprised to see all traces of seduction gone and his resting murder face back on full display.

"You need to get some sleep," he insisted, holding the laptop lid—and her hand—firmly in place.

"I'm not tired," she replied while trying, and failing, to slide her palm out from beneath his much larger one.

"You not only fell asleep in the car, but you look exhausted. Why won't you just lie down?"

She evaluated the stubbornness flaring in his dark eyes and gave up the struggle. "Look, that was a fluke. I don't sleep much, and even if I did, I'm not sharing a bed with you."

He released her hand and took a step back. "I said you were perfectly safe with me, Cora, and I meant it. No biting. No seduction. Just sleep."

"Never gonna happen."

He ran a hand through his wet hair, and the action dislodged a few water droplets that ran down the thick cords of his muscular neck. Now, *he* had a biteable neck, and she wasn't even a vampire.

"How about this?" he offered. "I need to make a phone call. If you lie down and at least try to fall asleep but are still awake when I come back to the room, then I'll leave you alone for the rest of the night. You can do whatever you want without interruption from me."

Cora pretended to analyze his offer. It was a sucker's deal because there was no way she would fall asleep in a crappy motel room with a dangerous vampire right outside the door. If it would get him off her back, though, she'd play along.

"Deal," she agreed and crossed the five feet to the massive bed. He eyed her warily as she slipped under the covers fully dressed and plumped the pillow beneath her head. Closing her eyes in an effort to convince him that she *was* attempting to sleep, she listened while he grabbed his keys and quietly shut the door behind himself.

*Phone call my ass*, she thought. He was probably heading out to find dinner since she'd firmly rebuked him.

Nestling into the surprisingly soft mattress, she waited for him to return so she could get back to her work. And she would get back to her work because there wasn't a snowball's chance in hell of her actually falling asleep.

# Chapter Seventeen

## Saiden

Saiden slid down the door of the hotel room and leaned his head back, his eyes lazily drifting up to the stars winking overhead. Allowing his hearing to amplify, he focused on the sound of Cora's breathing. He needed to wait until it smoothed out and he was certain she was deep into a REM state before he could walk away. He didn't know exactly how close he had to be for the relaxation effect of mate proximity to kick in, but he'd heard from Marquin that sometimes just the knowledge that Eliana was in the same house was enough to knock him out like a frat boy after a kegger.

Less than five minutes later, her breathing leveled out, and the gentle sound of soft little snuffles reached his ears. He wondered if she knew that she snored. It was sweet and cute, like little puppy chuffs. It had been difficult to pull the car over earlier because he hated to wake her up.

He was deeply thrilled that he did, though, just for the opportunity to hear her passionate explosion. It had taken all his willpower to stand there and let her describe the depths to which she found him attractive. If only she knew how little he cared about the apparent effect he had on other women. He only cared about the effect he had on her. And while it wasn't a declaration of love or a request to spend eternity at his side, it was a start.

Obscenely tight ass. He wouldn't forget those words as long as he lived. Every grueling second he'd spent training over the last three hundred years was suddenly very worth it.

She clearly desired him at least on a physical level, and while he wanted far more than just her body, for now he'd take whatever she offered. Not that she was offering anything currently, but the heat was there. It just needed fuel. If the way to her heart was through her panties, then he would gladly put in the work.

First, he really did need to make a phone call.

Confident that she wouldn't wake until morning, he sped over to his car and settled into the driver's seat. He tapped the start button in the center console and said, "Call Baylin."

He listened to the ringing sound for a second, waiting for his brother to answer. Baylin wasn't his biological sibling, but they both thought of each other as family. More so than the other members of their cadre they affectionately called cousins. Vamps were only allowed to turn one mortal, and Marquin had sired Saiden a couple decades after he and Eliana mated. They'd stumbled across him dying on the battlefield and said they knew right away that he belonged with them.

Then, less than a month later, Marquin came across Baylin in a pub in Galway. He'd been turned and abandoned, left as a newbie vamp to find his own way. Marquin saw a lot of himself in Baylin, so he brought him home, and Saiden and Baylin learned how to become vampires together. Three hundred plus years later, he still considered him his baby brother.

Since they always had each other's backs, he knew Baylin would take his call regardless of whether he was sleeping, fucking, or hacking.

The only three things Baylin was ever doing.

"'Sup, bro?" Baylin answered on the fourth ring.

*Thank goodness*, Saiden thought. The lack of a prominent Irish brogue told Saiden his brother was sober. Of all his family, Baylin adapted to the changing times better than anyone. It was part of his gift from Lilith—his ability to absorb, understand, and retain information at an astounding rate. As modern times brought modern advancements, he went from scholar to tech wizard and never looked back. Except when he was drunk. It was as if copious amounts of alcohol acted as a time machine, tossing him straight into the back alleys of Northern Ireland.

"Hey, I need a favor," Saiden replied in greeting.

"Name it." Baylin's tone was alert and his breathing steady which meant he was already in hacker mode, and Saiden hadn't interrupted either of his brother's other favorite bedroom activities.

"I have a woman with me, and I need—"

"Way to go, big bro," Baylin interrupted, and Saiden could practically hear him sending a virtual high five over the phone. "It's been what, two years, three years since you last got laid?"

Five, but that was so far off topic at the moment that he didn't bother to correct him.

"It's not like that," he gritted out, finding himself upset that Baylin had reduced Cora to a simple lay. He knew a mate's protective instincts were powerful, but he didn't expect to feel this murderous toward his brother over a simple offhand comment. It was probably a damn good thing he was warning them before he just showed up with her, and even better that Derrick was out of town. Baylin was usually respectful toward women, but Derrick would no doubt make a lewd comment and then Saiden would have to explain to Marquin why his cousin's spleen was splattered across the front steps.

"Dude, it's not a rogue, is it?" Baylin asked. "You know it almost never works out when you try to save them."

"You're lucky Marquin didn't feel that way when he first met you," Saiden shot back. He hated being reminded that his efforts to save rogues almost always failed, but Baylin hated being reminded that he nearly was one, so the retort was only fair.

"Yeah, yeah," Baylin muttered. "So, what's up?"

"You heard Marquin sent me down to compel that female who knew a little too much about our kind, right?"

"Yup," Baylin said, and Saiden heard him cracking open a can. He didn't even need to be there to know it was some foul-tasting energy drink with enough caffeine to send even a sloth into overdrive. He never understood how his brother could drink those things when vampires naturally had plenty of energy. It was like Baylin wasn't happy unless he was literally vibrating.

"Well, there was a hitch."

"A hitch?"

"Yeah. I tried to compel her and..." The words lodged in his throat. He really would have rather told his brother in person. In their world, this was pretty much epic level news, and it deserved more than a phone call. Given the givens, though, he had no choice.

"...and I couldn't."

The silence coming from the phone lasted for so long that Saiden had to check to make sure the call hadn't disconnected.

"Say something," he urged, sitting up ramrod straight in the car. It was killing him not seeing Baylin's reaction. He wanted his brother to be happy for him, but there was also a certain bone-deep sadness that hit when someone else found their mate and you were still waiting. He felt it himself more than once among a few acquaintances, but thankfully the couple had never been one of his own cadre. He couldn't imagine the soul crushing agony of having a newly mated pair living just down the hall from him.

"I am so fucking pissed," Baylin started.

Saiden cringed. He couldn't blame his brother. He should have been prepared for this.

"...that you aren't here right now so I can give you a massive freaking hug!"

A tidal wave of relief washed through Saiden, and he collapsed back into his seat.

"You're not upset?" he asked.

"Only that you told me over the phone, you jackass. Why aren't you here? I want to meet her. Is she amazing? I bet she's amazing. And I know she must have the patience of a saint to put up with you."

Laughing, Saiden pictured Cora's flushed face during her ranting earlier. "You might think that, but it's pretty much the opposite. And not the main reason I called. I need you to help me out with something, and you're not going to like it."

There was another bout of silence before Baylin asked warily, "What is it?"

"There's a slight problem with Cora. Well, two problems if I'm being honest, but only one you can help with. You know how Marquin sent me down here because you found her script with our secret? That's what she does for her career by the way, she directs horror flicks, and she's unnervingly passionate about it. You and I both know the film has to be stopped and the script destroyed, but the problem is that she's, well, let's just say she's less than willing to cooperate. I need you to hack her phone, her laptop, anything you can find and destroy all traces of it. Make sure to find anybody she's shared it with also."

"Dude," Baylin started, and Saiden could practically picture the judgmental face his brother was making right then. "You want me to go behind your mate's back and kill her dream? That's not a great start to a relationship, you know that right? It's been a while for you, but females still tend to frown on deception."

Saiden rubbed his face, exhaustion starting to weigh on him. "I'm well aware, and it kills me to ask this of you, but she's refusing to halt the movie."

"That doesn't make any sense, though. I'm guessing you haven't turned her yet since none of the fam is with you to help, but you'd think she'd be on board with protecting our kind since she'll be in just as much danger here soon."

Saiden sighed. "Yeah, that's the other problem I have."

"Oh? Don't tell me it gets worse?" Baylin asked, taking a slurp of his drink.

"She doesn't want to become a vampire."

Saiden really hoped his brother had a good protection plan on his computer because if the wet, sputtering laughter was any indication, he was going to need it.

# *Chapter Eighteen*

## Cora

"Five more minutes," Cora muttered when Jinx prodded her in the back. She nestled deeper into the covers that were wrapped tightly around her, cocooning her in a soft warmth. The gentle poke hit her lower back again, and she groaned. Didn't Jinx know how rarely she slept? What reason could she possibly have for waking her up?

Cora cracked one eye open, and the second immediately followed suit as her brain registered that she was not, in fact, in her own bedroom.

Everything came rushing back in, and she groaned again. She didn't know how he did it, but the sonofabitch had gotten her to fall asleep. It couldn't have been drugs; she didn't eat or drink anything yesterday beyond a power bar from her own purse. What magical voodoo did he do to knock her out?

Despite her best attempts, she really couldn't maintain her anger with him, though. Judging by the bright light streaming in through the faded hotel curtains, she'd slept through the night. She hadn't done that in well over a year.

She debated closing her eyes in an attempt to slide back into sleep—because if her body was willing then why fight it?—when she felt the subtle poke again. It was at that moment she realized she was not alone in the bed. And more specifically, her bedmate was snuggled up tight against her back with his strong arms wrapped around her midsection.

Cora shifted ever so slightly to confirm her fear then leapt out of the bed screaming. Scrambling away at nearly vampiric speeds, she crashed into the desk chair.

"Fucking hell," she cursed as the chair flew backward, taking her with it. She was mere inches from slamming into the floor when she was scooped up into Saiden's arms and deposited softly back on the bed.

Where she stayed for about two seconds before leaping to her feet and glaring at him.

"What the hell was that?" she barked, pointing at the bed as if there was any doubt what she was referring to.

He didn't even have the decency to look ashamed. He ran a hand through his hair, the long strands on the left side looking adorably messy from sleep, and gave her a lopsided grin so at odds with the harsh lines of his face.

"What the hell was what?" he asked with an innocence that had to be feigned. Not even an ancient vampire could be that naïve.

"You, on the bed with me, and... you know," she sputtered as her brain went on vacation and took her ability to form coherent thoughts with it.

"I'm afraid I'm still confused. I asked you to sleep, and you did. I told you I wouldn't bite you, and you aren't missing one single drop of blood in your perfect veins. I even kept my clothes on." He glanced down at his boxers. "Mostly. But you couldn't expect me to sleep in jeans. That's just cruel. I did keep my shirt on which seemed to be your biggest concern last night."

She gaped at him, her jaw hanging wide open. "Your shirt? That's what you think I'm concerned about? Your fucking shirt?"

He cocked his head, analyzing her like a strange new specimen. "What else would you be upset about?"

"That!" she screeched, pointing at his rather impressive morning erection that was barely contained by his underwear. Hell, if he moved the wrong way, the tip would pop out, and she'd never be able to look him in the eyes again.

He glanced down at himself, then let out an exaggerated sigh, but she couldn't tell if it was real or not. He picked his jeans up off the floor and gave her a wry smile. "I know, I know, it seems rather underwhelming, but you don't need to tease me about it. I haven't fed in a couple days, so I'm a bit lacking on blood for it to reach its normal size."

She didn't think her mouth could hang open any wider and yet... He considered that underwhelming? Less than usual? What the hell was normal for him, a freaking anaconda in his damn pants?

*Focus, Cora,* she chided herself. The more she thought about his manhood, the more she was able to visualize it and... Shit. She wasn't focusing at all. In fact, she was considering once more the benefits of throwing all her self-imposed rules out the window and giving in to what would most likely be a life-altering experience. She had limited time to be wild, so why not be crazy and indulge just once? Surely her no sex rule didn't apply when the guy looked like a Greek god.

She was half a heartbeat away from succumbing when she remembered that she was the one in charge, not the demanding little kitty in her panties that practically purred as it begged to be stroked by Saiden.

Shaking her head, she fixed her fiercest glare on him, which in comparison to his standard expression was about as intimidating as a mouse glaring down a tiger.

"I don't care about the size of your... your... you know."

His brows knit together, and he glanced down at the prominent bulge in his pants.

Was he honestly upset that she didn't care about his size? Freaking fragile male egos. Vampire or human really made no difference.

"I only care about the fact that it's awake and was clearly trying to get to know me!" Cora finished, her voice reaching a level of screechy that hurt even her own ears.

Saiden threw up his hands in protest and leaned back against the desk. "I wasn't attempting to take advantage while you were sleeping, Cora. I would never do that. I'm guessing you haven't woken up next to very many guys, though, because this is just biology. It always rises before I do."

She didn't know if she should be more upset that he basically called her inexperienced at sex—which was somewhat true but completely irrelevant—or the fact that he was so cavalier about what happened.

"And why did it wake up next to me? And by it, I mean you. Why weren't you on your side of the bed?"

He gave her a wolfish grin. "I don't recall that being part of the negotiations."

She racked her brain for memories of the night before. Okay, technically he only promised that he would leave her alone if she was still awake, and technically she had fallen asleep, but still...

"You said no seduction, so I figured no touching was implied."

His grin widened. "Then it's probably a good thing that you're a director and not a lawyer."

That did it. All the embarrassment, frustration, and indignation coalesced into a ball of pure rage that exploded inside her.

Stalking over to him, she hauled back her arm and punched him right in his devilishly handsome face.

"Fucking hell, that hurt!"

Wait, that should have been his line. So why was she the one rubbing her aching fist while he stood there clearly fighting the urge to laugh.

"Vampire," he remarked plainly, pointing at his chest. "Do I get props for letting you hit me though? I debated whether I should catch your fist, but it seemed like you needed to vent some of that pent up aggression."

*Do not punch him again*, she commanded herself while trying to ignore the throbbing in her hand. *It will only make things worse.*

Since any kind of physical retribution was out of the question, she resorted to what was basically her only option—shouting. "You freaking asshat! You are an ass with another ass as a hat. That is what you are."

Wow, that was embarrassing. Her brain really needed to return from the tropics because she couldn't even insult him properly.

Since she was still filled with righteous indignation, she got up in his face and continued her litany of grade school put-downs.

"You are the rudest, most arrogant, most disgusting, pig-headed—"

And before she could finish her insult that was undoubtedly headed nowhere eloquent, he grabbed her by the arms, hauled her tight against his chest, and kissed her.

# Chapter Nineteen

## Saiden

*Well this is a better use of that sassy mouth,* was the first thought that hit Saiden's mind as he pressed his lips firmly against Cora's. The second thought was less of a thought and more of a feeling as her taste swept through his brain and short-circuited anything resembling civilized cognition. He gripped her tighter, savoring the feel of her soft breasts against his chest, and his tongue darted out to beg entrance to her mouth. He was pretty much reduced to caveman level thinking.

*Want... Need... Mine!*

He couldn't even remember the last time he lost control like that and succumbed so completely to his arousal. Maybe it was spending the night breathing in the essence that was Cora. Or maybe it was some part of the mating bond screaming that she belonged with him. Either way, he needed her desperately, so he sent out a plea to Lilith that Cora wouldn't push him away. He would never force himself on anyone, let alone his mate, but he would need a six-hour cold shower if she rejected him right then.

Cora went stiff in his arms, and he waited to see if pleasure or pain would be the theme for his day.

She melted into the kiss, a tiny gasp slipping out of her, and right then he could have died a second time as a very happy vampire.

He seized the opportunity to seek out her tongue with his own, testing her interest in where things were headed. She tasted like berry-flavored sunshine, and he knew then that nothing else would ever be as delicious as her. He couldn't stop his fangs from lengthening inside his mouth or his cock from lengthening inside his suddenly too-tight jeans.

Every ounce of blood left his brain and fled south to his nearly painful erection. He ground his hips into her, craving the friction of her body against his and cursing whoever invented denim for making it so damn thick.

Her tongue tangled with his, and he could feel the stiff peaks of her nipples through the cotton of his t-shirt.

*More*, he thought, his head growing dizzy from the scent of her. He needed more of her body that he could touch and taste. Needed more of her skin against his own. Needed more of her soft whimpers as she sank into his arms.

Gripping her shoulders, he spun around to press Cora into the wall, his hand snaking up behind her so she didn't crack her head.

"Cora." Her name slipped from his lips on a moan, and his free hand slid under her shirt, seeking out those taught little buds. She arched her back against him, and he took the movement as an invitation to dip his hand beneath her bra, cupping the ample breast that perfectly filled his palm.

*So soft and warm*, he thought as his fingers circled her nipple, and his tongue demanded to take their place.

He began peppering kisses down the side of her neck as he rolled his hips rhythmically against hers, a mere taste of how good they would feel together if the clothing disappeared. He picked up the pace when she clutched him tighter, desperate to hear all the naughty little noises he could tease from her.

His other hand slid down to the waistband of her leggings, hovering right at the edge to see if she would deny him or grant entrance. When her hands tightened in his hair, and a tiny shiver ran down her spine, he let his fingers dip inside her pants to slowly begin the trek toward the bliss that awaited.

He was less than an inch away from the tiny bundle of nerves that would allow him to bring the most intense pleasure to his mate, when she seized up in his arms and cried out in pain.

That small, agonized noise hit him like a fire extinguisher, dousing his arousal and bringing his erotic pursuit to an abrupt end.

Moving at vamp speed, he leapt away from her, concern flooding him that he might have done something wrong. Harmed her in some way. He didn't taste any blood to indicate he nicked her with his fangs, but something had clearly flipped her switch from ecstasy to agony.

His eyes swept over her body as he took in her rigid posture, the slight twitching of her arms and legs as if she'd been electrocuted. Had he caused that?

*Damn it*, he cursed internally. He knew he shouldn't have kissed her. He hadn't meant to take that leap just yet when she was still so uneasy around him, but he hadn't been able to control himself. She was just so damned cute when she got all puffed up and fierce. And her insults were so adorably innocent, he couldn't stop himself.

Now he was paying the price for his lack of restraint. He couldn't bear the look of pain on her face as she leaned against the wall, twitching.

He took a tentative step forward. "Cora, what's happening? Did I hurt you? I know I shouldn't have kissed you without asking, but I just—"

"Shut. Up." Cora gritted out, and the words came out slightly slurred as if her tongue wasn't working properly.

Lilith help him, had he caused some kind of allergic reaction? Or maybe he was wrong and one of his fangs did slice into her. If she thought he'd been about to feed, then that might explain her unexpected shut down.

He watched her carefully for any signs of what was happening, and a few seconds later her body went slack and slumped to the floor. He caught her before she hit the hideous yellow carpet and eased her carefully to a seated position. Backing away, he perched on the bed and kept a watchful eye on her, waiting for any indication of what she needed or how he could help. He couldn't believe how badly he'd fucked the whole situation up. He kissed her one time, and she had a seizure.

Maybe he really wasn't good for anything other than causing pain.

"You can stop looking at me like I'm a leper," Cora said quietly after what felt like an hour of awkward silence.

"I'm not," he protested, wondering how she could have possibly come to that conclusion.

Cora stood up cautiously as if she didn't trust her own legs then walked over to her bag. She pulled out a change of clothes and headed toward the bathroom.

"Wait," he called out before she could shut the door. Was she just going to get dressed and act like nothing had happened?

He jumped to his feet and strode over to where she hovered just inside the bathroom, her small hand turning white as she clutched the door frame tightly. Bracing his hand on the door so she couldn't shut it in his face, he demanded, "Talk to me, Cora. What was that?"

"A mistake," she mumbled, refusing to look him in the eyes.

A flash of anger surged through him. "Like hell it was," he growled, capturing her chin and forcing her to look at him. "As far as I could tell, it was anything but a mistake right up until you started shaking."

He paused and squeezed his eyes shut for a second, forcing his breathing to slow and his frustration to dissipate. He might not know what just happened, but he did know anger was the wrong emotion for right now. Whatever she was dealing with, she didn't need his temper on top of it.

So much for playing it cool.

"Tell me," he asked, more subdued than before. "What did I do wrong?"

Her eyes shuttered, and all the rigidity left her body. Resting her forehead against the half open door, she whispered, "Nothing." Then added, "And everything."

She wasn't making any sense. "Cora, I—"

"Save it," she interrupted. "I don't want to talk about it. Just don't do it again. I'm going to take a quick shower, and then we can hit the road, okay?"

There was so much pleading in her eyes, he could do nothing but nod and step back.

Slowly, she shut the door, and moments later he heard the shower turn on.

Staring at the slab of wood that stood between him and his mate, he couldn't help but wonder if at some point in his very long life he managed to piss off a gypsy or a witch. Only someone with a curse hanging over their head could manage to fuck things up as badly as he just had.

# Chapter Twenty

## Cora

Cora didn't say a word for the first hour of their drive through Northern California. Thankfully, Saiden took his cue from her and remained quiet as well, though she could practically feel him itching to say something from the driver's seat. The silence was awkward, a heavy palpable feeling in the air, yet neither of them broke.

For as quiet as it was inside the car, her mind was the complete opposite. It felt like she was standing in the eye of a storm that threatened to smash her to bits with one wrong move. Or one wrong word.

She just couldn't stop thinking about that damn kiss. About how her body had melted into him without a thought or hesitation, as if she knew on some deep biological level that they were meant to be together.

When they kissed everything just felt...right. Like finally finding a place to call home after a lifetime of searching. The moment his lips touched hers, she forgot about everything and everyone. There was only him and her and the spark between them.

Which was complete insanity for so many reasons that she could probably write a self-help novel about it.

'101 Poor Decisions - Vampire Edition.'

The very fact that he was a vampire would comprise half the damn book. Sure, he seemed decent with his 'you'll be safe with me' lines, but that was the opening scene to like half of the horror movies she'd watched. When someone says you will be safe with them, you will undoubtedly NOT be safe with them.

Jinx loved to remind her that movies were not real life, but Cora was always quick to disagree. Movies taught you so many valuable lessons if you just knew which ones to watch. The romance crap where things end happily ever after? A steaming pile of bullshit with a side of lies. Films like Cabin in the Woods where everyone dies in the end because they made poor life choices? Now that's more like it.

And the reality was that even if he wasn't a vampire, and even if he didn't want to wipe her brain to eliminate her pièce de résistance movie script, getting involved with him was still a bad idea. He was going to live for hundreds of years, and she was... not, to say the very least.

If that single kiss was any indication, she had to stop things from progressing any farther. There was no rehab for the drug that was Saiden, and one more taste might lead to a lethal addiction. If her muscles hadn't seized up when they did, she would have been lost to him like the damsel who went to investigate a strange noise and was never heard from again.

Except she wasn't a damsel. She was a director. Which meant she was in charge of how things were going to play out, and there was no sex scene in her movie.

In her film, the vampire was the villain. He preyed on the young ingénue and killed her in the end because that's what happens when you think the snake is just cute and misunderstood. You get bit.

There was no way in hell he was getting his fangs in her. Literally or metaphorically.

Now if she could just convince her brain to stop playing their kiss on fucking repeat, it would be a lot easier to move on to the next scene.

Minutes later she got her wish, just not in any way she would have chosen.

There was a loud thunk that shook Cora in her seat, and suddenly the McLaren was limping along the freeway.

"Fuck," Saiden grumbled, the first word to penetrate their silence. He carefully guided the vehicle onto the shoulder and killed the engine.

"Please tell me you didn't just pop a tire."

The vein bulging in Saiden's forehead as he gripped the steering wheel hard enough to break it was answer enough.

"Okay, this is fine," she said. "I mean, you have a spare right?" Saiden's eyes slid over to her, and Cora felt her stomach bottom out. "Please tell me you're not the only person in the world who doesn't have a spare."

"This is a McLaren, Cora. It's designed for speed which means it doesn't carry anything that might weigh it down."

"What kind of tiny dick energy is needed to drive without a spare tire just so you can go an extra two miles per hour?" Cora squawked, scrubbing her hands over her face. "And why didn't you see this coming? I thought the whole purpose of your 'not-spidey sense' was to avoid situations like these?"

"First off," Saiden gritted out. "We both know my dick is anything but tiny."

*Don't blush. Don't blush. Don't blush.*

It was inevitable, though, and she blushed like a schoolgirl as the image of his bulging boxer briefs flashed in her brain like a neon sign.

"And secondly," Saiden continued, either not noticing or politely ignoring her bright, tomato-red face, "my ability only triggers for dangerous situations. Not minor inconveniences."

"I wouldn't exactly call this minor," Cora argued.

"When compared to what it's normally used for, I would say this is most definitely minor."

She hated that he had a point, but what was the purpose of having cool vampire powers if you still had to change a tire like any old mortal?

"So, what now? We have to wait for a tow truck to take us to a shop to get it fixed? That's going to take hours!" Cora banged her head against the seatback. She'd *wanted* to get this trip over with quickly before their kiss at the hotel. Now she *needed* to get it over with. Her ability to make smart decisions could only withstand so much when she was near Saiden and his damn animal magnetism. It was like feminism never existed when he was around.

"Relax, we're not going to wait for a tow truck."

Cora's tension did ease a little at the lack of concern in Saiden's words. He sounded so sure of himself that he probably had some vamp way to fix things.

"It would be pointless to call one anyway. No shop around here would even carry the right tires for a car like this."

And Cora's shoulders promptly ratcheted back up. "What do we do, then?"

"I think there's a patch kit in the trunk. I just need an air pump and that should tide us over until we get home." Saiden pulled out his phone, and a second later he held it up triumphantly. "There's an auto shop only twenty miles away."

"Are you serious? That'll take forever to get there and back on foot."

Saiden just raised one eyebrow.

"Right, vampire. You can run there in what? Two minutes?"

He rolled his eyes. "I'm not that fast, Cora. I can probably make it in five to ten, though. The question is whether I can trust you not to run off while I'm gone."

She flung her hands out, indicating the wide stretch of empty land on either side of the freeway. "Where am I going to go? The last town is miles behind us."

Of course the McLaren chose a barren stretch of I-5 to break down on. Couldn't have been helpful and waited til Stockton to crap out. Her best option for escape would be hitchhiking, but she was under no misconception that he wouldn't be able to immediately find her again.

Something sparked low in her abdomen at the thought of him hunting her down, but she promptly dismissed it. Now was not the time to unlock any new kinks that she absolutely should not be exploring.

Saiden's eyes flicked back and forth between hers, evaluating, then he sighed and said, "Fine. But lock the doors and stay inside. I'll be right back."

With that last ominous warning, he hopped out of the car and took off down the side of the freeway in a blur.

It took less than six seconds before she completely lost sight of him.

Pulling out her phone, she checked her e-mail to see if she had any new demo reels to watch, but the well of desperate Hollywood actors seemed to have already dried up. She started to send a check-in text to Jinx but decided against it. That would only lead to her friend asking questions, and Cora didn't want to lie to Jinx any more than she already had.

Tossing the phone back in her bag, she leaned down to start massaging the muscles of her legs. The little episode that morning was having lingering effects, and she really needed to do her usual morning yoga stretches. Asking Saiden for time to do that before they left would have required talking, and if they hadn't popped a tire, she would still be giving him the silent treatment.

Cora peered out the window and noted there was plenty of space between the McLaren and the fenced off field containing a herd of rather vocal cows. She could at least get a few good stretches in before Saiden returned if she was able to concentrate long enough to block out the mooing and the thrumming traffic whipping down the highway.

Stepping from the car, she wiggled her legs a little then eased forward into a front bend. She could barely reach the tops of her shoes lately, and today was no exception.

Fifteen minutes later, she was halfway through her series of sun salute poses, when the rattle of an engine in desperate need of repair broke through her carefully curated serenity.

"Need some help, miss?" a voice called out over the din of high-speed traffic.

She returned to standing and glanced over her shoulder at the guy making his way toward her from a beater truck that was likely older than her father. The owner of the junk heap clearly cared as little about his physical appearance as he did his truck's based on the hairy gut hanging over his oil-stained jeans. The prominent beer belly was only partially covered by a gray t-shirt that had probably been white when he bought it.

"One hell of a nice car ya got here," Beer Belly commented, running his dirty hands along the exterior.

"Can you not touch that? The owner would freak out if he saw." Flashes of Saiden picking the man up and flinging him into the field traipsed through her brain.

Beer Belly paused his exploration over the hood, ran one hand through his greasy brown hair, and flashed her a grin. "The owner, huh? That not you?"

"No. It belongs to a friend." Beer Belly's grin was starting to unnerve her so she added, "My boyfriend, actually. He's an MMA fighter. Super violent. Probably a good idea to keep your hands off. He'll be back any second too, so I don't need any help. Thank you, though."

To Cora's pleasant surprise, Beer Belly's smile dropped away, and he took a step back from the car. She always thought she was an awful liar, but maybe spending time around her cast was paying off if he believed her story.

Any delight she felt faded when Beer Belly didn't retreat to his junker, and the emotion promptly morphed into fear when he sauntered around the front of the car toward her side.

"Ya know," Beer Belly mused, his eyes crawling up and down her body in a way that felt much more lascivious then when Saiden did it. "A girl as pretty as you shouldn't be out here all alone. How's about I keep you company until this boyfriend gets back?"

Cora edged away, trying and failing to keep the unease off her face. "That's not a good idea. He can be really crazy sometimes. You should really leave now for your own safety."

Beer Belly matched her retreat with his own leisurely steps forward. "Ya know, I don't think you got a boyfriend. I think you're waiting for a tow truck all by your lonesome. So how's about I make you a deal? You give me the keys without a fuss, and I'll leave you be. If you decide you want to fight me... Let's just say I got a knife in my truck that can be very convincing."

Cora glanced around frantically, briefly calculating the odds of someone seeing her and stopping to help. The cars all raced by so fast that she doubted anyone who even noticed what was happening could slow in time to pull over.

"There aren't any keys," she replied, hoping she could stall long enough for Saiden to get back. She despised the damsel in distress mentality, but taking up kickboxing had never been in the cards for her. She made a mental note to keep a knife on her from now on if she survived.

Beer Belly cocked his head. "No keys? All cars got keys, darlin'."

"Not this one," she protested. "There's only a fob and a button in the center console. Take a look for yourself."

She honestly didn't think her obvious ploy would work, but she wasted no time bolting off into the field the second Beer Belly turned to look inside the window. Pumping her legs as fast as possible, she raced toward the half fence just off the side of the road. Likely designed for keeping the cattle in, it appeared low enough she could vault right over it and continue toward the tree line where she might be able to hide.

She was seconds from slamming her hands down on the wooden railing to propel her jump when a blood-curdling scream filled the air. Her steps faltered at the unholy sound, and she plowed straight into the fence, only to bounce off and land flat on her back. A position that gave her the perfect view as Beer Belly went flying through the sky and crashed to a heap ten yards into the field, the sickening crunch of bones breaking audible even over the traffic.

Cora scrambled to her knees and whipped her head around.

Saiden was back.

# Chapter Twenty-One

## Saiden

Saiden was going to murder someone. Most likely the cashier at the backwoods auto shop who didn't know his ass from a hole in the ground.

"Just one second, sir. I think I got this," the barely post-pubescent teen muttered as he tapped at his phone. "Sorry for the wait, but we just got this new square reader to take credit cards. Good thing you didn't show up last week when we were still cash only."

Saiden tightened his grip on the edge of the counter, only letting up when he felt the wood start to crack under the might of his frustration. His mate was alone on the side of the road. Everything in his body screamed to return to her, to just take the damn air pump and mail the store a check later.

The last of his patience dissolved right as the kid grinned.

"There it goes. You're all set, sir. Have a good day." The cashier handed over Saiden's credit card along with the air pump.

The effort required to not grab the item and blur out of the store was nearly herculean, but Saiden managed to control his steps until he rounded the small shop. After confirming there were no prying eyes around, he took off, pushing his vampire speed to the limit so he could get back to his mate.

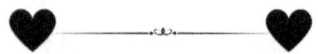

Saiden stared down at Cora, regretting his decision not to crush the man's neck with his bare hands.

When he'd arrived back at the car just in time to see his mate fleeing the advances of what could only be referred to as a hog in human form, something inside him snapped. Every bit of his training that told him to never kill a human vanished as the intensity of Cora's heartbeat thundered in his ears.

He'd reacted without thinking, dropping the air pump and snatching the man by the belt and back of his neck. The portly, unwashed assailant had to be pushing 350 pounds, but in a vampire's hands he was little more than a football begging to be tossed. Saiden was only too happy to oblige, so he'd sent the man spiraling toward the field and the cows he so clearly belonged with if smell was any indication.

Now that he was seeing his mate up close, he wished he could have watched the light drain from the man's eyes as he left this world, felt the body go slack in his arms, firm in the knowledge that this waste of space would never harm another female.

Kneeling down beside Cora, he slid one hand under her neck and the other under her back to help her up to a sitting position. He took in her red face, pounding heart, and mussed hair. Her shirt was torn near her stomach, and a glance at the fence confirmed a bit of fabric dangling from a nail. Thankfully, he smelled no blood to indicate that more than her clothing had fallen victim to the rusty bit of metal.

Which was the assailant's only saving grace. If his mate suffered even a single scratch, he would paint the freeway from here to Sacramento red with the man's blood.

He brushed a sweaty lock of hair out of Cora's face. "Are you okay?"

Cora ran her hands over her chest and arms before nodding. "Yeah, I think so." She glanced toward the field at the unmoving pile of grease-stained denim. "Is he okay?"

Saiden cocked his head. Only his mate would ever ask about the wellbeing of a man who just tried to do Lilith knows what to her. "Do you want him to be?" He assumed she was worried about the guy's injuries, but if it was the opposite and his mate wanted that asshole's heart on a platter, then his only question would be 'raw, fried, or al dente?'

Cora dropped her eyes, but not before Saiden saw a brief flash of indecision. "I don't want you to get in trouble for murdering someone," she answered.

Saiden knew there was more to it than concern about him getting arrested. His Cora had a little streak of vengeance in her. Good. That would serve her well if she became a vampire.

*When! When she became a vampire*, he corrected himself.

"I appreciate you looking out for me," he said, helping her to feet. "After this morning, I thought you might be perfectly happy if I was lying unconscious next to him. Which is what he is, by the way. Just knocked out. I'm not a doctor, but I believe he'll survive."

If Saiden was being honest, the man probably had 50/50 odds. As soon as they hit the road, he'd put in an anonymous call to the authorities. The last thing he needed was more death on his hands, regardless of how deserved it was.

Cora dusted off her pants with one hand, the other clinging to

Saiden's elbow. She took one step toward the car, and her legs wob-
bled.

He had her swept up into his arms before she could even think
about moving another inch.

"Hey!" She smacked his chest and wiggled in his grasp. "I can walk,
you know."

"No doubt. But I'm not taking any chances." He carried her back
toward the McLaren, shifting her weight into one arm so he could
open the door and gingerly set her down inside. He knelt on the
ground next to her, the low riding car at a perfect height to meet her
face to face. "What happened?"

Cora sighed, leaning back in the chair. "It's nothing. The guy
wanted your car, and when I wouldn't give it to him he decided to take
it. Along with me."

Saiden's fists clenched at his sides, causing him to briefly wonder if
he could break his own hand from the tension he felt. "Why did you
even get out? You should have just ignored him. The custom windows
are nearly bulletproof."

"I was sort of already out of the car when he arrived," his mate
admitted, refusing to meet his eyes.

*Don't yell. Don't yell. Don't yell.*

"And why were you out of the car when I specifically told you to
stay put?" he asked with thinly veiled outrage.

Cora's eyes snapped to him as if remembering that she was a fire-
cracker capable of exploding.

"Because you don't tell me what to do, Saiden! Did I make a mistake? Yes. But it was my mistake to make. It's my life and nobody else
gets a say in my actions, least of all a vampire I just met who's literally
trying to destroy my career."

Saiden flinched. She wasn't wrong, but did she always need to be so contrary?

"I didn't think that extended to common sense," he replied dryly.

"Well, it does," she shot back.

"You're going to get yourself killed acting so reckless all the time," he growled, unable to control his frustration.

Cora folded her arms defiantly. "Then so be it. But it'll be on my terms and no one else's."

"You should have let the asshole take the car," he argued. "What were you even thinking? No hunk of metal is worth your life, Cora. Not by a longshot. Or better yet, next time you could try listening to me and just stay inside where it's safe!"

The barely audible crack and sharp jolt of pain through his clenched fist confirmed that yes, his earlier thought was accurate. He could break his own hand. The gentle throbbing actually helped calm his anger, though. It gave himself something to focus on besides the aggravating creature before him who might have died if that cashier had taken even two minutes longer. It was a thought he wouldn't let himself linger on since he wasn't willing to waste twenty minutes waiting for even more bones to heal.

"You can chill out, Saiden," Cora replied icily, "because there won't be a next time. So just fix the tire, and let's get this whole thing over with." Closing her eyes, Cora settled back against the seat in a clear 'we're done talking' posture.

Saiden picked himself up and went in search of the discarded air pump. Finding it a few feet away, he dug out the patch kit and set to work.

Despite his years of accumulated knowledge, it would still take him some time to get the tire fixed decently enough that it would last the rest of the way. They had about five hours of driving left, and he highly doubted the next stretch was going to be any more pleasant than the last one, even without another blow out.

Lifting the car a few inches with his good hand, he spun the tire to find the damage while his thoughts drifted back to Cora's reaction. What kind of woman was terrified by him driving a few miles over the speed limit, yet let herself get caught unawares by strange men twice in less than twenty-four hours? Granted Saiden would never have harmed her, but Cora didn't know that when he ambushed her alone in a parking lot.

*"It'll be on my terms and no one else's."*

Her words rang in his ears. There was more to Cora than he was seeing on the surface, and if he was going to figure out a way to convince her to turn, then he better find a shovel and start digging.

Fast.

# Chapter Twenty-Two

## Cora

It took almost an entire hour for Cora to stop replaying her encounter with Beer Belly. All she'd wanted that morning was to stop reliving her kiss with Saiden. Now, she would gladly hop back into that memory if it would shut out the man's disgusting grin that kept invading her thoughts. The way he leered at her, his intentions painted on his face, still made her skin crawl, and she'd never forget the pure fury that had been pulsing off Saiden when he arrived. The way his nearly black eyes shone with the promise of death. The way his muscles flexed under his tight shirt, as if his entire being was itching to tear the man apart. The way his fists clenched so tightly that she was pretty sure a bone popped at one point.

She'd never been the type to go for alpha males, but damn there was something to be said about knowing a guy was willing to murder on her behalf.

It was those emotions that had inevitably reduced her to child-like stubbornness when confronted about her stupidity. It was much easier to get pissy than admit to herself that she'd never felt more alive—or more aroused—then the moments right after he saved her.

But why? That was the one thing she couldn't suss out. Why would he almost kill a man for her? And why had she seen so much fear hidden behind the fury in his eyes when he examined her. She'd honestly thought he would have been more worried about his car than her. She was just a package he had to deliver to Marquin. Sure, their kiss had been incredible, but not even she was naïve enough to believe her kisses could reduce a guy to violence. Where had all his rage come from?

It was that question that filled her head the rest of the way up north, only fading once she spotted an unremarkable green sign for Fall River Mills, and Saiden steered the McLaren off the main highway. Cora had been surprised when they took a right on Highway 299 out of Redding, not even realizing there were actual cities in the northeastern corner of California. She hadn't been too far off the mark since they hadn't passed anything that resembled more than a pitstop town for over an hour.

"Why the heck would you live all the way out here?" she asked, finally breaking their unspoken standoff over who would speak first.

"A number of reasons," he replied, slowing their speed to something more reasonable as they passed by an unimpressive collection of small-town shops and diners before turning off onto a smaller, unpaved road. "Privacy being a key one in addition to the local airstrip that is a necessity at times. Plus it's much easier to fend off questions from only a handful of residents as opposed to a larger city." A somewhat whimsical expression briefly rolled across his normally stoic face when he added, "Also, it's quite beautiful in the fall."

Cora gazed out the window, taking in the mixture of oak and pine trees that filled the landscape as they passed over a rushing river. "It's a shame I won't get to see it," she said honestly. The trees glowed in the golden light of the setting sun, and she could only imagine how much more beautiful it would be if the green boughs were mixed with yellow, orange, and red.

"Right, of course. You won't be here in a few months," Saiden replied, and something about his tone gave her pause. As if he didn't agree with his own statement.

They continued along the secluded dirt road for another ten minutes before a massive gate set into a huge stone wall prevented any further progress. She craned her neck to get a look at what lay beyond, but the blockade was too high to see anything other than a handful of towering pine trees poking up in the distance. Spreading out to the right and left, the wall disappeared into the thick forest leaving her unable to even gauge the potential size of their property.

Saiden pulled the McLaren up to the black wrought iron barricade and glanced up at a camera in the corner. A few seconds passed, and the gates began to glide open without so much as a whisper.

Beyond the entrance, a paved driveway split the dense woods, and Saiden easily directed the sports car down the narrow drive and past a few random small outpost buildings.

Embracing the twinge of excitement in her belly that she was actually going to get a look at the inner workings of a vampire's home, Cora was starting to regret the hours of silence that should have been spent asking questions.

Were they about to pull up to some crazy gothic castle? Who all lived here? He didn't have a harem of wives or blood servants, did he?

That last thought killed her budding sense of excitement, and it was reborn as a spike of fear as the damned reality of her situation struck her. Not only had she allowed herself to be taken into the literal middle of nowhere without telling a soul where she was going, but she was also about to blindly walk into a vampire's lair.

Surely he wouldn't have bothered with the whole charade just to turn her into some kind of thrall, right? He didn't need to go all the way to Los Angeles to find hot chicks to trap in his dungeon. Not that she considered herself a hot chick by L.A. standards, but she wasn't exactly homely either.

The car hummed along the drive for a couple minutes more before a break in the tree line appeared before them. As the car crested the small hill, Cora couldn't help but stare wide-eyed at the compound in front of her. Home was nowhere near the right word, nor would she even resort to belittling the residence by calling it a mansion. A small part of her was disappointed it wasn't a castle, but realistically she shouldn't have been surprised. America was woefully lacking in ancient gothic architecture.

Saiden pulled the car up the curved driveway in the courtyard of the main building and stopped in front of a set of imposing double doors. Cora was pleased to see that the entrance at least had a hint of dramatic flare to it with elaborate carvings set into thick slabs of black wood. The rest of the building, however, was all modern and sleek with lots of angled lines and not nearly enough windows. Taking up more space than a football field, it looked like a cross between a multi-million dollar mansion and a multi-million dollar prison.

Saiden stepped out of the car, and she followed suit, trying not to gape open-mouthed at the structure in front of her.

The doors pushed open, and one of the most beautiful women Cora had ever seen came running out. Tall and lithe with silky black hair cascading over the perfectly smooth, light brown skin of her shoulders, she could easily have been a model. Heck, most of the models Cora had met couldn't hold a candle to this woman's delicate elegance.

And all Cora wanted to do was kick the goddess in the cooch when Saiden ran up and threw his arms around her. Not a thought she should be having since this new person had done nothing wrong, but the way her body pressed up against his made Cora angry in an explicable way.

Saiden hugged the woman for a long moment, then released her to press a quick kiss to her cheek.

"I haven't seen you in forever," the beauty said, slapping him playfully on the shoulder with amusement twinkling in her almond-shaped eyes that spoke of a Pacific Island heritage. "You spend months on the road hunting rogues, and the only time you stop by home is when I'm gone? You could have waited for me in Seattle. I've missed you, Sadie."

*Sadie?*

"I know, I'm sorry," Saiden replied, appearing legitimately chastised as he shoved his hands in his back pockets. "All these new rogues are running me ragged. I was barely here for twelve hours, and I spent most of that time cleaning my weapons and sleeping. I didn't know I'd have to leave again before you got back."

"Yeah, Marquin told me about your special mission, which is the only reason I'm not kicking your ass right now. Though, we all thought you'd be back a bit earlier." She gave him what looked like a playful shove, but there had to be vampire strength behind it judging by how he stumbled back a step.

Was this his wife? Lover?

Cora had a feeling vampires were probably more open about their relationships, but would he have really tried to sleep with her if he had a woman at home?

Maybe. She still wasn't convinced he wasn't the villain in the story. She might be imposing human morals on a being that had none. Or at least not any that resembled hers.

Deciding she was done playing voyeur, Cora stepped forward. "Uh, hi," she said awkwardly, flinching when the woman whipped her head around.

The female swept her eyes up and down Cora for a long second then grinned.

It was incredible, that smile, like someone turned on the sun, and Cora's completely heterosexual body reacted in an intriguing way that she would have to revisit later.

"Is this her?" the woman asked Saiden in a gushing tone with enough bubblegum quality to her voice that made Cora think more cheerleader and less creature of the night. The cute white tennis skirt and baby blue tank top probably weren't helping either.

Saiden nodded, and the next thing Cora knew she was being swept up in her own hug. Any lingering doubts that this woman might be a vampire were squeezed out of her. Vamps really took bone-crushing hugs to a much more literal place.

"Hey, Tressa, you might want to let her go," Saiden cut in. "Cora is turning a rather suspicious shade of purple."

Tressa laughed and relaxed her hold, giving Cora a chance to take in a deep lungful of air.

"Tressa, is it?" Cora asked, stepping back and rubbing her sore arms. "It's, uh, nice to meet you. I'm glad to see Saiden's prickly demeanor isn't representative of all vamps."

Letting out a twinkling laugh that Cora could practically feel dance along her skin, Tressa said, "Oh, gosh no. Sadie here is a special kind of grumpy."

Saiden cringed. "I thought I asked you to stop saying that, Tress."

She turned and gave him a wide-eyed look of complete innocence. "Say what? Grumpy? If Cora has spent more than five minutes with you, she already knows." Tressa winked at Cora over her shoulder.

"That's not what I meant, and you know it. I've begged you repeatedly for over a hundred years now to not call me Sadie."

"Aww, is Sadie-Wadie worried about his image as a big bad rogue vampire hunter?"

"I'm remembering now why I left before you got to Seattle," Saiden replied, rubbing his face.

Tressa laughed again and grabbed Cora's arm, tucking it in her own as she led them toward the front door.

"Well, I'm going to show Cora around and find her some dinner since I doubt you fed her. You are more than welcome to stay here and practice your brooding, 'mkay, Sadie Bear?"

A groan came from behind Cora, and she didn't even try to fight the smile that spread across her face. She would need to remember his little nickname the next time he pissed her off.

Tressa leaned in and whispered conspiratorially, "Never let another vampire know if something annoys you. When you live as long as we do, you have to entertain yourself somehow." Standing up she called out, "Isn't that right, Sadie Cakes?"

A laugh bubbled up and out of Cora when Saiden's groan took on a louder, more pained quality. Much like when she kneed him in the nuts yesterday.

"So, are you his wife or girlfriend?" Cora asked hesitantly as they approached the front doors.

She really wanted to like Tressa. There was an infectious quality about the woman's energy that seemed to wrap around Cora and pull her in, like a planet orbiting a sun, unable and unwilling to break away. It wasn't enough to shake the jealous feeling that still gnawed at her insides, though.

Tressa halted abruptly, and it was only her strong grip on Cora's arm that prevented the otherwise inevitable face plant on the cement steps.

Glancing over at the now statue-still vamp, Cora couldn't quite place the look on Tressa's face.

Shock? Confusion? Disgust?

Seconds ticked by as Tressa evaluated Cora before throwing a glare back at Saiden. All teasing vanished from her voice as she asked, "Saiden, why does Cora think I might be your wife?"

Cora turned around to look at Saiden who thrust his hands back into his pockets in what she was beginning to recognize as his go-to posture when uncomfortable. His ability to shift from 'potential serial killer' to 'teenager struggling to ask a cute girl to prom' was doing funny things to her insides. Things that were getting harder to ignore or dismiss.

"We didn't really talk much on the drive here," he said with a shrug.

Tressa's eyes widened, and she looked back and forth between Cora and Saiden. "She doesn't know?"

Saiden shook his head, and Cora waved a hand in front of Tressa's face.

"Know what? Kinda feeling a little out of the loop here."

Something unspoken passed between Saiden and Tressa, but eventually the dark-haired beauty turned back to Cora and forced a smile.

The only problem with having a grin that lights up a room, though, is that it becomes glaringly obvious when it's no longer authentic. Saiden was hiding something from her, and Tressa wasn't happy about it.

*Well, that makes two of us*, Cora thought.

"No, I'm not his wife," the pretty vamp clarified, tugging Cora up to the top step. "I'm his cousin, more or less. But forget about him for now. Let's go find you some dinner."

As Cora allowed Tressa to pull her into the home, she tried not to think too much about how much relief swept through her from hearing they weren't together. She shouldn't care if Saiden had a girl already. It didn't impact her in the slightest.

Not. One. Bit.

She glanced back to see him lingering just outside the door, his eyes fixed intently on her, and it sent a delicious shiver down her spine.

Sooner or later, she really needed to start believing her own lies.

# Chapter Twenty-Three

## Saiden

Saiden hung back as Tressa dragged his mate into the house, mentally kicking himself for not forcing the conversation that morning. Or at any point during the painfully quiet road trip. He told Baylin last night that he was going to talk to Cora about the concept of mates before they arrived, but that plan took a header out a ten-story window when they kissed, and she made it clear she never wanted him to touch her again.

What was he supposed to say after that? *I know you don't want me to kiss you, but the universe knows that we belong together so any chance you'll get over that in the next few minutes?*

Trudging up the steps, he couldn't help but recount all the things he wished had gone differently. His violent outburst on the side of the road being at the top of the list since that had likely done him no favors in trying to convince her that vampires weren't soulless killers. At this point, Tressa was his best bet to get Cora onto Team Vamp. Nobody could spend time with his perky cousin and honestly believe that she was evil. Like all of his kind, she had a dark side, but for the most part she maintained a sunny disposition that could hopefully sway Cora's opinion about him. Then maybe he could casually bring up the topic of mates and judge her reaction.

Pausing just outside the door, he debated his next step. This whole process was supposed to go so differently. Normally when a vampire met his mate it was instant attraction on both sides. No seduction. No games. No convincing. Just an immediate feeling that the person in front of you was the other half of your soul, and no one else would ever come close.

Of course he had to be mated to the one female who would fight the process every step of the way. Maybe this was Lilith's idea of retaliation for hunting down his own kind. He'd assumed never having a mate was his punishment, but this was starting to feel like a much more painful kind of torture.

Heading into the main building, he swept his eyes around the parlor and spotted Cora and Tressa standing in front of the bank of floor to ceiling windows. He was pleased at the mesmerized look on her face as she gazed outside. It *was* the best view in the compound to take in the enormity of the estate grounds as it perfectly showcased the rolling hills, quaint babbling brook, and large meadow out back that often had a small herd of grazing deer. With the sun just dipping below the horizon, it made the whole place seem peaceful and so at odds with the oversized building most of them called home.

Marquin modeled the compound after the Palace of Versailles originally, but a couple decades ago he got on a modernization kick and resurfaced the entire exterior. Saiden thought it looked like a Swedish prison, but at least the inside still boasted the classic baroque style he'd grown rather fond of over the past century or so.

The sharp staccato clacking of heels on marble resounded through the long hall to his left, and Saiden turned to see Raven stalking toward him, her short hazelnut hair swishing violently around her face, fury blazing in her eyes.

Making a snap decision, he sped down the hall to intercept her before whatever she was so enraged about spilled into Tressa and Cora's conversation. Raven was normally a reserved individual, but when she got in one of her moods she could become the epitome of the evil vampire Cora was so convinced they all were.

Grabbing her by the arm, he yanked her into the library and slammed the door shut.

"Are you out of your Lilith-damned mind, you sodding wanker?" Raven barked. Much like Baylin's drunken Irish brogue, Raven's British accent always became more pronounced the angrier she got, and right now she had the Queen's English dialed up to an eleven. Although Saiden doubted Raven's expletives would be much appreciated in the royal palace.

"That depends on what you're referring to this time," he answered, sinking down onto a soft burgundy chaise. He'd been afraid he was the one responsible for her current acidic demeanor. It was the last thing he needed right now, but since what he did need was her help, he'd have to pacify her first.

"I'm referring to how badly you've bollocksed things up with Cora. First Baylin tells me that you have him hacking into her life behind her back, and now I find out you haven't even told her that she's your blooming *mate*? Why exactly does she think she's even here?" Raven folded her arms and glared at him like a mother admonishing a kid who got into the cookie jar.

Despite Saiden being a few decades older than Raven, something about her posh, upper crust demeanor and the sharp pantsuits she always wore made him feel like a child in comparison.

"I take it Baylin was spying on us again?" He should have known his brother would have tuned into the cameras the second he pulled up. Baylin probably sent a text to the entire cadre before he even set foot in the house. He loved his brother, but the guy gossiped like a twelve-year-old girl.

He forced himself to meet Raven's accusing stare. "I told her that I'd been sent to compel her because of her script, but since I failed I would let her plead her case to Marquin. I said he would ultimately decide if she could keep her screenplay or not."

The appalled look on Raven's severe face was almost comical.

"Please tell me that you are joking."

Saiden shook his head.

"And how exactly do you think she's going to react when she finds out the truth?"

He jumped to his feet and threw up his hands. "Not well, I'm sure, but what was I supposed to do, Raven? I honestly didn't even think she was my mate at first. She smelled off, and it screwed with my head. Was it wrong to lie? Probably. I just assumed that once I got her here Marquin would solve the dilemma, and I'd never see her again. Once I realized who she was to me, it was a little late to change my story."

Raven's face softened but maintained a healthy amount of skepticism. "And siccing Baylin on her?" she asked warily.

Saiden shoved his hands into his back pockets. "One of the first things she told me when I revealed that I was a vampire was that she didn't want to become one of us. She won't drop the film willingly, so I had no choice. At least until we can find some way to convince her... I have to protect our kind."

Raven's irritation fully drained from her eyes as she sat on the chaise and pulled him down beside her, patting his leg sympathetically. He would have preferred her rage. Pity was almost more than he could handle right now.

"You've really screwed the pooch here, haven't you?" she asked in a way that was less question and more statement.

"Most likely."

"She's going to be devastated when she learns the truth."

"Most likely."

"And she'll never trust you again."

"Most likely."

Saiden flung himself backward on the chaise, wondering when exactly he went from feared enforcer to distraught, lovesick teenager.

"I know she feels something for me," he told his cousin, his eyes tracing the intricate wainscoting in the room so he could avoid her pitying expression. "When I kissed her she kissed me back, and it was more than just a peck on the lips. It was filled with passion and desire. She *felt* the connection, I'm certain of it."

"Then what happened?" Raven prodded.

"Then she just seized up and said to never do it again. There's something wrong with her medically, but she won't tell me about it. I'm floundering here, Raven. She writes these horror films where the vampires are demonic villains and therefore believes that I'm just trying to sink my fangs into her neck. I'm afraid that I'm not exactly doing a good job of convincing her otherwise. Killing rogues is easy. Understanding women is... let's just say I need all the help I can get."

Raven sighed. "You know I'll do everything I can for you, Saiden." She regarded him with haunted eyes. "I owe you my life, even if some days I wish you hadn't saved me. I know how important this is. How important your mate is."

They both fell silent for a moment. He knew this would be hard for his cousin, and it meant the world to him that she would help.

"What do I do now?"

Raven pursed her lips. "Well, what have you done so far?"

Saiden described his time with Cora, and his efforts to sway her thoughts in a more positive direction about him.

His cousin let out a rather undignified snort of derision in response. "Are you telling me that you honestly believed the best way to woo her was to put on a Magic Mike show? Bloody hell, Saiden, she's your mate not a sorority girl. No wonder she doesn't trust you. Women have instincts like you wouldn't believe, and your little striptease told her more than enough about your 'intentions.' Did you honestly never once consider just telling her the truth? That every vampire has a mate, and she is yours?"

Saiden frowned. He had considered that approach but rejected it for being too absurd. Maybe another woman would have gone all moon-eyed at those words, but not his girl.

"You don't understand. She's not like other women."

Raven waved her hand dismissively. "Yes, yes, every vampire thinks his mate is a truly special and perfect creature."

Saiden barked out a harsh laugh and sat up. "That is definitely not what I said."

At Raven's quizzical look, he continued. "She's... difficult. It's like anytime I say or ask anything she has to clam up or turn belligerent. Whenever I get close to her I can't decide if I want to kiss her or strangle her."

"I imagine it doesn't help that you have considerably more experience with the latter than the former."

It was depressing how accurate her assessment was.

"I'm not charming or suave, Raven, but even if I was, she would likely be immune."

"I think you are underestimating modern day women, Saiden. Have you ever considered that charming and suave is not what she's looking for? That perhaps you should just be yourself?"

"Yeah, right," Saiden grunted, dropping his head into his hands.

"I highly doubt she's looking for an emotionally stunted, anti-social, violent, centuries-old vampire who prefers solitude and spends most of his time hunting and murdering other vampires because it's the only thing he's good at."

"Well at least you can add self-awareness to your list of personality traits," she teased in a rare display of amusement.

"Ha. Ha. Ha," he replied dryly, failing to see the humor in his situation.

"You have a soft spot for your family," Raven pointed out. "Perhaps you can bond over that?"

"She doesn't speak to her father, has no siblings, and I'm pretty sure her mom is deceased."

"I see," Raven mused. "You really do need more hobbies, Saiden."

"I'm well aware, thanks." He rose from the chair and held out a hand for his cousin. "I'm pretty sure Tressa will have Cora in the dining room shortly. Will you just go meet her and maybe talk to her for a bit? I'll take any advice you have."

Raven shook her head. "It's not going to be that easy, Saiden. You can't learn what makes a person tick in one meal. You have to put in the effort. I'll meet her tomorrow after she's settled down a bit. Let's not overwhelm the poor girl from the start."

Raven spun and strode toward the door. Pausing at the threshold, she tossed back, "I can give you one piece of advice, though. No more naked seduction. You're an attractive male, Saiden, but you don't want her to see you as a fling. Keep it in your pants, alright?"

Saiden nodded even as certain parts of him bristled at the suggestion. He could do it, though. He could fight the pull of the mating bond and keep his hands to himself.

After all, nobody ever said love was easy.

# Chapter Twenty-Four

## Cora

Cora hated to admit it, but she was having a really good time. She'd wanted to scream when Tressa first mentioned that Marquin was away from the manor and unable to speak with her, but since she had already resigned herself to staying overnight in Vampland based on how late they arrived, she gave in and allowed herself to enjoy the opportunity of a lifetime—seeing the inside of a vampire's lair. They referred to is as a compound, but that term was decidedly less exciting.

Tressa spent an hour showing her around the main house, indicating a few of the other buildings on the grounds that she might be interested in checking out in the daytime. Apparently they even had an Olympic-sized swimming pool somewhere. It was all a little strange given that she wouldn't be there long enough to see much of anything, but hanging around Tressa was relaxing. Like a friend she'd known for years.

Following the intriguing vamp through what felt like an endless number of hallways, Cora found herself fascinated by some of the history of the place. The original structure had been built in Lithuania, but Marquin had it torn down brick by brick to be reassembled here when he immigrated to the States. Tressa let slip that they even had a legit dungeon on the lower level, but despite several minutes of begging, she wouldn't budge on taking Cora down there. She said it was not appropriate for 'Girl Time.' Clearly Tressa had been hanging out with the wrong kind of girls.

The dungeon was promptly forgotten, though, as Tressa brought her to an expansive dining room. It wasn't the ornate chandelier or twelve-person table that caught her attention, but the massive spread of food. There had to be ten different dishes of pasta, ham, and roasted vegetables.

She didn't know how long she stood there gaping before Tressa nudged her from behind.

"Help yourself," the friendly vamp urged. "We prepared it all especially for you."

"For me?" Cora squeaked. "Why?"

Tressa directed Cora to a seat and handed her an empty plate. "We don't have many visitors, so our chef doesn't often get a chance to truly showcase his skills. I think he got a little overexcited."

"Talk about an understatement," Cora murmured, heaping a scoop of fettuccine alfredo on her plate. The motor lodge they'd stayed at had a poor excuse for a continental breakfast, and she hadn't wanted to ask Saiden to pull over for lunch. Her stomach was more than ready to dive in. It was five bites too late before she considered the fact she was eating food that could be laced with anything.

"Don't worry, it's not poisoned," Tressa remarked when Cora hesitated with her fork halfway to her mouth, sniffing the bit of pasta. "We're not going to hurt you. Besides, Saiden wouldn't have bothered bringing you all the way here just to murder you, so feel free to relax. Make yourself at home."

The words should have been comforting, a reassurance of her earlier assessment when she had come to the same conclusion, but the mention of Saiden and murder tossed her back into the memory of Beer Belly flying through the air, and the sickening crunch that followed. She knew full well what Saiden was capable of when he was angry. Could she ever really be safe when surrounded by vampires?

"She's telling the truth." Saiden's voice cut through her thoughts, and he strolled into the dining room to take a seat across from her. "Nobody here is going to hurt you."

Cora glanced between Saiden and Tressa. The two vampires couldn't be more different in terms of demeanor and appearance, but they both appeared equally genuine in their assertions of her safety.

The tension in her shoulders eased, and she continued shoveling food into her mouth, pausing every few seconds to remind herself to slow down. It was dangerous for her to eat fast as she knew all too well.

"Did you enjoy your tour?"

Cora looked up at Saiden's question and nodded. "This place is incredible, and I've never seen anything so grand before. It's hard to imagine people just living here like a regular home. It feels more like it should be a museum or something."

"Wait until you see the gardens tomorrow," Tressa gushed. "They're so gorgeous you could die."

Cora dropped her fork, cringing as a loud clatter echoed through the dining room.

"Not funny, Tress," Saiden said to his cousin who looked mortified by her own comment.

"I'm so sorry," she stammered. "I didn't even think."

Cora evaluated the panicking woman for a second. The spike of anxiety she'd felt from the offhand comment seemed to slither away, and she chuckled. "It's okay. I had the same reaction yesterday when I told Saiden he drove like a bat out of Hell."

"Well, that is true," Tressa pointed out, taking a sip of her water.

A silence settled over the table as Cora finished up the last of her pasta. "Aren't you guys going to eat?" she asked, eyeing the empty plates in front of Tressa and Saiden.

"I already ate," Tressa blurted out at the same time Saiden said, "I'll eat later."

"Okaaaay," she drawled, feeling a slight itch of discomfort when she remembered just who she was sitting across from. She should be thankful they weren't indulging in what was likely their standard dinner.

Cora set her fork down and stood up from the table. "I'm starting to feel a little stuffed. Could one of you show me where I can crash tonight? I promise I'll be out of your hair as soon as I talk to Marquin. He'll be back tomorrow, right?"

"Oh, definitely," Tressa said. "But let's worry about tomorrow later. Now, about your room..."

"I'll take her," Saiden interjected, pushing back from the table. "She will be most comfortable in the East Hall."

Tressa and Saiden exchanged a quick look, and Cora was starting to get annoyed at all the unspoken conversations those two had. Either they knew each other very well, or Saiden was hiding a telepathic ability because Tressa just settled back into her seat, seemingly happy to let Saiden take over.

Cora traipsed after Saiden as he led her around a few corners and down a long hall toward the east side of the mansion where he paused in front of a closed door.

"Listen, about your room..." he began.

"I'm sure it's fine," Cora interrupted. "As long as there's a bed, I'll survive. It's just one night."

"Right. Ummm... Okay then." Saiden pushed open the door and

gestured for her to enter.

Stepping over the threshold, Cora tried to keep the disappointment off her face. The room was so... boring. She'd honestly expected something a bit more gothic and dramatic, something that fit the rest of the home's antique interior. This room barely had anything on the lame beige walls, and the basic blue curtains looked like something she could buy on the cheap at any discount thrift store. One blocky dresser squatted next to a bookshelf loaded to the brim with classic hardbacks, and another sat next to an oversized bed that took up the majority of the space. With a deep mahogany frame and black comforter, it was the only thing even remotely dark and mysterious. So much for gaining inspiration from her surroundings.

"I know it's small, but..."

"It's fine," Cora cut him off, setting her overnight bag on the dresser beside the bed. "Like I said, all I need is a bed."

"I'm sorry it's not very nice. This room hasn't exactly seen a woman's touch. There's a bathroom through there," Saiden said, pointing out a door off to the side that she missed in her initial inspection. "Towels are in the cabinet if you want to shower. If you need anything, just open the door and yell. The rooms are somewhat soundproofed, so you should at least have some privacy here."

Cora nodded as she sat on the edge of the bed and waited for Saiden to close the door. When he leaned against the frame with no obvious intentions of leaving, she asked, "Is that all?"

He ran a hand through his hair. "Yeah, I guess. Unless you need anything?"

Cora eyed him, the casual way he rested with one arm on the frame, his muscular body taking up the entire doorway. The man wore death like an old familiar jacket, yet seeing him so relaxed made her want to dive inside and unravel his darkest mysteries. Cora could practically see herself getting up from the bed and crossing over to him. She imagined wrapping her arms around his neck and pulling his lips down to hers. She imagined forgetting for just one night all the things that were wrong with her, and all the reasons being with Saiden was a bad idea.

Unfortunately, her head had always been stronger than her heart. Okay, it was actually something a bit further south that was making demands, but rationality still won out.

"I'm good," she said quietly. "Thanks, Saiden. For everything. Not just the white knight routine this afternoon but bringing me up here at all. It means a lot that you're willing to let me have a chance. I'm guessing you don't do this often."

"Never," he confirmed, backing out of the room. "Good night, Cora."

"Good night, Saiden."

The door closed with a soft click, and she debated locking it behind him. Not that a lock would stop any of the vampires in this house. It might deter Saiden from showing up in the middle of the night for another cuddle session, though.

She got up and strode across the room. Placing a hand on the door she pressed her ear to the frame, listening for any noises on the other side. When she felt confident that Saiden wasn't still hanging around, she locked the door then headed into the bathroom to wash her face of all the grime from a day spent on the road.

Once she felt clean again, she shucked out of her clothing and pulled on a loose tank top. She should have packed pajama shorts, but her brain hadn't even considered how long this little trip might take. She'd just have to settle for sleeping in her panties and hoping there were no midnight visitors.

Flinging herself into the middle of the massive bed like a child making snow angels, Cora relished the softness of the mattress. She hadn't slept in a bed this incredible since she moved out of her father's place. If she was going to be stuck here, she could at least focus on the positives.

Crawling to the top of the bed, she snuggled under the covers and nestled back into the pillow.

It hit her the moment her face grazed the soft fabric, like someone just opened a doorway to heaven. She buried her nose in the pillow, taking another deep inhale to confirm her suspicion.

Yep. There was simply no denying the scent that coated every inch of the bed.

Leaping up, she crossed over to the nearest dresser, yanked open the top drawer, and stared down at the pile of familiar black boxer briefs.

That son of a bitch.

This wasn't a guest bedroom. This was his room.

She slammed the drawer shut and plopped back on the bed. She was completely and utterly screwed. If she demanded another room after saying 'anything with a bed was fine', then he would want to know why. A question for which she had no believable lie.

Slipping back under the covers, she hoped maybe her senses would have adjusted to the smell and dismissed it, like when you visited the home of someone with pets.

No such luck. It was like someone bottled the essence of Saiden and soaked the entire bed in it. Every pillow she tried overwhelmed her with his scent. She still couldn't quite pinpoint exactly what it was he smelled like, though. It was familiar, sweet, and extremely comforting. Yet at the same time, there was also an underlying scent of something wholly male and delightfully musky.

She couldn't resist; she wrapped the blankets around herself as her thoughts drifted back to their kiss. To how he made her light up with desire.

The memory played out in high definition, plastered to the backs of her eyelids. It would be smarter to pull out her laptop to focus on anything else, but she didn't want to be smart anymore.

Remembering what Saiden said about the soundproofing, she decided that just for a few minutes she could let herself indulge in the fantasy.

Slowly, her hand slid down the length of her body and beneath the lacy waistband of her panties. Seeking out the throbbing between her legs, Cora let her mind fill with images of Saiden.

He had just saved her from the assailant on the side of the road, only in her fantasy, he didn't treat her like a fragile piece of glass afterward. Instead, he bent her over the hood of the McLaren and smacked her ass.

"I told you to lock the car, Cora," Fantasy Saiden growled. "Bad girls get punished."

"Saiden…" she moaned when strong hands yanked her leggings down, and thick fingers began to stroke between her legs, playing with her dripping pussy but never entering her. Teasing her, then backing off.

Night had fallen over the landscape of her mind, and not a single car passed by on the freeway. It was only her and Saiden and the pleasure he taunted her with yet refused to deliver on. Even in her fantasy, the man was aggravating.

Back in reality, her own fingers slid through her wet heat and circled her clit, matching Fantasy Saiden's movements.

"Do you want to come, Cora?" he purred in her ear. "Do you want me to make you scream?"

"Yes," she begged, rubbing her ass against the rigid length she knew could grant all her wishes.

A finger slipped inside her, and then a second one. She arched her back, encouraging him to move, but he held his hand still. The stretch was exquisite, yet nowhere near what she craved from him.

"Do you promise to be a good girl from now on and do what I say?" he asked, his breath tickling the nape of her neck.

"Yes," she cried, willing to offer up anything if he would just fuck her instead of fucking *with* her. "I'll be good. I promise."

With a deep, amused chuckle, Fantasy Saiden started thrusting his fingers in and out, while her own hand mimicked the speed in the real world. She drowned in his scent, and it was like she could feel him there with her. Right there. Driving her closer and closer to the euphoria she craved.

"In that case," he murmured, his tongue swirling over the shell of her ear, "scream for me, Cora." His thumb swiped roughly over her clit, and the pressure was the perfect amount to send her careening over the edge.

Inside Cora's mind, she shouted Saiden's name to the heavens in a declaration that felt like something had just been set free inside her. But in Saiden's bedroom at the back of the compound, only a small whimper sounded when her orgasm exploded.

Sweat cooled on her forehead as Cora lay on the bed, panting softly as the fantasy faded away far too quickly. Rolling over, she took another deep inhale of his pillow and groaned.

She really needed to leave first thing in the morning because resisting Saiden was about to get a lot harder.

# Chapter Twenty-Five

## Saiden

Saiden didn't even bother knocking on Baylin's door when he reached his brother's suite in the west wing of the compound. He just barged in, shouting, "Baylin, you in here? I've got a bone to pick you."

With the bedroom through an archway at the back, the expansive front room of Baylin's suite was wall-to-wall computers, monitors, and a stack of blinking boxes that Baylin referred to as servers.

Screechy death metal music blasted from massive speakers, making Saiden cringe. He never understood why Baylin listened to that garbage, let alone so loudly. With vampiric hearing he could play it at the lowest setting and still catch every word. Not that Baylin's harsh music had words. At least none Saiden could understand.

Sweeping his eyes over the room, they landed on his brother sitting at the security monitors, enthusiastically bobbing his head to the music between sips off a Red Bull.

"How dare you," Saiden growled.

Baylin swiveled in his chair, ran a hand through his wavy russet hair, and kicked his feet up on the desk as Saiden approached.

"How dare I what? Is this because I told Raven that you were home?

I figured you'd want her to know. Also, welcome back. Nice to see you too, bro."

Saiden glared at his brother, ignoring the sarcastic greeting. "You know that's not what I'm pissed about. You spied on my conversation with Tressa out front, then immediately tattled to Raven that I was keeping the mate thing from Cora. You could have let me speak to her first. Explain my reasoning before she fully engaged murder mode. You know how she gets about mates."

Baylin shuddered and tapped a button on his keyboard, silencing the pulse-pounding screams that were setting Saiden's teeth on edge.

"Yeah, I know," he replied. "But given you don't have a ton of time before Cora starts asking about leaving, I figured you'd want the cousins to get right to work on Operation Vamps Aren't Jerks."

Saiden groaned and yanked a blood bag from the oversized silver cooler at the back of the room. "Choose another name, will you? I'm not referring to anything involving my mate as Operation VAJ."

Baylin smirked. "I thought it was funny."

"Yes, hilarious," Saiden replied dryly. "And I thought I asked you to stop spying on me all the time. You really need to get a life, Bay."

"Nah," Baylin dismissed. "I'm good. I know how to find companionship when I want it, but otherwise I'm happy with my computers. Much less of a hassle than females."

"You're not wrong," Saiden muttered, jamming his fangs into the blood bag and sucking down the entire thing in three deep pulls. He tossed it in the trash and leaned back against the wall, far too antsy to sit down. "Since I know you've been watching everything, what do you think about Cora?"

"I like her," Baylin replied. "She's got sass. Way out of your league, though. Lilith was really shooting for the moon with this one."

"Tell me about it. This mating bond is screaming for me to go back to her, but I know she'll just kick me out if I try."

"Really? I thought you two..." Baylin waggled his eyebrows suggestively and made a few thrusts with his pelvis.

Saiden scowled at his brother's lewd gesture. "Not exactly. She freaked out when I kissed her, so I don't see anything else happening anytime soon."

"Why'd you put her in your room then?"

"Because it's the only place where I'm certain that you can't watch her." Saiden glared down at his snoopy little brother. He knew Baylin was a good guy and would never violate Cora's privacy, but he couldn't risk it. If Baylin so much as caught a glimpse of her getting undressed, he wouldn't be able to control his actions.

"Come on, you know I'd never do that," Baylin protested. "I might be digging through her entire life and monitoring everything she does and says online, but even I have my limits."

"I know," Saiden replied, trying to actively unclench his jaw. "It's just the protective urges. I've never felt anything like this."

"Yeah, Marquin warned me that you might be a little touchy. Well, more so than usual."

Saiden rolled his eyes. "Have you encountered anything useful yet?"

Baylin pulled up a file on his computer and scanned through it. "Nothing earth shattering. A few parking tickets. Decent grades in school. I'm still digging."

"Thanks, I appreciate it. Anything that might help me understand why she's so anti becoming a vampire would be helpful. Considering she's a fan of horror movies, you'd expect her to jump at the chance."

"Nah, only you would think that," Baylin said, closing the file. "The rest of us know people are more complex. Something you'd be aware of if you spent any amount of time around them."

"I spend plenty, thanks," Saiden replied, frost coating his words.

"Now if you don't mind, I'm going to go sleep on the floor outside my own bedroom just to feel close to my mate."

He pushed off the wall and headed for the door.

"Have a nice night," Baylin called, his words swallowed up by a fit of laughter.

Saiden stalked down the hall back to his room, keeping his steps light as he got closer. He doubted Cora would hear him given that the room was sound treated, but he didn't want to risk it. He had no believable lie for why he was going to be curled up on the floor like a guard dog.

He stopped outside her door and let his senses expand to take in the sounds inside the room. Not even soundproofing could block out vamp hearing if they were close enough, and surely it wasn't snooping if he was just confirming she hadn't tried to slip out the window. A flimsy excuse given their security system would have alerted them if that was the case, but an excuse nonetheless.

A tiny moan reached Saiden's ears, and his entire body stiffened, his cock more so than anything else. It was the same sound that had been playing in his brain on repeat ever since that morning when he had his hands on her body, his fingers dancing over her delicate skin.

What exactly was happening in his bedroom?

He pulled his senses away from the intriguing noise just long enough to confirm none of his family were in the East Wing. He didn't want anyone hearing the sounds Cora made. Not if she was doing what he hoped she was doing.

He'd never been so hard in his life, and all he wanted was to kick open the door and replace her hands with his own. She was his mate. He should be the one making her moan. His own hand started to drift toward the zipper on his jeans, but then he remembered where he was.

*Fuck.*

His eyes shot to the ceiling and scanned along the hall until they landed on the blinking device pointed right at his door. He flipped his brother—who was almost always watching—the middle finger, then ripped off his shirt to toss it over the lens. Jerking his phone out of his pocket, Saiden sent Baylin a quick text threatening to destroy every computer he owned if he so much as thought about coming over to fix the camera.

Keeping only half of his senses focused on listening for approaching footsteps, Saiden pressed his ear back against the door.

Cora's soft moans were still going, and he reached his hand down to rub at the painful bulge in his jeans. He knew what he was doing was wrong. Listening to her. Violating her privacy. Touching himself to the sounds of her pleasure. He should be disgusted with himself that he would stoop to such levels. And yet...

"Saiden..."

The hand that had been palming his cock through unbearably thick jeans froze at the sound of his name coming from inside the room. He had hoped it was him she was thinking about, but to have confirmation? To know his mate was on the other side of the door touching herself to thoughts of him. It was his undoing.

He wrapped his hand around the knob, ready to yank the entire door off its hinges to get to his woman. Whether it was the mating bond or just Saiden's own desire fueling his actions was anybody's guess.

The only thing that saved him in the end was the soft tap of approaching heels.

He dropped his hand from the door and flashed across the hallway, leaning casually against the wall as if doing nothing more than simple guard duty.

Tressa rounded the corner a few seconds later, and he blurred over to meet her before she stepped within earshot of Cora's room.

"Hey, Tress. What's up?"

His cousin eyed him suspiciously, her gaze briefly dropping to the erection still very obvious even through his jeans.

"I could ask you the same thing, Saiden. Bay told me you blocked one of his cameras?"

"Yeah, it just felt weird having surveillance right on her door. Privacy and all that."

Fuck, he was such a hypocrite.

"Right," Tressa drawled. "And you needed to remove your shirt for that?"

He shrugged. "Just used what I had."

"Okay then," she said with a knowing smirk, turning to head back the way she came. "Oh, Saiden? You might want to listen to your own words. If you think Cora might not like having a camera on her door, I doubt she would appreciate anyone listening in either. Just a suggestion."

Tressa disappeared around the corner, and Saiden slumped against the wall. He couldn't believe what he had been about to do. There was no doubt in his mind that Cora would not have responded favorably to his bursting in on her.

Shit. He had just come within seconds of blowing any chance he had with her.

Pushing off the wall, he headed toward one of the actual guest rooms. Mating bond or not, he simply couldn't sleep outside Cora's room. Not after their kiss. Not when he knew how much more could be happening. He'd just suck it up and maybe spend the night doing weapons inventory and maintenance. It was his least favorite task but guaranteed to be an effective distraction.

Right after he took yet another really cold shower.

# Chapter Twenty-Six

## Cora

Cora slept like shit. She'd really hoped that maybe something was shifting in her body after passing out so easily in the car and then again in the hotel room, but last night had been back to the usual tossing and turning. Not even the orgasm she'd given herself relaxed her enough to drift off. In fact, it might have made things worse. All she could think about afterward was how much better it would have been with Saiden's fingers instead of hers.

She'd felt like he was there at first, like she could sense his presence nearby, and it drove her wild. Then it faded, taking the relaxation that had accompanied her release along with it.

It was like her body craved him and nothing else would do. More than once she'd debated going in search of him just to see how he would respond. He'd made it clear he was attracted to her, but he also hadn't tried to make a move when they were alone in his room. It was only that reminder that kept her butt in the bed. On the off-chance that his interest in her had been a fleeting amusement, she wasn't about to risk her dignity by throwing herself at him.

She opted instead to let herself suffer all night long until birds outside began their morning song, and a knock on her door had her dragging her ass from the luxurious bed. She was surprised to see not Saiden but Tressa on the other side, holding a tray of croissants and orange juice.

"Breakfast?" the chipper vamp offered.

"Uh, thanks," she said groggily, taking the overflowing platter of pastries and setting it on the dresser. "You didn't have to do that."

"Sure, I did," she beamed. "You're our guest, and I thought you might enjoy a little room service."

"Thanks," Cora repeated, unsure of what else to say since her brain was running on zero hours of sleep.

"My pleasure. I'd love to show you the gardens after you've eaten and dressed. How about meeting me at the front of the compound in an hour? Does that work?"

Cora blinked, about to decline the perky vampire's offer when a tiny hint of warmth rolled through her brain. A smile tugged at her lips. Everyone here had been nothing but nice to her so far. Hell, she'd received better treatment here than she had at most hotels. Of course she could join Tressa on a morning stroll.

"I'm in," she said with a grin. "I'll meet you up front as soon as I'm ready." She paused, considering the long trek Saiden had taken her on last night. "Or I will if I can find wherever 'up front' is in this place."

"Oh, it's easy," Tressa insisted. "Take the last left at the end of this hall, followed by a right, and you can't miss it. You'll get used to the layout eventually. We all did. See you in a bit!"

Cora watched Tressa flounce off down the hall then returned to her room to snag a quick bite and a shower. The flaky croissant was so buttery and delicious that she completely forgot to worry about what Tressa had meant by 'eventually.'

Tressa hadn't exaggerated when she said the gardens were incredible. They must have gone on for acres, featuring some plants that Cora was pretty sure shouldn't be growing on this continent. Regardless, she allowed herself to get swept up in the magic of the beautifully manicured hedges, the flowers with vibrant colors, and the thick luxurious grass that had her tossing her shoes next to Tressa's so they could roam barefoot.

Hours later they returned to the house and were joined by a British vamp named Raven. Intense but still kind, the new woman seemed very keen on getting to know Cora which made little to no sense. Cora was a boring human, and these were vampires who lived multiple lifetimes and visited countless places. She could only imagine what they had witnessed. World Wars, the Industrial Revolution, not to mention they might have gotten to meet Bela Lugosi. How cool would that have been?

Her fascination made it easy to forget that they were dangerous vampires and not just slightly strange girlfriends she'd known for years. Currently they were lounging on a back patio, sipping chocolate martinis in the dappled shadows of oak trees, and it was all just so... normal. By the time she was on her second drink, she'd nearly forgotten about Saiden and the quasi-kidnapping.

"Thank you, Donna," Tressa said when a portly woman in her early sixties with more gray than brown in her tight bun placed a tray loaded with crackers smothered in brown paste on the table.

Cora wrinkled her nose at the smell. "As good as your taste in drinks is, your taste in snacks leaves a lot to be desired. What even is that?"

Tressa laughed. "It's chicken liver crostini. One of Saiden's old family recipes from Sicily. I can have Donna bring you something else if you'd like. I'm sure it's way past lunchtime, so you're due a proper meal."

Cora's belly rumbled, and she couldn't deny drinking martinis on an empty stomach was one of her less than stellar ideas. The two bites of croissant she had hours earlier weren't absorbing anything.

"I guess I could eat, and I'm open to just about any kind of food." She eyed the liver dish, wondering if it was worth attempting. "Well, almost any kind."

"Donna," Raven called, and the older woman reappeared as if by magic. "Would you bring our guest something a little more appropriate for a young American human? Thank you much."

Cora waited for the woman to leave then asked, "So does everyone here know that you're vampires?" The mansion had appeared empty when they toured last night, but she glimpsed a couple humans in the kitchen this morning, and Donna never seemed far from Tressa's side since they came back from the garden.

"Of course," Tressa replied. "This is our home. We don't want to hide who we are, and the humans who work for us would never betray our truth. In fact, most of them have lived here for generations. We pay them exorbitantly well, and they get to enjoy all the luxuries of this place. Plus, they all know whenever they are ready to leave that we'll simply compel the details of their time here from their minds and send them off with a generous severance package. They retain only the knowledge that we were excellent employers, and we would love to have them back should they ever want to return."

Tressa popped a cracker in her mouth as Raven added, "Donna was with us for nearly a decade when she was younger, then she left to become a concert pianist. She only returned once her arthritis set in.

You should ask her to play for you some time. She's still quite good."

"Yeah, I'll have to do that," Cora said, wondering exactly how long they planned to keep her there. She got the impression it would be a quick conversation with Marquin then back to her life one way or the other.

Shit, Marquin.

She knew she kept forgetting something. Damn delicious chocolate martinis making her all fuzzy headed. Cora couldn't even remember the last time she'd gotten drunk since she usually called it after a single beer. Alcohol wasn't recommended with some of her medications, but for some reason when Tressa had suggested cocktails on the patio she'd agreed without hesitation.

"Hey, so do you guys know if Marquin is back yet? I'm supposed to plead my case to him." Cora looked around as if Marquin might be hiding behind one of the Grecian statues that flanked the French patio doors.

The look Tressa gave Raven was so fast that Cora almost missed it.

"What?" she asked warily, afraid her good time was about to come crashing to a halt.

"Marquin is going to be away from the compound for a bit longer," Raven said, taking another sip of her martini.

"What?" Cora barked, jumping to her feet then immediately regretting the action when the world tilted sideways. Gravity dropped her into the chair before she could fight back.

"It's okay," Tressa soothed, and Cora blinked at the raven-haired beauty across the table.

*Heh. Raven wasn't the raven-haired one*, she thought, chuckling to herself.

Wait, this situation wasn't funny. Angry, that's what she was.

Except she couldn't manage to keep a firm grasp on her anger. It just kept slipping through her fingers like fine sand.

"So, where is he," she asked. Before one of them could answer, Donna reappeared carrying a plate loaded with mini burgers and breaded cheese sticks. All other thoughts vanished from Cora's mind when the smell of fried food reached her.

Bless Donna and her vamp-loving heart.

Cora grabbed a slider and tore into it. Through a mouthful of food, she proclaimed, "Donna, you are a goddess."

The older lady just gave her a wan smile then disappeared back into the house.

Swallowing the tiny burger, she grabbed two of the cheese sticks. You'd think she hadn't eaten in days with how viciously she attacked the appetizers, but there was just something so enticing about comfort food that it was practically begging to be devoured in seconds.

Cora shoved a hunk of melty mozzarella into her mouth, and the taste of fried bread had just hit her tongue when, to her complete horror, her throat seized up.

Gasping for air, she clawed at her neck, but things only worsened when her face began to spasm, her bottom lip pulling uncontrollably to the left side.

*Not now*, she pleaded. *Please, not now.*

"Are you alright?" Tressa's concerned face swam in Cora's vision and someone, probably Raven, pulled her chair back from the table, giving her space to stand.

Not that she was able to get up. In fact, Cora knew that hunching over was the exact opposite of what she was supposed to do, but she just couldn't fight the rising panic that crippled her body.

"What's wrong with her?" Raven demanded, appearing next to Tressa. Both women kneeled in front of Cora, their faces painted with worry and confusion.

"I think she's choking," Tressa replied, her voice laced with trepidation. "I don't know how to do the Heimlich. I think you're supposed to pound on their chest? Or is that CPR?"

"Oh, for Lilith's sake," came a soft voice from somewhere behind Cora.

A pair of arms slid around her midsection and lifted her off the chair as if she were no weightier than an infant. Her unknown savior gave two sharp thrusts, and a chunk of melted cheese flew from her mouth to land smack in the middle of the liver crostini platter.

Between the alcohol and the nearly dying, Cora lost all sense of control over her body. She swayed and tilted in the breeze for a moment, then she was falling backward, the blue sky suddenly the only thing in her field of view.

She waited for the painful strike of impact, but her body made contact with the stone patio so gently that somebody must have laid her down. She remained there unmoving while the clouds above danced in and out of focus.

What was in that martini? Had they drugged her? Or was she that much of a lightweight now?

Her eyes blinked shut for a second, and when they reopened, there was a new face staring down at her. The woman glowed with a holy light, her long blonde hair creating a frame of gold around the edges of Cora's fuzzy vision so all she could see was smooth pale skin, icy blue eyes, and rosy lips.

*An angel*, Cora thought, finally succumbing to the fatigue that dragged her off unwillingly into a deep sleep.

# Chapter Twenty-Seven

## Saiden

"Someone's crankier than usual this morning," Baylin commented as Saiden stole the blood bag straight out of his hand. "And here I thought that you covered up my camera so I wouldn't see you sneaking into Cora's room."

Saiden grimaced. "No. As much as I wanted to, Raven said no more seduction."

"And you listened?"

Ignoring his brother's shocked face, Saiden just shrugged. "Nothing I was doing worked. So yeah, I listened. I left Cora alone last night."

Baylin let out an amused snort. "Well, that explains the four hours of footage I found this morning of you in the weapons locker. What happened to sleeping on the floor outside her door?"

"I was going to but then..."

Saiden's hand that was gripping the blood bag squeezed tighter when he thought back to the sounds that had been coming from his room, and he forced himself to relax before the bag popped and re-decorated his brother's room in red. "I just changed my mind. Okay?"

"Fine, fine," Baylin defended, throwing up his hands in protest.

"No need to get testy with me just because your testes didn't get any action."

"Baylin," Saiden growled, his voice infused with the very real threat of violence.

"Aaand I'm shutting up about that." Baylin mimicked zipping his lips. "Care to share where you've been all morning then? I saw you dip out at dawn."

"Tressa said she was going to spend time with Cora, and I would just 'mess shit up,' so I took the McLaren to Joe in town. He's going to order a new tire, but it'll probably be a few weeks."

Baylin gasped in mock surprise. "Whatever will you do in the meantime?"

"Drive one of the other ten vehicles? Not all of us are attached to our toys like you are." Saiden tilted his head at the bank of high-end monitors.

"Hey now," Baylin protested, running a hand gently over the nearest computer. "These aren't toys. These are my babies. Not to mention incredibly useful for keeping an eye on your girl."

"Please tell me you haven't been spying on her all morning."

His brother grinned mischievously. "Not *all* morning. Only the last hour or so after Raven joined in. Like I was going to miss that show. And look, they're having a wonderful time."

He gestured to one of the monitors, and the moment Saiden's eyes landed on the screen his heart skipped at least three beats.

Laughing. Cora was laughing.

"Turn on the sound," he whispered, mesmerized by her brilliant smile as she chatted with Raven and Tressa.

Baylin obliged, and Cora's giggle filled the air of the massive tech room. The sound stirred something inside him. His mate was happy, and just the sight of her laughing made him... elated. As if her joy was his joy. He'd never felt such absolute contentment before.

Sinking back into the oversized black gaming chair beside Baylin, Saiden punctured the pilfered blood bag with his teeth. He stared transfixed at the monitors as Cora sipped martinis on the back patio while he sipped his O+ in Baylin's room. She was on the completely other end of the compound, yet he felt her as if she was right there with him. His hand drifted down to rest on his right thigh, wishing he was caressing hers, and something warm bloomed in him when Cora mirrored the action on the screen in front of him. Almost as if she could feel his hand on her.

"Tell us more about you, Cora," Raven said on the monitor.

Saiden watched his mate bite her lip before responding. "Like what? I'm just a human. Aren't we all kind of the same to you?"

Tressa leaned forward, placing a hand over top of Cora's. "Not at all. We want to know everything about you, Cora. How did you get into directing horror movies? It must be a fascinating way to make a living."

Cora chuckled, and Saiden felt another jolt of happiness race through him again. "I mean, I wouldn't call it making a living," she said. "More like accepting poverty status to pursue a dream. I graduated film school a couple years ago and directed a few shorts that did decently on the festival circuit. I'm currently working on my first feature with my best friend Jinx..." Cora paused and glanced around. "Which, by the way, I think I'm supposed to talk with—"

"Jinx, you say?" Tressa asked, cutting Cora off. "What a fun name. I bet she's wonderful."

Saiden held his breath, hoping Raven's tactic would work. The last thing he needed was for Cora to start pressing about speaking with his sire. As soon as that happened, she would realize the whole thing was a ruse.

"Did you warn Marquin last night?" he asked his brother, relaxing only when he saw Baylin nod out of the corner of his eye.

"Yeah. He was pretty upset that I was the one who told him you found your mate, but once he calmed down he agreed to play along. He's going to stay out of sight for now, so you have some time."

Saiden fought back the guilty feeling in the pit of his stomach. Marquin was the closest thing he had to a father, given that his human one abandoned their family shortly after his sister was born. He really should have been the one to share the amazing news. More than anyone, Marquin worried about how disconnected Saiden had become, and the fact that he found his mate probably thrilled his sire. He'd need to carve out time to go explain everything.

After he watched his mate just a little bit longer.

On screen, Cora's face scrunched up for a second then relaxed back into something peaceful and easy. It was an expression Saiden had seen on countless human faces over the years.

*Lilith bless you, Tressa*, he thought.

"Jinx is like my sister," Cora gushed, once again smiling and chatting happily. "She's also my assistant director, but we grew up together like family. She lost her hearing in a freak accident when she was twelve, and we started watching horror movies more and more because there wasn't as much dialogue as other kinds of films. Plus she said the silence often made it creepier. The more we watched, the more we fell in love with the genre and wanted to make our own."

"I'm sorry to hear your friend went through that," Tressa said. "That must have been hard for her to adjust to."

Cora took a sip of her drink then nodded. "It was. Her left ear eventually healed enough that she could pick up some sound, and she has a hearing aid that helps. She's not the type to let anything keep her down, though, and we make a great team. She's amazing at details like scheduling, and I'm better with big picture ideas like plot and visual style. We moved out to L.A. together right after high school."

"From where?" Raven asked casually, lifting her glass to her mouth then setting it back down. Saiden wondered if Cora would even notice that Raven wasn't actually drinking. Alcohol didn't affect vampires much since their increased metabolisms burned it right off, and it took so much for them to get drunk that Baylin was usually the only one who even bothered. The drinks must have been Tressa's idea since she spent considerably more time with humans and would have had the best idea at how to get one to open up.

"I grew up in Beaverton," Cora answered on screen. "I do miss it sometimes. Not the rain of course, but the trees. Not many of those in L.A."

Saiden glanced at Baylin who mouthed, "Oregon."

Tressa clapped her hands excitedly. "You should see it here in the fall. It's absolutely—"

Baylin flicked a switch, and the sound cut off. "I don't recommend spying on her too much, dude. She's already gonna be pissed about everything else. You don't want to add snooping on her girl time to the list."

Saiden sucked down the last bit of blood then tossed his empty bag into the trash by Baylin's desk. He probably would have spent all day watching Cora talk with his cousins. Anything to learn more about her when she wasn't in defensive mode. His brother wasn't wrong, though. He shouldn't be constantly spying on her. He'd already messed things up worse than a toddler left alone with finger paints and lollipops.

"You're right, for once," Saiden conceded, dragging his eyes from the screen and Cora's animated gestures. Whatever she was describing had her eyes lighting up like the Eiffel Tower on New Year's, and he wondered if she had ever been to France. Or anywhere in Europe for that matter. He'd love to show her his hometown in Sicily sometime. Palermo looked quite different these days, but the Collesano farmhouse he'd been born in still stood. Thanks to Baylin's incredible skills, the deed was even in his name. As far as the world at large knew, they were all basically their own great, great grandkids. Except with a handful more greats in there.

"Anything new turn up in your Cora search?" Saiden asked, turning his attention back to his brother. He figured Baylin spent all morning continuing to scour his resources. His brother could uncover things you wouldn't even find on the dark web.

But when Saiden's eyes met Baylin's, he suddenly regretted asking the question. The freshly ingested blood coursing through his veins curdled at the sight of his brother's grimace.

"What?" he asked, fear ramping up inside him. Almost nothing caused Baylin to lose his sense of carefree frivolity. Anything that made his brother's face contort in pain and sympathy was not going to be good news.

"I did find something you should know," Baylin began slowly, as if each word out of his mouth drew razors across his skin.

"Tell me," Saiden demanded, his panic level reaching heights beyond what he thought himself capable. Whatever his brother uncovered they would deal with, but it had to be tragic for him to not immediately spill the details.

Baylin let out a pained sigh. "You know how you thought she might have a medical condition? Well, she does."

"And?"

Baylin rubbed his face, and if Saiden wasn't so terrified that he could barely move, he might have considered brutally maiming his little brother for dragging it out.

"And?" he demanded again, his voice growing louder and infused with the kind of menace that sent most rogue vampires fleeing in terror.

"And you might not have decades to convince her to become a vampire."

"What does that—" Saiden's question died before he could finish asking it because the monitor over Baylin's shoulder caught his eye, showing his mate shaking and clutching at her throat.

He was out of his seat and racing down the hall before it even dawned on him that he never got a full answer from his brother.

# Chapter Twenty-Eight

## Cora

It was the harsh whispers that eventually pulled Cora from sleep. She recognized the male voice, but the vaguely familiar ethereal tone of the female wasn't one she could immediately place.

"What in Lilith's name did you do to her?" the male snarled.

"Calm yourself, Saiden. I understand that you are frustrated, but you do not speak to me in that tone."

"I apologize, Eliana. I'm just scared. It was a little concerning to see my m—"

"Hush now. Cora is awake."

Damn. She'd kept her eyes closed in the hopes of hearing a little bit more. She should have known she couldn't fool vampires.

Cora cracked her eyes open, blinked a few times at the bright light assaulting her retinas, then evaluated her situation.

Spacious bedroom larger than her apartment? Check.

Massively oversized four poster bed with gossamer crimson curtains? Check.

Rich mahogany furniture and wine-colored velvet drapes? Check.

So pretty much exactly what she would expect from a vampire's guest suite—gothic and opulent. She knew Saiden was holding out on her when she got dumped in his bedroom.

The only thing she didn't expect was the two very concerned faces peering at her like she had just narrowly escaped the clutches of death.

"Uh, hi," she said awkwardly, trying and failing to sit up in bed. Glancing down, she realized someone had tucked her under the covers, and that someone must have been a vampire because the blankets were secured tighter than any human could achieve. It was actually making it a little hard to breathe.

"Cora, we are so pleased to see that you are awake," the female intoned in her gentle, melodic voice.

There was something so hauntingly beautiful about the way the woman spoke. As if the words slipped out of her mouth on a glittering celestial cloud, danced through Cora's brain, then floated off into the ether, leaving a faint tinge of sadness in their wake. Cora's memory finally filled in, and she connected the face to the voice. It was the one she'd heard on the patio right before she was saved.

The woman really was an angel.

"What happened out there?" Saiden growled, but Cora dismissed Sir Grouchy in favor of staring at the divine being in front of her. If her arms weren't securely fastened at her sides, she would have reached out to touch the woman's face to confirm that she was real and not a heavenly illusion.

Cora smiled sheepishly at the captivating female. "Is there any chance you could loosen the blankets? They're a little restrictive."

In a flash, Saiden had both the comforter and sheets off the bed and in a pile on the other side of the room. He moved so fast that Cora was surprised she didn't go flying along with them.

It was a little overkill, but at least she could breathe easier again.

Saiden lowered himself onto the bed beside her, his face twisted in such a deep expression of worry that Cora couldn't quite fathom anyone else looking at her that way. Not even her family or friends had ever shown that level of concern after any of her episodes. She squirmed under the discomfort of his unrelenting stare.

*Geez,* she thought, *it was just a little light choking, no big deal.*

Unable to bear the intensity of Saiden's gaze any longer, Cora looked back over to the otherworldly female. The woman practically glowed from within, the mirror opposite of the dark prince staring down at her.

"Are you an angel?" she blurted out before her brain could catch up to her mouth and inform her of the ridiculousness of her question.

The woman just laughed, and the sound was magic personified. It was like a melody that couldn't be properly heard by human ears. Something spellbinding that swept you up into its arms, wrapped you in a cocoon of shining white euphoria, then gently set you back down, only for you to mourn the loss of it so keenly that you would slice out your own heart just to hear it again.

Saiden turned to Eliana and muttered, "Is there any chance you'll give us some privacy? I won't get a proper answer out of her if she's drowning under your spell."

The female smiled beatifically at Saiden and nodded. "Of course. I will leave you to tend to your... mortal." Turning her enchanting face to Cora, Eliana leaned down and pressed a faint kiss to Cora's forehead. "Despite the unpleasant circumstances, it was lovely to meet you, Cora Lee. I do hope to see more of you in the future."

Cora watched the angel float out of the room, and a hypnotic urge filled her, demanding she follow this woman to the ends of the earth.

"It will pass," Saiden reassured, placing a hand on her shoulder, gently pinning her down until her muscles relaxed and she eased back into the mattress.

"Who was that?" Cora asked, dragging her eyes away from the door to look at Saiden.

"That was Eliana. She is Marquin's mate."

Cora nodded absently, still in a daze. The fog faded away after a second, and she regained her full senses once more.

Damn, that woman was like walking ecstasy. How did anyone get anything done with her around?

"*What* was she?" Cora breathed out, propping herself up against the fluffiest pillow she'd ever touched.

"She is a vampire like me, more or less. She's just a little extra in many ways. She is considerably older than any of us in the compound, but we don't know her exact age, nor do we ask. I've been told that she was never exactly human the way you are. That even before she was turned she was a feared and respected seer. After she died..." Saiden scrunched up his face in thought for a second, and Cora couldn't help but think how disarmingly cute he looked when he was struggling for words. Like he briefly forgot he was supposed to be mean and scary.

"Let's just say she's not quite a vampire either. She's something special. All of us have an aura, an emanation that causes humans to be, at the very least, intrigued by us. Eliana's aura is unlike any other. She rarely leaves the compound because of the effect she has on humans and vampires alike."

"But you don't feel a pull to her?"

Saiden shrugged. "I did at first but not anymore. Eliana is, for lack of a better word, like a mother to me. Marquin is my sire, and she is my sire's mate. It's a bit difficult to feel so enamored by someone who is a parental figure as well as the one most likely to lecture me any time I mess up. Not that messing up is a common occurrence."

Cora searched his face for any hint of deception or teasing and found none. "That was your *mom*?"

It kind of made sense in a weird way. Eliana spoke to Saiden in a manner that was similar to how she imagined a mother would speak to her child.

Saiden laughed at her comment, and she really wished he hadn't. Every time he laughed his features relaxed into something less intimidating, and it made it that much harder to remind herself of what he was. That much harder to resist him.

Which is probably why she didn't pull away when he leaned forward and brushed her hair away from her face.

"What happened?" Saiden asked, the question tender and compassionate this time.

Cora sank into herself. The last thing she wanted to do was discuss her illness, but she doubted he was going to leave her be without some sort of explanation. "It happens sometimes if I eat too fast. My throat spasms, and I start choking. Jinx has done the Heimlich on me three or four times by now, and I'm never supposed to eat meals alone because of it. I'm sorry if I scared your cousins."

"Don't be sorry, Cora. We were all just worried about you. You stopped breathing then passed out. The girls said you only had three drinks."

Cora tried not to look too embarrassed. It would be easier to pretend they drugged her, but she knew three martinis would have done it. She must have lost count somewhere along the way.

"I don't drink much," she explained. "Or ever, really. The trauma combined with the booze was probably just a little too much of a hit to my system. I'm sorry if I made a scene."

Saiden gave her a heated look. "If you do not stop apologizing, Cora, I'm going to have to punish you."

The way he said 'punish' made her think it would be less chained in a dungeon and more handcuffed to a bed.

She gulped as the visual of a naked Saiden 'punishing' her took up rent inside her brain and signed a lifelong lease. It was becoming increasingly difficult to keep track of the naughty new desires he was unlocking inside her. If she found one more, maybe she'd win a new vibrator to help deal with all of them.

"Got it, not sorry," she corrected, and a flash of disappointment crossed his face. Almost as if he hoped she would apologize again.

"So now will you tell me what's going on?" he urged. "I know I have not been human for a long time, but I'm pretty sure throat spasms are not a common occurrence. Not to mention the muscle twitches when we kissed. Something else we still need to circle back to."

Shit, why did he have to bring that up again? The one time she was content to sweep something under the rug, he had to call attention to it. She debated her two options and decided she preferred airing her dirty medical laundry over airing her dirty thoughts about him.

"The twitches and spasms are symptoms of Huntington's Disease."

She waited to see if he recognized the illness. Some people did, and she had to deal with a disgusting level of pity. Others didn't, and the pity was staved off only until after they went home and googled it.

Saiden's blank look indicated he would be one of the latter.

"I see," he replied carefully. "And this Huntington's Disease, how exactly does it affect your life in the long run?"

She would have preferred the internet gave him the answer to that particular question, but since that didn't seem to be an option, she might as well rip the bandage off. She was going to bring it up eventually when she pleaded her case with Marquin anyway.

"It doesn't affect me in the long run because there is no long run," she answered, forcing herself to look him in the eye.

"I'm dying, Saiden."

# Chapter Twenty-Nine

## Saiden

Baylin was exactly where Saiden left him, only this time when he barged in it wasn't irritation coursing through him. That was far too mild of an emotion. Even anger wasn't up to snuff.

No, this was pure, unfettered rage.

"You knew!" he shouted, crossing the tech room in the blink of an eye.

Baylin didn't even fight back when Saiden ripped him from the chair and slammed him up against the wall, knocking over a Monster energy drink in the process. His brother's eyes slid down to the amber liquid spilling over the keyboard for a second and then he met Saiden's piercing gaze head on.

"I tried to tell you," he replied calmly.

Saiden didn't know if it was the sedate tone or the words themselves that infuriated him to the point of exploding. He slammed Baylin against the wall a second time and relished in the cracked plaster that rained down like a winter snowstorm.

"You tried to tell me?" he bellowed. "You don't try to tell someone something. You just do. You open your mouth and say the words. It should have been the first thing you mentioned the moment I walked through your fucking door this morning. You don't hide something that monumental from someone you claim to care about."

"Like you're doing with your mate?" Baylin commented blandly, refusing to meet Saiden's fury with any of his own.

The words gutted Saiden because he couldn't deny the truth of them. At least Baylin *tried* to tell him. He hadn't even attempted to let Cora in on everything he was keeping from her.

Releasing his brother, Saiden stepped back and fell roughly to his knees. "How long?" he whispered, the anger draining from his body to leave nothing but a broken male crumpled on the floor. "I know you looked into it. It's what you do. How long does she have?"

"It's hard to say," Baylin began. "She has Juvenile Huntington's Disease. The symptoms first appeared when she was seventeen. A comment in her chart from the most recent doctor's visit indicated he doesn't believe she has much beyond a couple years left. The symptoms are progressing and will likely make it hard for her to maintain any kind of normal life within a year or so. Maybe less."

*Years.* If he couldn't convince his mate to turn, he would lose her to illness in only a few short years. And in only a single year she would no longer be his fiery, obstinate Cora. A year was nothing. A drop of water in the ocean of a vampire's existence. There and gone in a blink.

"There's no cure?" he asked, his eyes still shuttered since he refused to open them. The longer he kept them closed, the longer he could deny the reality unfolding before him.

"No," Baylin confirmed, that single solemn word acting as the final nail in the coffin of Saiden's hopes. "No cure."

Saiden finally opened his eyes when a hand touched his shoulder, and he stared up at Baylin. There was only compassion in his brother's storm gray eyes. Compassion and pity. It broke him, and he let out an anguished sob.

Saiden had never cried before. Not once in his life. Not when his mother died of consumption. Not when his little sister was abused and murdered while he was away fighting in The War of Spanish Succession. Not even when he'd been captured and tortured for weeks by a band of rogue vampires in Marseille. Not once did a single tear roll down his face.

Life was long and difficult and tragic things happened to everyone sooner or later. The longer you lived, the more tragedies you witnessed. In the end, all you could do was play the hand you were dealt. Getting weepy never solved a single problem.

But knowing he would spend an eternity without his mate shattered something inside him. Something he'd spent over three hundred years burying so deep that he had almost forgotten it existed.

His heart.

Saiden sobbed on the floor, tears gushing down his face in salty rivers of sorrow, and Baylin just held him through it all, knowing there was nothing he could say to ease Saiden's suffering. They sat there for a long time on the cold marble tiles. One brother hurting, while the other did the only thing he could do—be there for him.

"Please tell me you aren't giving up."

Raven's sharp voice cut through his cloud of despair. Saiden looked up to see her looming over him, hands on her hips, and not an ounce of compassion on her stern face.

"She said she would never want to be like us," he choked out. "She called it a curse."

Before, when he assumed he would have a few decades to change her mind, he'd thought there was a decent chance she'd come around. If he spent enough time showing her that being a vampire wasn't anything like the movies, surely she would have eventually relented. But now?

The clock was winding down, and he was no closer to his goal.

"You need to convince her then."

Saiden wiped the tears from his eyes, not even embarrassed that she had seen him so thoroughly broken.

"A year, Raven. That's all the time I have left before the disease starts to take her from me."

"I know, Saiden. Baylin sent me a text." Raven grew quiet and knelt down beside him. "And a year is still more than I got with my mate."

The harsh biting words were a low blow, and Saiden knew she had intended it as such. The only way to get through to him.

It happened before the rest of the cadre even met her, but everyone knew the story. She had become a cautionary tale of sorts. Raven was nearly thirty when she'd been turned into a vampire and forever trapped at that age, but her mate was only twenty-three when she finally met him a century later. They decided to wait a bit before turning him since he didn't want to spend an eternity with a baby face. After all, what was a few years compared to the millennia they had waiting for them?

Six weeks later, Raven's mate was mugged and stabbed in the back alleys of London on his way home from the market. He bled out on the dirty cobblestone road, all because the men wanted to steal the watch on his wrist that didn't even work.

Raven was a ghost when Saiden met her a decade later. A shell of a vampire that wanted to die so badly she picked a fight with a rogue in the hopes that someone else might end things for her.

Saiden saved her before the rogue could finish her off, then he spent years helping her find her way back to some semblance of a meaningful existence.

Now she would have to do the same for him.

"I don't think I'll survive if I lose her, Raven."

"I know it feels that way now, but should it come to that, I am certain you will survive," his cousin replied, holding out a hand to help him up. "You'll just wish you hadn't."

It took Saiden's cousins almost an hour to calm him down enough to formulate some type of plan. In the end, it was harsh words from Raven that had his agony fading and his will to fight rising.

"Are you acting like the kind of vampire who would even be worthy of a mate like her?"

It was all he needed to remember exactly who he was—one of the most feared rogue hunters in all of North America. And the reason he was so feared, the reason he knew other vampires whispered about him in hushed tones, was because of his tenacity. When he was on a hunt, it didn't end until either he or the rogue was dead. And after three hundred years, he remained undefeated.

Saiden would not let this break him. He couldn't. The moment he accepted the situation was the moment that she was already gone. He would fight for her right up until her very last breath if that was what it took.

The first step, they'd all decided, was finding out exactly why Cora was so prepared to die. Was it that she really hated vampires that much? Or was there something else driving her decision?

If he could just convince her to turn, then he could spend the rest of his very long life trying to make her realize how perfect they could be together. He just needed that time.

"Do you really think this will work?" Saiden asked Raven and Tressa as he went over the itinerary in his hand. He trusted his cousins completely and fully understood that he knew less about women then he did about synchronized swimming, but still...

"It's perfect," Tressa gushed. "We took care of all the reservations and even found a pilot who can meet you at the airfield in half an hour. Trust me, women love grand gestures like this. Stick to the plan, keep everything secret until the last minute so she can be surprised, and I promise she'll be melting into your arms before dinner."

"I thought I was supposed to be myself? Isn't that what you said before, Raven?"

His cousin ran a comb through his hair, swooping the long strands artfully off to the side of his face. "Of course you should be yourself. But that doesn't mean you can't be yourself while indulging in a romantic evening out."

"Okay," he agreed reluctantly, tugging on the stiff button-down shirt they'd stolen from Derrick's closet. He glanced at himself in the mirror and tried not to cringe.

A light blue collared shirt, black tailored pants, and shiny loafers that were at least two sizes too small. He looked posh and refined. Exactly how one might envision those misunderstood vampires in romance novels. And he wanted nothing more than to rip it all off and throw on a pair of jeans and a t-shirt.

But love requires sacrifice—or so the girls had told him—and he would dress to the nines every day if it meant Cora would be by his very uncomfortable side.

Saiden put the mantra on repeat in his brain as he strode down the hall toward the guest bedroom where he'd left her, the tight shoes pinching his toes the entire way. He just hoped Cora wasn't too upset. She opened up to him about her disease, and he'd immediately made some lame excuse about a security check to race from the room.

Staying hadn't been an option, though. Not when her words had crushed him like a boulder, burying him under an avalanche of emotion that he couldn't possibly process in front of her. She wouldn't understand why he was so upset, why her words made him feel like someone had sucked all the air from the room.

He would just have to make it up to her. It was what the entire evening was about. Helping her to see him in a different light. Turning a corner and putting all that pesky kidnapping stuff behind them.

A fresh start... so long as she would allow it.

He took one last glance at the list the girls had made him promise to follow to the letter.

It had to work.

*It will work*, he told himself. After all, any woman would be crazy to say no to all of this.

# Chapter Thirty

## Cora

"No."

Saiden's jaw dropped, and if Cora hadn't been so pissed, she might have laughed. The fish out of water look really took all the menace out of his dark features. You couldn't really be afraid of someone when all you wanted to do was lift their chin to see if it would squeak like a rusty hinge.

He had to be crazy if he thought she was going anywhere with him. It had hurt her more than she wanted to admit when he bailed earlier. She had a lot of reactions to her illness over the years, but not once had someone gone stone faced and left the room so fast you would think they were being chased by hellhounds.

But that was exactly what Saiden did, tossing a hasty, "Sorry, I need to go check in with security real quick," over his shoulder.

He'd just left her there, sitting on the bed and wondering why she felt like she should be apologizing to him for something.

Now he showed up looking like a smooth-talking playboy asking to take her out? She scoffed. Sure, she'd go out with him. When vampires took up sun tanning.

"What do you mean, 'no?'" he demanded, blocking her from leaving the room.

She'd waited like an idiot for hours to see if he would return. If maybe he really did need to just check in with someone, and then he would come right back. She'd stared at the clock, watching the minutes tick by, occasionally scrolling through the social media apps that she despised. When she finally realized it was naïve o'clock, she'd climbed from the bed and slipped on her ballet flats. She would find one of the nice female vamps and demand to speak with Marquin. Her film wasn't going to direct itself, and somehow she'd wasted almost an entire day letting them sidetrack her with fun and friendship.

Vampires weren't friends, though. She was nothing more to them than their food source, and you don't cozy up to your Big Mac.

Crossing her arms, she stared Saiden down. She was under no misconceptions that she could move him if he didn't want to be moved, but she'd also been told she could freeze a guy's dick off with her resting bitch face. Granted the guy who told her that was mostly pissed she had refused his drunken advances, but all the same, she knew she could pull off 'Don't fuck with me' with very little effort.

Unfortunately, she was facing off against the king of 'Fucking try me,' and all Saiden did was cross his own arms in a mimicking posture and ask, "Why not?"

Cora would not pay attention to how that small movement pulled the shirt taut against his chest and arms, placing his muscular physique on full display. Nope, she wouldn't look. Not even one tiny glance.

Locking eyes with him, she said, "Do I need a reason? I just don't want to go anywhere with you. You do realize that you basically brought me here against my will, right? All I want is to talk with Marquin then get back to my normally scheduled life. Sorry, but I don't have time to indulge the whims of a bored vampire."

A muscle ticked in his jaw as they played a dangerous game of who would bend first. It wasn't going to be her; she was certain of that much. Stubborn was her middle name. Okay, technically it was Eunice after her grandmother, but she should probably legally change it to stubborn since that was way more appropriate.

It felt like they spent an hour in their unspoken battle of wills, but in reality probably no more than a minute or two passed before Saiden's shoulders dropped in defeat.

Mentally, she thrust her fist in the air and celebrated her victory. Something about beating a vampire in a game of intimidation just felt really damn satisfying. It almost put her in a good enough mood to agree to go out with him.

"Listen," he began in that gentle tone that could easily be her undoing if she let it. "I feel bad that I brought you here without realizing Marquin would be unavailable. I'm just trying to make it up to you. I thought we could get out of the compound for a bit, have some dinner, and maybe catch a show. I know a great place."

When she didn't budge, he added, "You can stay angry at me all night if you want, but you need to eat. And hanging out here with a bunch of lame vampires won't be any fun. Come out with me. Please."

It was the 'please' that did it. How that single word seemed to have a burr to it, as if it was something he wasn't accustomed to saying. She searched his eyes, noting some new emotion in their dark brown depths. Something... desperate. Her response mattered to him a great deal.

You'd think she had the memory of a goldfish the way she kept forgetting all the awful things he'd done just because he gave her a soulful look.

"Fine," she conceded, dropping her arms. "But I don't have anything as nice as what you're wearing, so any place you take me better be okay with my attire."

He leisurely scanned her body, and the way his eyes went molten with heat made her feel like she was dressed in a silken ball gown instead of gray leggings, purple ballet flats, and a baggy black t-shirt that touted, 'I'm the Director so I call the shots.'

"I think you look beautiful, Cora."

Her cheeks flushed, and she tucked her arm behind her back, not wanting him to see the little muscle twitches that picked the worst time to show up. Based on his earlier reaction, it would probably be best to just not bring up anything about her illness with him. Some people could be so touchy about the subject of dying. You'd think as a vampire who routinely murdered others he'd be way more relaxed about it.

"Shall we?" Saiden held out an arm.

Reluctantly, she curled her hand around his elbow. "I guess we shall, Sadie Cakes."

It was almost worth agreeing to go out with him just to see the grimace on his face.

"Are you going to tell me where we're going?" Cora asked, settling into the convertible Aston Martin DB11.

She was afraid to even ask how many expensive sports cars they owned. When he'd guided her out the front door, this one sat in the same spot they'd left the McLaren. She liked the other car despite its unreliable tires, but the new shiny silver convertible was winning her over as they took off down the road, wind whipping through her messy hair.

Now if she could just stop thinking about how one of these cars alone would finance not only her film but three more after that, then she might actually be able to enjoy herself.

"It's a surprise," Saiden answered coyly. He waved at a security camera and moments later they passed through the imposing front gate.

"Not a huge fan of surprises," Cora said. The last major surprise in her life was learning that her father had hid her predisposition toward Huntington's from her. After that, she preferred things to be a little less unexpected.

Although, she had to admit that learning about the existence of vampires wasn't turning out so awful. Provided they let her leave soon with her veins and mind still intact.

"Well, I'm pretty sure you'll like this one," he replied confidently.

"Well, I'm pretty sure you can't know that for sure," she shot back. "And besides, don't you still owe me a third question? I'm calling it in. I want to know where we're going."

He chuckled and gave her a heated look. "I thought you said you didn't want it. Something about shoving it up my obscenely tight ass, if I recall correctly?"

One at a time, her fingers curled into her palms until two tense fists lay at her sides. Trust an ancient vampire to have a memory like Fort Knox. "I lied," she argued through teeth clenched nearly as tightly as her hands. "I want it."

"While I would love to give you everything you want, Cora, I think you'll enjoy this more as a surprise."

"Saiden," she pressed, shoring up her voice with steel rebar. "Unless you want this outing to be another kidnapping scenario, I need you to tell me where we're going."

He said nothing, merely running his hands idly along the steering wheel, and Cora contemplated her options for getting out of the vehicle with her limbs intact.

Before she had to resort to drastic tuck and roll measures, he caved and pulled a folded sheet of paper from his shirt pocket.

"Here," he said, handing it over. "That's everything planned for tonight. And I'll even let you keep your third question for something vampire related. If you still want it."

Cora snatched the paper from his hand and scanned the itinerary. It took all of ten seconds for her to come to a conclusion.

"Saiden, stop the car."

"What?" he asked, glancing over at her. "Why?"

"Saiden, stop the car."

His brow wrinkled in confusion. "Cora, what's—"

"Saiden, stop the motherfucking car right this second!"

He slammed on the brakes, and she braced herself as the convertible skidded to a stop on the gravely forest road. Turning slowly to face him, she tried to figure out the best thing to say. The best way to explain her reasoning for wanting to crumple up the piece of paper in her hand and drop it in a bottomless well where it could never hurt anyone else. She needed to phrase her words carefully, so she didn't sound ungrateful, but at the same time she had to make it clear just how far off the mark he was with his plan.

"Are you out of your fucking mind?" she bellowed.

Not quite the eloquence she was going for, but it got the point across.

"What?" Saiden blustered, his expression reminiscent of an actor whenever she called 'cut' in the middle of a scene. He really had no clue where the bad was in this insane outing of his.

She waved the paper at him. "Do you seriously believe that this is making things up to me? Because honestly? I wouldn't wish this on my worst enemy."

He ran a hand through his hair, transforming the gelled strands on the side from 'too stiff for even the wind to move' to 'sexy, tousled bedhead.'

"I thought this was what you girls liked? Fancy meals and grand gestures."

Cora scoffed. "Maybe other girls. Look, I know you've only known me a couple days but come on. Did you really think I would like any of this?"

He sighed. "No, not really. Tressa and Raven set it all up. They said it'd be perfect, so I figured it was worth a shot."

Why the hell were his cousins planning out their evening?

"Yeah, it's pretty much the exact opposite," she replied. "First off, I hate flying. So locking me inside an airborne death trap to head over to San Francisco? Bad start. Second, I despise fancy food. If it's not fried or dipped in chocolate, then I'm uninterested. And third, the Opera? Seriously?" Cora looked down at her outfit. "How did you even think you would get me inside looking like this?"

"You would be surprised what money can buy."

Cora snorted. "Well maybe that was your first problem. You can't solve everything by throwing money at it."

"That's for damned sure," he muttered under his breath.

She sat back in her chair, shifting so she could stare at him. With his head dropped and his shoulders sagging, he looked like a kicked puppy. For some reason he had been so excited about taking her out, and now she felt awful about the dejection on his face.

She sighed, really hoping that she wouldn't regret her next words.

"Okay, here's the deal. You said Tressa and Raven decided this, yeah? I'll give you one more shot. If *you* had planned to take me out somewhere, where would you go?"

A wide grin lit up Saiden's face, and Cora felt like she could live for days on that smile. It called to her, hypnotized her, promising her the happiest of days and most sinful of nights. It was a smile that she would follow to the ends of the earth.

A moth chasing after her flame.

# Chapter Thirty-One

## Saiden

*Derrick is going to kill me,* Saiden thought when he bit into his slice of garlic pizza, and a massive drop of grease landed on his thigh. He didn't know much about fashion, but he was pretty sure Armani was one of the high-end brands that his cousin had specially tailored. Saiden didn't want Cora to feel uncomfortable as the only one eating, though, and he would gladly destroy Derrick's entire wardrobe if it meant he could prevent that.

Besides, it wasn't like his cousin couldn't afford to replace them. At least Saiden had taken the shirt off. In fact, the minute Cora said she wanted nothing to do with his original plans, he'd started unbuttoning the uncomfortable garment. His black undershirt was decent enough for where he was taking her. The tight shoes followed right after, and he thanked Lilith that he always kept a spare pair of boots in most of his cars. Had plans not shifted, he doubted he would have made it to San Francisco before he lost all feeling in his toes.

But better than removing the overly stiff shirt, better than removing the painful shoes, was the look on Cora's face when he pulled the convertible into The Old Merc. More than just the best pizzeria in the

Fall River Valley, the Merc was one of those small-town places where you could just relax, kick your boots up, and not give a shit about anything for a while. Plus, he'd known the owner's family for years, so he didn't even need to bribe them to get the corner TV changed to some horror flick that Saiden had never heard of. Cora squealed a bit, so he imagined House on Haunted Hill must be somewhat decent. He wouldn't know because his eyes never left her face for a second.

He cherished the moments when her attention was fixed on the television because it gave him the opportunity to just stare at her. To memorize the soft lines of her face. The slight glow to her amber eyes. The way her lip twitched when someone screamed on the TV. Almost as if she enjoyed the scenes where the characters made dumb decisions and were murdered for it.

His bloodthirsty little horror fiend. She was more suited for the life of a vampire than anyone he'd ever met. And yet...

He rubbed absently at his chest, trying to banish the painful thoughts. He told himself he wasn't going to think about it. Wasn't going to put that kind of pressure on their time together.

There would be plenty of opportunities for panicking later.

The credits started rolling on the film, and Cora kicked back in her chair, rubbing at her tiny tummy like a grizzly bear ready for their winter nap.

"That might have been the best pizza I've ever eaten," she proclaimed with a near sexual tone to her voice.

He hid his amused grin behind a napkin as he wiped at his mouth, wondering if she realized how blissed out she looked.

Now if only he could get himself ranked higher than greasy food on her list of moan-worthy things. He was pretty sure after last night that he was on the list somewhere, but she had yet to tackle him with the same ferocity as melted cheese on bread.

"And you know what was so good about it?" she said, leaning forward conspiratorially.

"What?" he asked, meeting her in the middle of the table.

"We didn't have to get on a damn plane for it."

He laughed as she settled back into her seat, but something tickled at his brain. A curiosity he couldn't quite shake.

"Why do you hate flying so much?"

Cora seemed fearless about so many things that her aversion to something viewed as universally safe was mind-boggling.

A shadow clouded her face, and he kicked himself for being the one to put it there.

"I didn't always," she answered softly. "After I was diagnosed, my dad flew me all over the country to see the best specialists he could find. I think eventually I started to associate airplanes with needles and doctors, and it just grew from there. Now I'm terrified to even set foot in a plane. It really sucks because going on trips with my dad when I was younger was one of my favorite things. It's always sad when you lose something you love, you know."

Oh, he knew. She had no idea how much he knew.

He wanted to ask more questions about her father. Baylin relayed how her mother died in a car accident when Cora was still a baby, but her relationship with her father was the one thing his brother hadn't figured out. How one day they were happy and the next she moved down to L.A. with Jinx, never to speak to him again. Her father wasn't vampire wealthy, but he certainly had the means to keep her living in a much nicer place than the hovel he'd seen. Given what he'd spent on specialists trying to help Cora, Saiden doubted her dad just decided to randomly cut her off. Which meant Cora had done the severing. What did her father do to warrant such a reaction?

And how could he avoid the same fate?

"Did you want dessert?" he asked, trying to move their conversation in a less depressing direction. "This place has the best strawberry pie you've ever tasted."

It wouldn't smell half as good as Cora did, but being surrounded by her scent all night had him craving one of the few human foods he indulged in on a semi-regular basis.

Cora let out an agonized groan. "Why didn't you tell me that before I ate so much? Strawberry pie is my favorite dessert, but if anything else goes in my belly, I'm going to look like Violet Beauregard."

He didn't get the reference, but the intention was obvious. He'd have to bring her back there another time for pie.

If he managed to get another time.

Glancing out the window, he noted the sun was maybe an hour from setting. "Do you need to go sleep off the food coma or are you up for a little more fun?" he asked, hoping she didn't hear the edge of nervousness in his voice. If she wanted to go back to the compound, then he would take her, but he really hoped he'd done enough to warrant a little more time. "If it's not too taxing on you. I don't want to push if you need to rest because of..."

He'd promised himself that he wouldn't bring up her illness, but he had to make sure he didn't do anything to make it worse. He would spend the whole night studying up after she went to bed, but in the meantime he would have to trust she knew her own body.

"I'm fine," Cora glared. "You don't need to walk on eggshells around me. I'm not a porcelain doll."

He observed the little flare in her eyes. There was his obstinate girl. He could work with that.

"Oh, yeah?" he asked casually, leaning back in the chair far enough to balance on two legs. "Prove it."

She scoffed, but he didn't miss the twinkle of excitement in her eyes.

"And how do I do that?"

He grinned. "Come with me."

# Chapter Thirty-Two

## Cora

"When I asked you earlier if you were out of your fucking mind, the answer to that question should have been, 'Why yes, Cora. Yes, I am.'"

It was the only logical reason that he would have looked at her with such amusement when he'd told her to jump.

When Saiden had first dragged her from the car in the middle of nowhere and started off down the overgrown pathway, she was worried he might be taking her somewhere to finally murder her. It would have been one hell of a long game considering he could have done it at almost any other point, but she saw no other reason he would bring her out into the woods.

Until they arrived at the waterfall. The setting sun cast an orange and red glow across the top, almost as if the water was fire spilling down the side of the cliff, and it was incredible to witness.

There had been one couple splashing at the base of the falls, but they left the moment she and Saiden arrived. When she asked why, he simply shrugged and said that people around there knew his family valued privacy.

Before she could ask anything else, he'd swooped her up into his arms and dashed up the steep side of the falls. Depositing her at the top of the cliff, he'd grinned and said, "Jump."

Clearly laughing at her assessment of his mental faculties, Saiden started stripping off his shirt.

*So that's why he brought me here,* she thought. He was back in seduction mode.

Except it didn't feel like it. He wasn't casting her heated glances or slowly pulling the shirt up to reveal each of his defined abdominal muscles one by one. No, this felt like a different Saiden. Relaxed and carefree. Like he genuinely just wanted to go for a swim and nothing more.

Which would have been fine if said swim wasn't at the bottom of a hundred-foot drop.

"Come on," he protested. "It's only forty feet."

Hrmph. Looked like a hundred.

"Seriously," he continued, yanking off his boots. "It's not like I'm asking you to jump off Burney Falls. Now that might warrant the very dubious look you're giving me right now."

"That's easy for you to say; you're a vampire. You could jump off here or Burney Falls or, hell, even Niagara and you'd be fine. I'm not quite as invincible as you are."

"You could be," Saiden commented under his breath, but the words were still loud enough to reach her ears.

Eyes widening, Cora froze in place. Had he just offered to turn her into a vampire? Or was it just an off-the-cuff comment with no real sincerity? And why was he even bringing it up? She'd made her thoughts on that matter crystal clear.

She wanted to blame the uncomfortable silence for the idiotic decision she made next. Cora had never done well with those awkward quiet moments, but she also never realized she would risk her life to get out of one.

"Fine. I'll do it," she announced, slipping out of her ballet flats.

Saiden's head shot up so fast that she didn't even see him move. One second he was bending over to pull off his pants, and the next he was staring at her with the intensity of a cougar that spotted an injured deer.

"The jump," she clarified in case he thought there was any chance she was referring to his potentially non-existent offer to make her a vicious creature of the night.

Not that she was really thinking there was any accuracy to the term anymore. It was hard to think of Tressa and Raven as either 'vicious' or 'creatures' after having sipped martinis and snacked on hors d'oeuvres with them while basking in the afternoon shade.

She really didn't like the way her world view on vampires kept shifting. It was a lot easier to think of them as evil. Evil was something you ran from, not toward. You didn't sleep with evil. And you definitely didn't feel a warm pulse in your lower belly when evil slipped his pants off and stood in front of you wearing nothing but those damn tight boxer briefs.

It made her more than a little self-conscious, his perfect body with olive skin and defined muscles in places she didn't even know could have muscles. Her pale, thin figure that she never minded in the past suddenly seemed so lacking. Really the only thing the illness hadn't taken from her was her breasts. Those were still a solid handful, even for hands as big as Saiden's. Something she knew all too well.

Okay, she was getting wildly off track. If she didn't get her clothes off and her ass in the water soon, then her clothes were going to be coming off for a very different reason.

Turning her back to him for some unnecessary modesty, she slid off her leggings and t-shirt. Glancing down, she was glad she had absentmindedly packed her black lacy underwear. This would be a whole lot more awkward if she was standing in front of him wearing her granny panties with the hole in the waistband. It was like her body had subconsciously urged her to let something happen while she was here.

On the other hand, her body had like three recall notices so she wouldn't be paying much attention to it anytime soon.

Bracing herself, she turned back around to face Saiden.

Who was gone.

What the hell?

She frantically searched around, trying to locate where he'd run off to. Had he seriously abandoned her in the woods? She'd only been worried about him biting her before, but now she had to add being mauled by a bear or cougar to her list of fears.

"Saiden?" she squeaked out, hating how high and timid her voice was. She'd watched the Conjuring in her pitch-black apartment, alone, and not even flinched once. She didn't usually do the scaredy cat thing.

That was a movie, though, and this was real.

"Saiden?" she called again, trying to squash the little quiver in her voice.

"Down here," he called, his voice muffled by the rushing falls. Cora whipped her head around and raced toward the cliffside, stopping herself inches away from flying over the edge.

Glancing down, she saw Saiden swimming lazily in the turbulent pool.

"How did you get down there?" she demanded.

"The same way you will. I jumped."

She didn't know if it made her feel better or worse that he'd already made the leap. Either way, there was no backing down now.

Should she be doing something like this in her condition? Probably not. But life was short, and hers was shorter than most. She'd told him she wasn't a broken doll, and she meant it.

Cora took a deep inhale and squeezed her eyes shut.

And then she jumped.

# Chapter Thirty-Three

## Saiden

From the moment Saiden laid eyes on Cora, he knew there was something special about her. Once he realized they were mates, he knew he wanted to spend the rest of his life with her. But it wasn't until he watched her fly off the cliffside and plummet into the pool below that he truly fell in love with her.

It hit him like the last piece of a puzzle snapping into place, and suddenly the entire picture changed. She was everything he never knew was missing in his life. Someone who would challenge him. Would stand up to him. Someone who was fearless and never backed down from anything he tossed her way. The kind of person who understood that sometimes life shits in your breakfast, so you just grab a protein bar and go about your day.

She was fiercely unbreakable.

She was his perfect match in every way.

She was...

Not swimming to the surface.

Ice cold panic sank its teeth into Saiden's heart, and he dove under the water to search for Cora. In a calm lake, he would be able to see for a mile, but the churning of the waterfall obstructed his view. Stilling himself, he heightened his other senses to seek out any noise that could be his endangered mate. It was useless, though. Thunder from the falls dominated even his vampiric hearing.

He dropped to the bottom of the pool, groping for anything that wasn't rock or silt. As a vampire, he could go without oxygen for nearly ten minutes, but the way his heart was pounding, he doubted he would last sixty seconds.

She couldn't be dead. He thought only having a year with her was torture, but this was unbearable.

Bursting up through the surface, he screamed, "Cora!"

"Yes, Saiden?"

Her voice came from behind him, and he whipped around so fast a mortal would have snapped their own neck.

Lounging on a large rock just outside the pool, Cora gave him a feline grin. "You weren't worried or anything, were you?"

"I... I..." He couldn't form words. His brain lacked all ability to process the situation. He had never been so thrilled to see someone alive while simultaneously tempted to murder them.

Cora cocked her head. "It's almost like someone vanishing without a trace is a little terrifying. Wouldn't you say?"

He blinked at her, still dumbfounded that she had eluded him. "How?" The single word response was all he could manage.

"I swam off to the side once I hit the water and waited to see if you would dive in after me. Huntington's has severely limited my ability to hold my breath, but dang, Saiden, you didn't even give it thirty seconds before you started panicking. If I didn't know better, I'd think you cared."

She didn't think he cared? She was joking, right?

With a predatory slowness, he swam toward the rock, drinking in the tableau before him: Cora leaning back on her elbows, a slight arch to her lithe body, the setting sun throwing up a halo of golden light behind her glowing auburn hair. She called to him, like a siren of old, and he would gladly give himself to her charms, smiling the entire time she pulled him under.

He emerged from the pool, water droplets fleeing his skin as if they could feel the unrelenting storm inside him, and stalked over to her.

Peering down at him from her perch atop the massive stone, Cora quirked an eyebrow. "Did you have something to say, Saiden?"

She was playing with fire and thinking herself immune. Soon enough, she would learn his desire burned hotter than the most intense inferno.

"No," he stated. He was done talking. Done holding back.

In a flash, he leapt onto the rock and pounced on her, crushing his lips to hers.

For a single terrifying heartbeat, he thought she might pull away when her body stiffened. Then she relaxed, and all her soft curves melted against his hard muscles.

Cora pressed up into him, and a tiny moan escaped, so similar to the one from the night before yet so much more arousing to be present for it. To be the cause of it.

The time for soft kisses and romance had long passed. His tongue warred for dominance against hers, and she met him on the battlefield with a passion to rival his own. She would have stolen all the breath from his lungs if he didn't gladly surrender it. His skin tingled everywhere they touched, and it made him shiver in the best way possible. As if fate itself was confirming, *Yes, this is the one for you.*

"Saiden."

She broke their kiss just long enough to let his name slip from her lips, then her hands tangled themselves in his hair, and one of her legs curled up and over his waist.

She was there with him, she wanted this too, and it was all he needed to unleash himself.

His cock swelled at the feel of her writhing in his arms, and he gripped her ass to pull her tighter against him, content to never let her go. The wet fabric of his boxers was an improvement over the thick jeans from last time, but it wasn't enough.

He needed to feel every inch of her skin.

He needed to be inside her.

He needed to know what she tasted like when she screamed his name.

Cora had teased a starving lion, dangled a plethora of delights in front of him, and now he would feast.

# Chapter Thirty-Four

## Cora

Cora tried furiously to remind herself of all the reasons she'd refused to give in to Saiden, but the moment he looked at her with the kind of heat that threatened to burn her alive, they all fluttered away like ashes in the wind.

Dying in his arms suddenly didn't seem like such a bad way to go.

Abandoning all her reservations, Cora allowed him to fully claim her.

Lightning arced under her skin, and she pressed herself tighter to him, sending the tiny shocks into overdrive. A moan slipped out, and she didn't know if it was from the pleasure or the pain.

She didn't care. She just needed more.

If this was what it was like to be with a vampire, she understood where all the romance novels came from. Being in his arms just felt safe. It felt right. It felt like she had always been destined to find her way to him.

It was almost embarrassing how badly she craved him right then.

"Saiden."

His name fell from her lips, a wanton plea for him to take more of her.

All of her.

Wrapping a leg around his hip to pull him closer, she pressed her aching pussy against his rigid cock. She was grateful for the swim since the water hid how wet her panties would have been otherwise.

Not that she needed to hide her arousal. She was done hiding from Saiden.

She was done hiding from life.

He growled something incoherent in her ear, but she understood his intention all the same. They weren't teasing this time. Weren't dancing around their attraction. There was something primal happening, a need inside them both that couldn't be, *wouldn't be*, denied. Her muscles could spasm however much they wanted, but all she would feel was Saiden.

She reached between them to slide her hand inside his boxer briefs, and nearly stopped breathing altogether when she felt him. She knew now what he meant earlier about his cock being underwhelming when he was low on blood. He must have fed at some point because he had gone from unquestionably large to 'Oh dear God, am I insane to try this?'

Of course she was insane. She was out of her fucking mind, and there was no turning back.

She curled her hand around as much of his girth as possible, loving how his cock twitched and his hips thrust forward. As if her touch alone might drive him to madness. She circled a thumb around the tip and tried not to blush at the drop of moisture that was not water. There was something empowering about knowing he felt just as strongly for her as she did for him.

A tiny prick of pain nipped at her lip, and she pulled back in time to see his fangs slide the rest of the way out. A drop of blood dangled off the edge of one tooth. Just a single drop, waiting to be sucked into the ecstasy that was Saiden's mouth or lost to the cold, hard ground where it would dissolve into nothing.

If she gave herself over to him, he could take whatever he wanted. Could take her completely. Yet for some reason, she wasn't afraid anymore.

She was intrigued.

She leaned forward and let the tip of her tongue dart out to snag the drop of blood, surprised that she didn't entirely hate the coppery taste.

Saiden fixed an intense stare on her throat when she swallowed before dragging his eyes up to meet her heated gaze. He must have seen at least some apprehension on her face, though, because he pressed his forehead to hers and whispered, "I won't hurt you. I promise."

Her hand squeezed tighter around his cock, and the resulting moan sank into her skin, fueling the heat throbbing between her thighs.

"What if I want you to?" she offered breathily.

His eyes shuttered, and his body stiffened. "Don't say that if you don't mean it, Cora."

She released him so she could slide both hands up and around the back of his neck. Leaning forward, she licked a water droplet off the thick muscular column of his neck.

"Look at me," she ordered, her breath hitching at the beauty in his eyes when he did. "I want to experience all of you, Saiden, and I do mean *all*. So shut up and make me forget about everything else in this world for at least a little while."

He shook his head. "I can't bite you, Cora. The way you taste... What you mean to me... I might not be able to stop."

"So then don't bite me," she offered. "You're more than just a vampire, Saiden. Show me what it means to be with *you*. Just you. Just for tonight."

He winced, and she didn't know if it was because he wasn't able to separate sex and blood, or if it was something else. She didn't even have time to ponder it because between one gasp and the next, he wrapped her in his arms and shot them over to a spacious green meadow on the other side of the pool, somehow shucking his briefs in the process.

He lay her out on the soft, mossy ground and parted one thigh with his knee. He stared at her for a long moment, drinking her in like he was a dying man and she was his salvation. She couldn't think too much about that look though, what emotion was shining through as he possessed her with his eyes.

The last rays of sunlight danced over his skin, casting his features into a mixture of glowing peaks and shaded valleys. The contrast was hypnotizing, like he was a fallen angel come to claim her.

She let out a whimper when he bent down and sucked one of her nipples into his mouth through the thin fabric of her bra. His tongue flicked and swirled around that taught bud, teasing it while his hand slid down her stomach to cup the space between her thighs. He brushed his palm along her throbbing clit, and Cora rolled her hips against his hand, grinding into his fingers to chase the satisfying friction she'd dreamt of the night before.

When he pulled back, she cried out at the loss of sensation.

"These are in the way," Saiden growled before tearing her panties off with his teeth. His behavior was animalistic, skating the edge between violent and erotic, and if he didn't fuck her soon, she might honestly start begging.

Saiden had other ideas, though. Ideas she got fully on board with when he licked a line straight up through the center of her pussy. Back bowing, she threaded her hands through his dark hair, gripping the soft strands as she bucked and writhed against his face.

And then he showed her exactly what it meant to be pleasured by a vampire.

She screamed when his tongue kicked into overdrive, practically thrumming against her clit in a way that not even her high-end vibrator could achieve. The intensity bordered on excessive, yet she would die a not-so-little death before she stopped him.

The orgasm exploded inside her, and she cried out in ecstasy, riding his tongue until every last ounce of release had been wrung out of her.

She lay on the ground, spent, weak, and thoroughly satisfied.

"That was..." Her mouth tried to speak, but her brain was so drenched in oxytocin that it hung up a 'back in ten minutes' sign and completely abandoned her.

"I'm glad you think so," Saiden purred as he crawled up her body, leaving soft kisses in his wake. "That was just the beginning."

Staring down at him, she sucked in a breath when he gripped his impressive erection and rubbed his cock over her swollen clit. Her body shuddered under the overpowering sensation, the lightning under her skin shooting down her body to create another thunderstorm between her legs.

"Beginning?" she croaked out. He was really going to test her belief that dying in his arms wouldn't be a bad way to go.

Saiden grinned as he positioned himself at her entrance and teased her with just the tip of his cock. "Oh, Cora. I'm going to embed my scent so deeply into your skin that no amount of time will ever let you forget me."

Forget him? Like that had ever been an option to begin with. Saiden was not someone you forgot. Saiden wasn't a person; he was an experience. Fucking him was like being swept up into a tornado. All you could do was hang on and hope to survive.

He thrust into her with one smooth motion, sinking himself completely to the hilt. The slightest hint of pain fluttered through her at how wide he stretched her open, but then he started rocking his hips, and there was only euphoria. All-encompassing euphoria that demanded her complete surrender.

She chased that feeling as he pushed himself harder and faster, reaching a spot inside her she thought was a myth. His mouth latched onto the soft space above her collarbone, and his fangs scraped against the sensitive skin. She shuddered, wishing for just a minute that he would let go and take all she had to offer.

"Fuck, Cora," he moaned when he pulled back. "Do you even know how much you drive me crazy? I want to murder any man who has even looked at your sweet pussy."

It should have scared her. His declaration. Because if any guy could make good on a threat like that, it was Saiden. But the shiver that ran through her wasn't fear. It was exhilaration. And it took her to the edge once more. She wanted to say something, but she had no words to describe how he made her feel.

At least not any she was ready to give voice to.

All she could do was wrap her legs around his torso and lock her ankles, deepening the angle and bringing him flush against her. Then she dragged her nails down his back. She didn't care if any scratches healed immediately. She wanted to leave her mark on him in some small way, even if just for a second. Because the mark he left on her would last for the rest of her days.

His answering moan sank into her skin, and she did it again.

He wrapped an arm under her back and pulled them both upright until she was all but bouncing on his cock as he lifted her up and down.

She couldn't take it any longer. She grabbed his face and slammed her mouth against his, letting her tongue graze his fang. Letting him taste just one more drop of her lifeforce.

Saiden threw his head back and growled, "You're killing me, Cora. I need you to come for me now. I need to feel you clenching around me."

Then he reached down to flick her clit with his thumb, and she was lost to him. A second orgasm rolled through her in a crashing wave of pleasure she would gladly drown in.

Moments later, Saiden shouted his own release in a deep roar that felt like he was announcing his claim to the world, and the pure warmth that filled Cora was unlike anything she'd ever felt before. Unlike anything she would ever feel again.

Hope to survive? Talk about naïve.

She was already gone.

# Chapter Thirty-Five

## Saiden

The last vestiges of day surrendered to night's tranquil embrace while Saiden lay next to Cora in the small grassy meadow. He'd been worried at first that things might be awkward after, but she'd let him curl her body into his side and leisurely stroke her arms as they shifted into idle post-coital chatter.

At one point he felt her shiver, and he dashed up to retrieve their clothes from above the waterfall before she even realized he was gone. Her underwear was beyond saving, so he only handed over her leggings and shirt, hoping she didn't notice that he pocketed the wet scraps of fabric.

Once dressed, he lay back down, waiting with strained breath to see what she would do. A blissful sigh eased out of him when she molded her body to his once more, this time wrapping her arm up and over his chest to snuggle.

"Tell me something about yourself," she said, resting her cheek on his shoulder. "You're like this big mystery that I don't know anything about other than the one rather notable fact."

"That I'm an incredible lover?"

She laughed and playfully smacked his arm. "That's not what I meant." She paused, then added, "Even if it is accurate."

He was pretty sure he found his new favorite color when she blushed a little, and the crimson hue of her cheeks accented the strawberry scent enveloping him like a cloud. He didn't even notice the medicinal tinge anymore. All he smelled was her. If he closed his eyes, he could practically imagine himself sitting in a berry field, feeding slices of pie to Cora. It was tempting to lick the side of her face and see if she tasted as good as she smelled since he had already experienced just how delectable other parts of her were.

"It's just a little weird," Cora continued. "I feel like I've known you for years, and yet I don't actually know anything."

Saiden knew exactly what she meant. He could barely remember his life before Cora, and he couldn't imagine his life without her.

"I like to crochet," he offered, needing to lighten the mood before he did something stupid like confess his eternal and undying love.

"No, you don't," she said with a giggle, and the sound was sweeter than any music.

"I'm serious," he replied, nuzzling the top of her head. "I spend a lot of time on surveillance just sitting around. If I don't keep my hands busy, I'll go insane. Don't tell my cousins, though. I'd never live it down."

Cora propped herself up and gave him a dubious look. "You're not messing with me?"

"Not even a little bit," he said, removing a stray twig from her tangled hair. "My little sister used to knit all the time a few hundred years ago. I like crocheting better, but it still reminds me of her."

She blinked at him a couple times as if the factoid short-circuited her brain cells.

"What do you make?" she asked once the gears seemed to reset themselves.

"Little animals usually. Sometimes I come across human children when I'm hunting rogues, so I'll leave one with them for comfort until Tressa arrives to wipe their memories."

Cora's eyes searched his face for so long that the scrutiny started to make him uncomfortable.

"What?"

She shook her head, then lay back down on his chest. "You just keep surprising me is all."

"And that's a good thing?"

She sighed. "Honestly? I'm not sure yet."

He stroked her hair and slowed his breathing so his rising chest didn't disturb her too much. "What else do you want to know?"

She was quiet for a moment, and he listened to the sounds of rushing water mixing with the crickets chirping nearby.

At heart he was a predator, more dangerous than any of the other nocturnal forest creatures emerging from their dens to begin their evening hunts. There was a peacefulness to the night that he could never find in the day, as if the shadows settling over him forced a pressure to drop away from his chest. With night vision better than any of the owls watching over them, he was just as at home in the dark as any human was during the day.

Eventually it would become too cold for her, though. Or she would be too nervous to be in the woods late at night. Until that time came, he would cherish every second of contact with her.

"I guess tell me more about this whole rogue hunting thing," she said a minute later. "When you first brought it up, I thought you were just a method actor trying a little too hard to get the role. Now that I know the truth, I'm kinda curious about what it all entails."

He let his gaze lock on the stars above him for a second, searching for the answer in their glittering brilliance. He didn't remember what it was like to look at the night sky as a human, but he knew it was a damn shame that Cora couldn't see what he could—a tapestry of constellations spreading out over a blanket of swirling sapphire and violet. An explosion of stardust, like grains of twinkling salt tossed up into the sky with abandon.

To his disappointment, the stars didn't hold the guidance he was looking for. The answer to her question was easy, but what he struggled with was how much truth to reveal. Too much, and she might bolt like a rabbit. Too little, and she would think he was hiding things from her.

In the end, the reality of the situation made the decision for him. He had precious little time with her, so best to get it all out in the open that way he could judge her reaction and determine the amount of damage control needed.

"There are laws within our society," he began slowly, keeping his tone soft and casual as if discussing the Treaty of Ghent.

*Nothing too disturbing here, just a little lesson in how much of a murderer I am*, he thought.

Damn, he would kill for Tressa's calming ability. She could tell a person their entire family had been brutally massacred, and they'd take the news no worse than hearing they stepped in dog shit.

"One of those laws," he continued, "is regarding the creation of more vampires. Secrecy is paramount to our existence, naturally, but it's also necessary to control the population. If vampires were allowed to go unchecked, siring more and more of our kind, eventually we would have no food source."

He felt her stiffen and kicked himself for phrasing it like that. He made it sound like vampires looked at humans the way Cora looked at a hamburger. Like mortals were little more than twitchy, irrational, anxiety-filled cows.

*Smooth, Saiden. Smooth like butter filled with pop rocks.*

"I guess I can understand that," Cora accepted, relaxing slightly, and he thanked Lilith that she reacted to things better than the average high-strung bovine.

"To prevent the inevitable downfall of our kind, a bunch of vamps got together long before I was born and established two rules. The first being that no vampire can sire more than one other vampire, and the human they choose has to be willing. It keeps our population relatively low and still allows us to turn our mate."

Cora ran a hand leisurely over his chest, and the casual relaxed motion almost caused him to shiver with delight. He wanted to stay there with her forever, hiding from the pain of reality.

"You said that word before. 'Mate.' I'm guessing you aren't referring to the Australian definition?"

He chuckled. "No. A vampire's mate is essentially the other half of their soul. The only other person who could happily endure spending eternity at their side. It's a supernatural bond that transcends reason and science. More than love, more than devotion, it's a connection that can't be explained, only felt. When a vampire meets their mate... they just know."

"It sounds wonderful," Cora replied, her voice full of awe and maybe a hint of wistfulness.

"It is." Saiden gulped, wondering if it was the right moment to tell her. "Or so I've heard," he added, chickening out.

A heaviness settled over them until Cora eventually broke the silence. "What's the other rule?"

Saiden ran his fingers down the curve of her hip, wishing they could go back to the conversation about mates so he could try again to tell her. "Rule two is the obvious one. Not telling anyone about our kind."

"Which is why you brought me here; you need Marquin to wipe your existence from my brain."

There was a sadness to her voice that nearly broke his heart. He wanted to believe it was for him. That she hated the idea of being forced to forget their time together.

He knew better than that, even if he wished he didn't. All she wanted to do was make her movie before she died, and he was likely nothing more than a pleasant distraction for her.

He cleared his throat. "Yeah. That's why."

She nodded. "So, a rogue vampire is what then? Someone who broke the rules?"

"Essentially," he replied. "Sometimes it's a vampire that isn't being careful and is letting mortals learn about us. Most of the time, a rogue is one making more of our kind beyond their allowed single turn. Oftentimes that behavior just ends up breeding more vampires who don't know about our rules. A rogue might change three mortals then grow bored and abandon them. Those three don't know anything about how to survive, so they resort to what little they've heard about vampires from books and movies—brazenly killing and feeding. Then they go make more like them. It's a self-perpetuating cycle, and it's my job to stop it."

"You hunt them down and kill them," she said. A statement, not a question.

Saiden stiffened. "I do."

"And do you like it?"

He pulled away from her hold and stared at her. He doubted she could make out too much of him in the dark, but he needed to see her face. Needed to see what she truly thought of him.

"No, Cora. I don't. Do you honestly think me so evil that I would enjoy killing anyone, regardless of the situation?"

She bit her lip and wrinkled her brow for a second before her face relaxed. "No. I don't think that. I'm sorry. I didn't mean to be offensive."

He settled down and guided her head back to his shoulder. Back to where she belonged. His mate.

"I hate it," he whispered into the night. "I hate that it needs to be done, and I hate that it's gotten worse lately. Mostly, I hate that I'm good at it."

"I hate that for you," Cora whispered back, their words melding in the darkness.

"Thank you," he said, unsure of any other adequate response. "I don't think I'll ever stop doing what I do, because I still hold onto the hope that I can save some of them. The other enforcers don't even try. They've become so desensitized that the rogues are little more than animals to them. I've seen firsthand how wrong that can be if you get to them early enough." He paused. "I just wish it wasn't the only thing in my life."

"That makes sense," Cora murmured, her voice taking on a sleepy tone. "I hope you find your mate someday. I hope she's so amazing that you can forget about all the bad in your life, Saiden. I hope you can just be happy for once."

Her words were a curse and a blessing.

"I hope so too," he whispered, clutching her tighter. "I hope so too."

# Chapter Thirty-Six

## Cora

It was nearly midnight when Cora finally cried uncle, admitting she was a little too cold and a lot too tired to stay at the falls any longer. The drive back up to the compound was quiet, but the silence wasn't awkward so much as contemplative. Both of them seemingly lost in thought.

She tried to force her brain toward safer subjects, but it kept bouncing back to Saiden and their discussion about mates. The reverence in his tone when he spoke about them. The longing and sadness that practically emanated from his body.

The conversation had sparked something in Cora that she couldn't quite put her finger on when they'd been laying in the clearing. Something that bothered her, and the feeling had only grown as the night wore on. As he told her more about his cousins and his early life in Sicily. As she told him about the first short film she ever made, and how she learned the hard way that fake blood can dye your skin.

Whatever they talked about, that feeling was still there in the background, demanding she pay more attention. It kept pestering her like an itch that needed to be scratched yet some doctor had said 'whatever you do, don't scratch it.' Knowing she shouldn't examine the feeling just made it tug harder.

Saiden expertly navigated the dark forest roads with an ease that spoke of a lifetime spent making the drive. He kept the headlights off, telling her he could see just fine and didn't want to blind any woodland creatures. It was such a considerate thought, so at odds with what she thought a vampire's nature should be.

Cast almost completely into darkness and with no other conversation to focus on, Cora mistakenly let her thoughts wander back to the moment when she told Saiden that she hoped he found his mate. The moment when he'd responded with, "I hope so too."

The unrelenting feeling she'd been fighting so hard to ignore flared to life once more, forcing her to accept it for what it was.

Jealousy.

But that was even more absurd than the fact that vampires existed to begin with. They had sex one time. Or maybe five times. She never understood how people counted that. Did the multiple orgasms he'd overwhelmed her with earlier each count as their own time? Or was it more like one movie but broken up into different scenes?

Wow. Her brain was really struggling to think of literally anything except the reason why she was jealous.

She cared about him. At some point during all the kidnapping and soulful confessions, she'd started to think of him as something more than a vampire. She'd started to think of him as just a guy. A guy she might like to date. A guy she could maybe even love one day if so many things were different.

She forced the sigh to stay locked inside her throat and not escape out into the wild where Saiden might ask what she was thinking about. There simply was no future between them in any capacity. Even if she wasn't dying, she was still human and would never be anything but human.

Which meant as soon as she spoke to Marquin, Saiden would be wiped from her mind forever. That thought threw a smothering blanket of sadness on the flaming jealousy burning in her stomach. She didn't *want* to forget Saiden, even though she *should*. After all, if they couldn't be together, then wouldn't it be better to Eternal Sunshine his obscenely tight ass from her mind?

Her brain begged for a razor to cut out every trace of him, yet her heart vehemently denied that request. If she was going to die soon, then she wanted to keep the memory of this experience. Wanted something to clutch onto and revisit when things started to get bad.

Of course, the likelihood of Marquin approving that request was so laughable it deserved its own Netflix special.

Cora was still struggling with her emotions when Saiden guided the Aston Martin up to the main gate. He stopped the car, waved at the camera, then sat back, waiting for someone to let him in.

A minute went by and nothing happened.

Cora glanced over at Saiden who now sported a rather deep frown. He was lucky vampires didn't need to worry about Botox with how prominent those ridges became when he was stressed.

"What's wrong?"

"Nobody's opening up," Saiden observed warily, a tight edge to his tone.

"Maybe they're on a break or going to the bathroom."

He shook his head. "No. Anytime Baylin isn't monitoring, he turns the tablet over to one of our human security teams. Even if they were otherwise occupied, they would have it nearby to check any motion notifications. Something's wrong."

"Oh, come on, Saiden," Cora scoffed. "I get that being a vampire means you take security seriously, but humans do have to use the restroom sometimes. Plus, it's the middle of the night. They probably didn't expect anyone back."

The muscles in his back bunched, and the longer they waited, the more his concern started to bleed over into her. Cora swept her eyes over the ground outside the window, but there was nothing to see save for an ominous pitch black nothing. The only light around was the faint red blinking just below the camera.

Another minute passed, and that light too went out.

"Shit," Saiden cursed, pushing open the car door. He stalked over to an electric panel beside the gate and pulled it open. He jabbed at a few buttons until a mechanical whirring cut through the hauntingly silent night. Slowly, the gate started to slide open.

"If you had a code why not use it from the start?" she asked when he returned.

"It's an emergency override," he replied, easing the car forward down the drive. "If you open the gate using that code, then it won't shut again. It's a manual fail safe in case something goes horribly wrong. The doors open, and the system locks them so our human employees can't be trapped inside."

A tremor ran through Cora's body. She placed a hand on Saiden's arm and looked up at him. "We're not in any danger here, are we?"

His expression gave nothing away, no hint of the severity of the situation beyond that touch of concern carving deep frown lines. "Nothing immediate," he replied. "I would know if that were the case. There might be a valid reason for everything, but I wouldn't be good at my job if I didn't take every potential threat seriously."

"Okay," she said, sinking back into the seat, her heart beating faster than a hummingbird's. She should have asked more questions about his threat awareness ability. Like whether or not it included people around him.

Saiden pulled the car up to the main building and cut the engine. The entire place was dark, not a single flicker of light in sight. Maybe it was all just a power outage?

Yeah, right, like she hadn't seen enough horror movies to recognize the wide-open front door for what it really was.

"Saiden, what's going on," she asked, trying to hide the wobble of fear in her voice. She was a horror film director, damnit. She ate fear for breakfast.

His eyes darted from the home to the grounds just beyond. "I'm not sure," he replied.

She wondered just how much more he could see with his vamp vision. Whatever he saw, he clearly didn't like because he handed her the keys.

"Listen to me, Cora. I want you to lock the doors and keep the engine running. If you hear anything other than me telling you it's safe, I want you to get out of here. Drive into town, and hide somewhere near a lot of people. I'll come find you when everything is clear."

She blinked at him. "How will you know where I am?"

"I can smell you a mile away, Cora. I'll find you. I said you were safe with me, and I meant it." He paused for a second as if debating, then leaned in and pressed his lips to hers. The kiss was fast and intense and over before Cora even knew what happened.

Then Saiden was gone, vanished into the night.

She stared out into the dark around her, wondering if she should be worried that she might never see him again.

Cora raised a finger to her swollen lips, still able to feel him there, and allowed his last words to run through her mind.

*I said you were safe with me.*

Only she wasn't with him now.

It was that thought that was still rolling through her brain a minute later when the car door was yanked open, and something clubbed her over the head.

*Shit*, she thought as an inky blackness rolled over her vision.

*Why do I never remember to lock the doors?*

# Chapter Thirty-Seven

## Saiden

He took on nests of rogue vampires without hesitation. He put himself into the most dangerous of situations on a near daily basis, and not once did he feel the slightest whisper of fear.

Because he'd never had anything to lose before.

Saiden crept stealthily through the halls, keeping his threat awareness on high alert. Three to four seconds was all the warning he normally got, but for a vampire it was more than enough time to avoid most attacks. With his ears straining for the slightest sound, he searched for anything to indicate the presence of his family or the intruders.

Nothing. Which meant either the house was empty, or everyone inside was already unconscious.

Or dead.

Saiden shook his head. He couldn't think like that. He could only focus on the facts at hand, and the facts were that he didn't smell any blood.

He sped down the hall to Baylin's room, hoping for a clue as to what occurred. He wasn't surprised to find it empty, but he was surprised to see the overturned Rockstar slowly dripping the last of its liquid onto the floor. What happened here happened fast and not long ago. Baylin would never abandon an energy drink voluntarily.

Beyond that, the room held no clues as to what could have caused a hasty departure.

A sharp icy feeling rolled over Saiden's head, and he went preternaturally still, recognizing the ghost-like tingle that alerted him to danger.

Spinning on his heels, he sank into a half crouch, left arm rising to block the incoming attack he'd sensed.

Nothing happened, though. No blow landed. No foe was even present. Only heavy silence filled the manor.

*What the hell?*

His ability never failed him before. Never gave a single false signal in three hundred years. But if there was no danger around him then...

His heart jackhammered in his chest, and an overwhelming urge to go check on Cora swept through him. He needed to see that she was safe first. Then he would worry about his malfunctioning gift.

He turned to leave the room when a sound finally reached his ears. It was just a faint thud. Could have been anything really. But there was no mistaking the soft, pained grunt that accompanied it.

*Lilith, no.*

His ability had been trying to warn him about Cora. About his mate who was still out in the car.

He dashed at top speed back toward the front door. Bursting out into the night, he skidded to a stop on the marble steps when he saw what awaited him.

Cora hung limply from the arms of a female vampire. More worrisome was the fact that it was a vampire he'd never seen before.

Everything about the girl screamed innocence. From the blonde curly hair, to the pink sundress, to the chubby cheeked face that made her appear barely eighteen. She looked like she should be asking a boy to the Sadie Hawkins dance, not holding his mate with one arm while the other hand gently caressed Cora's neck.

"Hello, Saiden," she greeted, her voice filled with so much cotton candy sweetness that it made his teeth ache.

His body itched to race forward, to grab Cora and get her to safety. Then, and only then, would he come back and destroy whoever the hell this bitch was.

The only thing stopping him was the long, sharp nails dancing along Cora's pulsing jugular. Nails sharp enough to rip out his mate's throat faster than he could dive forward to stop it.

So he stood there, frozen in fear, and doing his best to let none of the turmoil shredding his insides show on his face.

"Who are you, and what are you doing with my dinner?" he asked, feigning indifference in the hope of bluffing his way to an advantage.

If he thought the girl's voice was syrupy, then her laugh might induce diabetes. It filled the air and floated on the breeze, a tinkling melody that nestled into your ears and forced the widest and happiest of grins to your face.

Wasn't that interesting. Saiden had thought Cora looked like a siren earlier, but this vamp really was one. It gripped him, that laughter, begging him to dance and play with her.

Luckily, he'd spent centuries learning to suppress Eliana's pull, so this Mary Sue wasn't sinking her psychic claws into him anytime soon.

"Nice trick. That normally work for you?" he asked, taking a slow step down the stairs. He stopped advancing when the blonde's grin turned wicked, and she pricked Cora's throat. It destroyed Saiden to stand there and watch as a thin rivulet of his mate's blood slowly dribbled down to bloom across the collar of her t-shirt.

"It does, yes," the girl replied. "Especially with the younger ones, and normally those are the only ones I care about. Or 'cared' I guess, since you came along and murdered them."

Saiden thrust his hands into his pockets, the perfect image of calm and collected. "Oh, yeah? You'll need to be more specific. I've killed a lot of young vamps." He gave her his own wicked grin. "Some old ones too."

*Oh, she did not like that*, he thought as the blonde's face contorted into rage. He could practically feel the fury rolling off her. She wasn't fooling anybody with her loveable prom queen act.

Her voice lost all its light and laughter, instead twisting into something inhuman and feral. "You really don't care, do you?" she growled. "They're all just nameless faces. You just waltz in, murder them, then curl up in bed as if you spent the day gardening. Is that all we are to you? Weeds to be plucked? A blight on your refined vampire society? You probably don't even remember Montrose."

Saiden pretended to pick some dirt out from under a fingernail. Oh, he knew Montrose. He would never forget Montrose. It happened about five years ago and was the first and only time he had been too late to prevent a nasty situation. Three rogue baby vamps had killed a couple humans in Montrose, Colorado, and a janitor found the bodies stuffed inside a furnace that was down for unscheduled maintenance.

The city lost its mind when the mangled corpses were discovered. Police pulled a fingerprint off the deceased, and that was it. By the time he arrived in town, Baylin alerted him that a SWAT team was already on the way to the vamp's still registered address. If his team had found the rogues sooner, he might have been able to save them. They weren't insane from what he could tell. Just three young men living in the suburbs that didn't know any better. But the cops needed a killer to give to the press, so he did the only thing he could do with little notice. He placed a few sticks of dynamite at the back of the house, and once the police verified there were people in the home, he lit the fuse.

Boom. No more serial killers plaguing the town.

It still ate at him some nights. How they never even knew it was coming. Never had a chance to decide they wanted to be different.

If this woman sired those vamps, then he could understand her anger. It didn't change anything, but a hint of empathy was there.

Saiden's senses never left Cora as he ignored the blonde's rant and acted oblivious about Montrose. Cora's heartbeat started to slow, the stream of blood down her neck flowing steadily. He estimated she had less than a couple minutes before she bled out completely which meant he needed to piss this vampire off. Needed to force her to make a mistake.

He shrugged his shoulders in an exaggerated movement. "Why would I remember a specific kill? They're all just rogues. It's not like they matter."

Bullseye.

An unholy shriek ripped from the girl, and she shook Cora like a ragdoll.

It took all his energy to keep up the casual façade when he wanted nothing more than to pull his mate from the psychotic vampire's grasp and hide her away somewhere safe where she'd never suffer so much as a papercut for the rest of her life.

*Please help me, Lilith*, he pleaded. Less than one second was all he needed to tear the vamps head from her shoulders, yet it might as well be an hour so long as her nails continued to dig into Cora's flesh.

"To you!" the blonde screeched. "They don't matter *to you*. But they mattered to me. They were my children, and you murdered them because we don't want to follow your stupid rules. Why do you get to decide, huh? Maybe it's time for someone else to be in charge."

Saiden held up his hands in a placating gesture. "Then take it up with the Ruling Coalition, and leave me to my meal. I get cranky when people steal my food."

"Oh, is that what this is?" she asked, digging her nails in tighter so two more thin streams of blood raced down alongside the first.

Cora wouldn't survive the torture much longer.

Blood dripped onto the blonde's shoes, but she didn't seem to notice or care. "This human is just a snack to you? That's funny because I've been watching you for a while now, and you don't do 'snacks.' In fact, if scent is any indication, then I'd say this lovely creature was your mate." She took a deep inhale. "Yes, you smell delicious together."

The words drained every bit of blood from Saiden's face, and he dropped his mask of indifference. If the vamp knew what Cora was to him, then there was no point in trying to hide it. It was time for intimidation.

"If you know who I am then you know exactly what I'm capable of. The kind of torment I can inflict. If she dies, there will be no limit to my wrath. You will beg for a death that will never come. I will spend every waking second of eternity ensuring you remain in a permanent state of unending agony."

"Hmmm..." the blonde mused, tilting her chin and staring into the dark as if considering something. "See, the problem is that we find ourselves in a bit of a pickle. You murdered three of my children, and I've spent years tracking you down for my revenge. It only seems fair that I get to murder someone you love. In fact, I'm the one with the raw end of the deal because I'm only going to kill one person. I'm willing to call it square, though, given that this one happens to be your mate."

She bent down and ran her tongue down the length of Cora's neck, lapping up the small bit of blood that pooled in the hollow at the base of Cora's throat.

"I must say, Saiden, she tastes delicious once you get past that mortal medicine. If I were you, I'd have a hard time turning her and losing all that precious human blood. Consider this a favor from me to you. I'll remove the temptation."

"There is nowhere you will be able to hide if you do this," he threatened through clenched teeth.

"Maybe that's true," the vamp acknowledged, idly stabbing another hole in Cora's skin. Then another. "Maybe it's not. Maybe I don't care."

He couldn't even see Cora's neck anymore, it was so covered in a thick sheet of bright crimson blood. She might not even survive another sixty seconds.

He had to do something. He refused to watch her die without a fight.

Coiling every muscle in his body, he slid one foot back to rest against the stair, preparing to pounce.

"Oh, you'll care," he purred. "You know, I think I'm going to kill you the same way I did your children. Do you want to hear about it? How I shattered their legs and tore their arms from their shoulders. How I poured gas over their twitching bodies and set them ablaze. How I watched their skin slowly blister and peel while they screamed for help. They died begging for you, thinking you might come and save them, but you never did."

His words, despite being completely fabricated, had the intended effect. The vamp curled her fist in anger pulling those sharp claws away from Cora's delicate throat long enough for him to make his move.

The marble step cracked like a starter pistol as Saiden pushed off the step, flew through the air, and tackled Cora out of the vamp's grasp. Letting his senses guide him toward the best possible outcome, he twisted his body midair and wrapped himself around her. He braced for impact as the force of his launch propelled them into the surrounding forest.

They crashed into a poor oak tree a dozen yards from the edge of the driveway, sending a fracture line up through its center. Saiden didn't even feel the pain of the broken ribs or his freshly dislocated shoulder, the entirety of his focus on the bleeding human in his arms.

Her heartbeat was so weak he needed his vampire hearing to even know it was there. Seconds. His mate would be dead in seconds if he didn't prevent it.

"Guess you have a choice to make," the blonde called, and Saiden whipped his head up to see her standing next to the Aston Martin with its keys spinning around one manicured finger. "What'll it be? Save the girl or get revenge. We both know that I win either way."

Then she blew him a kiss and hopped in the car.

He barely registered the door slamming and the vehicle speeding off down the road because none of that mattered. Cora was dying. Not in a year, not in a couple years. Now.

He had the ability to change her fate, but if he did she might never forgive him. Not that he could blame her. Forcing his existence on someone who didn't choose it wasn't the same as signing them up for a yoga class. Her entire world would change in ways that she already stated she didn't want.

Maybe he really was the monster Cora thought he was because at that moment Saiden simply didn't care. She could hate him for a thousand years so long as she did it with breath in her lungs.

Sealing his lips to hers, he let his vampiric Essence flow out of him.

Saiden hadn't been conscious when Marquin turned him, and he had never been around for a new siring before. They were so rare that many vamps never witnessed one. Still, every vampire innately knew what to do. From the time they were turned, they could feel the Essence inside them, itching to be released and shared with another.

He just didn't realize it would be so beautiful.

Keeping his eyes open and his lips on hers, he held his breath while the faint purple glow emerged from his skin, surrounding them in a cloud of pure energy. Stunned, he watched as the last hints of Essence floated out of him and started to pour into Cora, draping her in a cocoon of pulsing violet light.

His perfect, beautiful mate.

Then she took one last shuddering breath and died in Saiden's arms.

# Chapter Thirty-Eight

## Cora

Cora dreamt of a circus.

The dream state was obvious straight away, and not just because Cora would never go to a circus—she found the animal cruelty outweighed any potential joy—but because the place she found herself in was not a normal circus. The lights shined a little too bright, and the depths of the shadows were a little too prominent. Something moved in those dark places, and though it skulked just out of sight, there was no denying that she could sense its presence.

Whatever it was slipped away, and Cora found herself lost to the flashing lights and the infectious sounds of laughter and frivolity.

Large plumes of purple cotton candy floated through the air, yet nobody else seemed to notice them. She bumped into one, and it exploded into sugar crystals that rained down over the long black dress that clung tightly to her body.

The outfit was all wrong for a fun night out at a circus. Midnight crushed velvet with flared sleeves and a low-cut bodice. She looked like a less boobilicious Elvira.

*Take it off,* she thought.

She wanted to. She wanted to rip it from her body, preferring to go naked over this gown that was all wrong for her. The fit was too tight, too uncomfortable. She shouldn't be wearing it, but when she reached behind her back there was no zipper.

Frantically, she clawed at the stretchy material, but it wouldn't budge. It was as if the dress was now a part of her, fused to her skin. Something she could never take off.

*Wrong. Wrong. Wrong.*

The words echoed through her brain as she stumbled through the crowd, trying to find the exit. She dashed from one end to the other, the circus seeming to close in on her while also expanding in all directions.

No exit. There was simply no exit. Only sparkling lights and calliope music. Groups of people laughing. Everyone having an amazing time.

Didn't they know it was all wrong?

Pushing through the crushing throngs of delighted circus goers, she stopped abruptly when she found herself in front of a metal cage. Inside, a white tiger paced back and forth, occasionally stopping to snarl or growl at some unseen thing in the distance.

*Don't pet the tiger*, she thought. *Bad idea.*

And yet... It was so mesmerizing. So majestically beautiful with its restrained violence. A predator this fierce shouldn't be trapped. Shouldn't be caged.

*Let it out.*

The new thought wasn't hers. She didn't know where the voice inside her head came from, but it was familiar and comforting. A voice that promised everything would be alright in the end. All you had to do was trust it.

So, she did.

Reaching up to the thick metal bolt, Cora slid the latch over and pushed open the door to the cage.

The tiger stalked over to the threshold and stared down at her. Something ancient and primal danced in the depths of its dark brown eyes as they searched her face.

It really was so beautiful.

And then the beast pounced.

# Chapter Thirty-Nine

## Saiden

"Bianca Holgrem."

Saiden snapped his head over to where his brother sat in front of the computer monitor. "You found her?"

They had been searching for almost an entire day for any information about the blonde vamp that attacked Cora. Baylin had been able to pull only a single blurry still from the security cameras before the system went dark, and he'd been running it through an enhanced facial recognition program for the past ten hours.

Granted it would have been more like twelve hours except Saiden wasn't particularly helpful in providing details at the beginning. His family showed up at the compound shortly after he started Cora's transformation, but he didn't even bother asking where they'd been or what happened. All he cared about was his mate.

Without so much as a word, he'd taken her into his bedroom and stayed locked to her side for the first couple of hours. Turning someone into a vampire wasn't an instant process. It could take anywhere from half a day to three days depending on the human, and the entire time they needed a slow trickle of Essence to keep the initial influx burning until completion. It was why vampires almost always had family nearby before a change. That way someone could step in and take over when the sire needed a break.

Tressa was with Cora right now, but Saiden couldn't fight off the urge to return to his mate for much longer. He'd stepped away once to tell them everything he knew about the attack, and a second one shortly after to demand answers from his family. He may have also made a handful of idle threats against their lives and limbs, but his fury at them died off when he was reminded that his cell would work better if he kept it on him. He'd been so wrapped up in his date with Cora that remembering something as trivial as a phone had fallen to the wayside.

It was all Eliana, they'd relayed once he calmed enough to see reason. She'd seen something and pulled all the vamps from the compound at the last minute, leaving only the humans inside, clueless as to what was happening. Minutes later gas filled the house, knocking everyone out, and Bianca showed up.

It was all too easy. Had to be an inside job, they'd determined.

Tressa was the one who eventually caught Donna trying to sneak out the back of the property. It took little effort to wring the confession from their housekeeper, and the sound of hearts breaking could be heard throughout the compound. She had been like family to them, and no one could fathom any possible reason for her betrayal. Until they could figure out not only the how but the why, she was currently enjoying an indefinite stay in their five-star dungeon.

Saiden had made them all promise not to touch the human. Not until he had his chance first.

"Yeah," Baylin said, pulling Saiden's attention back to the task at hand. "I think so. Is this her?"

It would be a thousand years before he'd forget the face of the one who stole his mate's life. The one who stole his chance to convince her to turn willingly. This Bianca had ripped everything away from him, and staring at the grainy snapshot on Baylin's monitor caused an intense kind of anger to flare to life that he hadn't felt in a long time.

The overwhelming urge for violence coursed through him. Not because it was his job and not because it was necessary. No. He wanted to fulfill every promise of pain he'd made to Bianca last night. He wanted her to suffer.

"Where is she?" he gritted out, clenching his fists so tight he might break his own bones again if he didn't calm down.

"Unknown," Baylin replied as screen after screen flashed up on the monitor.

Too fast and complicated for Saiden to understand, he collapsed into the chair next to his brother and tried to force the tension from his muscles. He needed to think rationally right now. Later, he promised himself. Later there would be blood. Oceans of it.

"Let me check one other thing..." Baylin trailed off, his eyes glued to the screen as his fingers danced over the keyboard with supernatural speed. "There!" he exclaimed triumphantly.

Saiden leaned forward. "Did you hack into the Ruling Coalition's database?" He didn't know much about computers, but he'd seen screenshots before and was confident that he was looking at the Coalition's internal dossier on Bianca.

"Nah," Baylin dismissed, scrolling through the document and sipping his Celsius energy drink. "After the third time I broke their firewall, they just gave me access. Said it was easier than trying to find a programmer skilled enough to keep me out. We have an arrangement. I don't use the database for anything nefarious, and so long as I do the occasional tech job for them here and there, they let me keep my head. It's all good."

"Right," Saiden grunted, pinching the bridge of his nose. "I'll ignore the fact you've been hiding that from me if you can tell me where to find her."

Baylin chuckled and continued scanning the document. "She's been on their radar for over a hundred years, it looks like. Originally born in 1878 in Stockholm, she was sired by somebody named Gunther Larsson in 1897. Looks like he wasn't her mate, so the reasoning for her turn is unknown. After that, she was a perfect vampire until she lost it in 1905 and murdered her sire. She's been tied to seven different minor rogue outbreaks throughout Europe, but they've never been able to catch her. It's her siren gift, apparently. Most enforcers end up dead or incapacitated, and she escapes to do it all again."

Saiden pushed himself out of the chair and paced anxiously around the room, waiting for his brother to tell him something helpful. Bianca murdered Cora. He didn't care what her life story was. Didn't care what drove her over the edge. He just wanted to make her pay.

"There's some sort of flag on her file," Baylin continued. "It's not labeled, though. I can dig a little deeper, but your pacing isn't exactly helping my concentration."

"So have another energy drink," Saiden growled, but halted his attempts to wear a hole in his brother's floor. He grabbed the back of Baylin's chair and leaned in to take a look at the file, his nails slicing into the leather upholstery with little pops while his eyes passed over Bianca's grainy picture.

Baylin tapped at a small marker on the screen. "Found it. That red flag indicates she is NCM. Non Compos Mentis. It means the Coalition believes her to be insane more or less. Completely unpredictable. No enforcer is allowed to go after her alone." Baylin cast Saiden a dubious look. "That means you too, bro. No cowboy shit. I know what she did but—"

"You have no idea just how much damage she did," Saiden snarled, pushing back from the desk. "Knowing I've lost my mate is tearing me up inside. I feel like the other half of my soul has been ripped out."

"You don't know that you've lost her," Baylin offered. "She might be okay with it."

*Sure*, Saiden thought, *and maybe you'll take up drinking tea.*

"Does it say where she was last spotted?"

Baylin scanned the screen. "Looks like she was seen entering the U.S. from Canada about a decade ago but nothing since. She's an expert at avoiding detection. I can run the photo through a wider database of traffic cameras, but it will take a while."

Saiden spun around and started toward the door. "I'm not waiting for her to get away. I doubt she went far, and I'm going to find her."

"How, Saiden?" Baylin called after him. "You going to knock on every door between here and the East Coast?"

"If I have to," he replied, halting long enough to grab a blood bag. "But I'm starting with Donna. My mate is in there hooked up to an IV because she nearly bled to death, and any minute she's going to wake up to a terrifying new life. I don't care how long Donna worked for us. I don't care how much everyone loved her. If I need to break every bone in her frail human body to get the answers I want, then I will."

"She's human, remember? You can always try compelling the answers from her," Baylin pointed out, his words stopping Saiden at the door.

Rotating slowly to face his brother, Saiden's lip curled up into a snarl. "She doesn't deserve the easy way out."

The amount of concern Baylin showed should have made Saiden pause to consider if he was going too far, but he already knew he'd gone off the rails. Now it was time to get back on track.

"I'm going to swing by Cora's room to check on her, then I'll be in the dungeons if you find anything else."

Saiden spun on his heels and sped away before his brother could try to dump more useless logic on him. Baylin hadn't tangled with Bianca, so he didn't know just how accurate the NCM flag was. It also meant she wouldn't leave her toys behind. She wanted to keep playing with Saiden, wanted to keep breaking him, so she had to be nearby. Somewhere.

He was halfway down the main hall when a strong hand clamping on his shoulder halted his movement, and his momentum nearly forced his feet out from under him. Regaining his footing, he turned to see Marquin standing behind him with a dark expression.

*Lilith save me, what now?*

Saiden didn't think he could handle any more tragedies. He was about to tear his skin off if he didn't get back to Cora for at least a little while.

"We have a problem," Marquin stated grimly.

Of course they did. When it rains it pours. Except in his case it felt like acid.

"What's wrong?" he asked, scratching at his arm. The prickles under his skin were getting worse. A sire wasn't meant to be away from their changing progeny for this long.

"The Coalition knows."

Saiden's entire body locked up at the three words nobody ever wanted to hear. "Knows what exactly?"

"About Cora."

All the fight left Saiden, and his body deflated alongside any remaining trace of hope. Slumping back against the wall, he slid down to the shiny marble floor. That was it, then. Game over.

"Who told them?" he asked weakly when Marquin knelt beside him.

"Anonymous tip," his sire answered, taking the blood bag from Saiden and setting it aside. "Probably your blonde attacker wanted to twist the knife a little deeper."

Saiden sat quietly for a moment. He should have known Bianca would try something. It was his job to anticipate his enemies' next move, and while he'd known she would do something, it hadn't occurred to him just how deeply she would bury the knife. Some enforcer he was.

"I knew the risk," he stated, forcing himself to meet the sadness in Marquin's eyes. "And I would do the same thing again a million times over. I couldn't just let her die."

"I know," Marquin agreed solemnly. "I never told any of you, but when Eliana saved me as a rogue I was in the process of trying to end my own life. I wanted nothing more than to be spared this tortuous existence. But I was her mate, and she refused to let me go despite knowing how I felt about being a vampire. It was her love that changed my mind in the end. I owe her everything, Saiden. Perhaps someday Cora will feel the same."

Someday. He'd spent so long clinging to the hope that someday they would get the chance to be happy. The problem with someday is that you rarely get to see it. The only thing you could ever count on was today.

"How much time do I have?"

Marquin sighed. "The Praetorians arrive Sunday morning."

Shit. Less than a day and a half. Might as well be in twenty minutes for all the good it would do him.

"Options?"

"Plead your case, I guess. But you know the laws, Saiden."

Of course he knew the laws. He was the one who enforced them. He closed his eyes and wondered for a second who the Coalition would bring with them. Andre was based out of Bucharest these days, close enough to their headquarters to easily join them. Or maybe they'd call in one of the other North American assets. Sanya always liked him since they'd worked a few high-profile cases together. Not that she would be any help. She knew the job the same as he did.

Didn't matter. None of it mattered except Cora.

He pushed up off the floor, and Marquin followed suit.

"So what now?" his sire asked.

"Now, I'm going to see my mate."

# Chapter Forty

## Cora

*And then the beast pounced.*

The scream ripped from Cora's throat, loud and guttural, as if it might ward off the creature intent on ripping her to pieces.

"Cora? Cora, please calm down."

Words. Someone was saying words, but all she could do was throw her arms in front of her face. Words couldn't save her from vicious teeth and claws.

"Cora, please, look at me."

*Saiden?*

The sound of his voice slipped through a crack in her broken psyche and soothed enough of the terror for her to take a deep breath. Air rushed into her lungs, and her eyes popped open.

"Saiden?" she croaked out, recognizing the brilliant brown eyes in front of her. She tried to focus on him, but everything was bright. Too bright. And there were so many people, all shouting. Why was everyone shouting?

"It's okay, Cora. Just breathe and focus on my face. Everything will be alright."

She wanted to do what he asked. She trusted Saiden. Cared about Saiden. But the voices were so loud, and the harsh explosions of light fried her retinas. It was all too much. She had to get away from there. Get somewhere quieter.

She tried to scramble away from Saiden, but he held her down on the bed.

A memory sparked. The bed. She knew this bed, recognized the black comforter. And, oh God, the scent. It was like she could smell nothing else but him.

Saiden's bedroom. The compound. She was back in the mansion with Saiden. So why wasn't he helping? Why was he holding her there?

"Tressa, do you mind pitching in a little?"

Saiden's words skated through her mind, triggering more memories. She knew Tressa. The sweet female vampire who looked like she belonged on an island soaking up the sun instead of hiding from it. She was the one who was all big laughs and wide smiles. Fun and happy, like a spring day.

"I am trying, Saiden. It's just not working."

"What do you mean it's not working?"

"What do you think I mean, dumbass? She's clearly not calming down."

Arguing. Why were Saiden and Tressa arguing? They liked each other. Cousins. Family. Were they arguing over her? Was that why everyone was shouting? Did she do something bad?

Bad. Compound. Cousins. Bad.

The floodgates opened and memories started pouring in. There was an attack. They came back to the compound, and something was wrong. Everyone was gone. Saiden went to investigate, and then...

She racked her brain, sorting through all the visuals, trying to decipher dream from reality.

There was nothing. Empty. A black void slowly being filled with images brighter than the sun and noises louder than a nightclub.

"What are we supposed to do now?" Saiden barked, and Cora flinched at the cacophony threatening to pierce her eardrums.

"Too much. It's all too much." Her voice trembled through the spinning and whirling. Like one of the circus rides. Maybe she was still there, still in the circus. Saved from the dangerous tiger only to be trapped inside a tilt-a-whirl of sensations designed to smother her under so many lights and sounds that she could never leave.

"She's overloading," a calm British voice filtered in from somewhere off to the right. "I've seen it happen before. She wasn't prepared ahead of time, so she has no idea what's happening. Let me put her back to sleep, and we can move her somewhere dark and quiet."

Sleep? No, she didn't want to go back to sleep. That's where the beast waited for her. The Circus of the Damned. She couldn't go back there.

Cool hands cupped her cheeks, and a porcelain face blocked out some of the strobing lights. A female with harsh features and chestnut hair evaluated her.

Raven. She knew Raven. Raven was a friend. But why wasn't she helping her then? Why wasn't anybody here helping her?

"Sleep," Raven urged. "Be at peace and sleep."

"No," Cora yelped, wrenching herself from Raven's firm grip and scrambling backward until she slammed into the headboard. Trapped. She was trapped in this torture.

"What the hell, Raven?" Saiden growled, and Cora tried to focus on him again. It would be a lot easier if he would just stand still.

"Bloody hell," Raven muttered. "Either something is off with me and Tressa or... or I have no idea what's going on."

The others went quiet for a moment, and the brief silence allowed

Cora to think clearly long enough to beg Saiden, "What's happening to me?"

"Are you all really this naïve?"

A new voice. One that was peaceful, calming, and it flipped a switch inside Cora's brain. Slowly she turned to the bedroom door. *Angel*, she thought as she stared at the ethereal beauty. Eliana, she corrected a moment later as that memory clicked into place in her mind.

Then Saiden's mom flicked a switch on the wall and tossed a blanket of gray over the world.

Not an angel, but a savior all the same.

"Cora," Eliana said slowly. "I need to put these in your ears, okay? It'll help."

She nodded slowly. Help. She needed help.

Eliana pushed little bits of orange rubber into her ears, and all the screaming dulled to a low thrum of voices.

Not a circus anymore. Now it felt like a packed theater right before the movie started. Dim and mostly quiet with a smattering of hushed conversation.

Cora slid herself off the headboard so she could relax back against the pillows.

"Do none of you remember your turn?" Eliana asked, glaring at Saiden and his cousins who stood with their heads drooped. "Do you not remember how heightened everything was at first, and how the Essence is still coursing through her, shifting and changing her mind and body? The transformation will interfere with any other Gift for hours yet. I swear, I thought you were all smarter than this."

A mom, Cora realized. Not a vampire. Not an angel. Just a mom scolding her misbehaving children. She'd seen it happen in movies but never in real life. She never got to have a mom. Never got scolded.

She'd missed out on so much growing up. Would miss out on so much more when her illness took her.

Her illness.

"Am I dying?" she asked no one in particular. The doctors tried to prepare her, but they'd also said symptoms could be highly unpredictable. Was this what they meant? Was her body failing her already?

She thought she had more time.

"No, Cora," Saiden assured her in a hushed tone as he sat on the bed. "You're not dying, I promise."

His eyes were larger than normal. As if hope and love filled them up like a balloon close to bursting.

"Saiden, what's going on?" she asked, focusing on those vibrant irises. She remembered indulgent brown eyes with a fleck or two of gold, but now she found herself tumbling into wide pools of dark chocolate strewn with lacy ribbons of caramel and bursting with golden stardust. They were still his, just even more exquisite.

"I need you to listen very carefully, and try to remain calm," he replied.

Those words were about as effective as tossing water on a grease fire, Cora decided when the thudding bass in the room cranked up a notch, and she realized it was the sound of her own heart.

Her heart shouldn't be that loud, though.

"Something happened," Saiden began in a low, steady voice. The kind of voice you only use when things have gone so far south that you might as well buy a piña colada and enjoy the beach.

"We were attacked last night," he continued.

She knew that, but it didn't have anything to do with her. She remembered something was wrong at the compound, but she was fine. She stayed in the car. She...

She didn't lock the doors.

Fear detonated inside her like fireworks. Everything was high pitch whistles, burning cinders, and shattering explosions. Saiden was still talking, but she couldn't hear him. Didn't want to hear him because what he was saying wasn't possible.

Too loud.

Too bright.

Her mouth hurt.

She shook her head. Not possible. She was still dreaming. Maybe if she could find her way back to the circus, she could force herself to wake up. Maybe...

Too many maybes. None of them actualities.

She forced herself to look at Saiden. To look deeper into his eyes than she would have ever thought possible.

"Please tell me I'm not..." The words caught in her throat, and tears crept into the corners of her eyes. "Please tell me you didn't..." No amount of pushing or pulling would dislodge the question. Once she asked, once she knew, it became real.

But it couldn't be real. What she was considering was simply impossible. And she wasn't scared of impossible things. She ate impossible things for breakfast. Or was that fear she ate? Both, she decided. Clearly, she had a very big breakfast.

*So just ask*, she commanded herself. Get assurance that the impossible is still impossible, then deal with whatever is actually happening.

"Am I a vampire?" Cora asked, the question holding more weight than the words deserved to be burdened with.

No taking them back now, though. They were out in the world, prepared to determine her fate.

Unfortunately, fate was a raging C U Next Tuesday who'd made it her mission to continually fuck with Cora year after year. She saw the answer in his eyes long before the soul-damning word escaped his lips.

"Yes," Saiden whispered, the single word so quiet that the very fact she heard him was confirmation enough.

Something erupted inside her like a volcano, demanding to be re-leased. It dug its claws into her throat and coated her lungs in acid. Higher and higher it rose, ready to be unleashed on the monster in front of her. *Murderer*, it screamed. *Killer*. It climbed up and up, and when she could hold it in no longer...

Cora threw up her very big breakfast.

# Chapter Forty-One

## Saiden

Saiden closed the door to his bedroom, and the resounding click of the lock sounded like a jail cell swinging shut on his life.

He stalked over to his bathroom and flicked on the shower. There were a lot of pros to being a vampire, but the heightened senses kind of lost their shine when the love of your life vomited blood and bile in your face.

Not that he didn't deserve the gore-filled puke explosion. He more than deserved it. Not to mention all the other things she'd said to him before Eliana politely suggested that he give Cora some time alone.

It killed him to walk out the door. To leave her in the hands of his cousins. But he lost his right to make demands the moment he turned her against her will.

He would clean himself up instead, and focus on the only thing he could.

Revenge.

Saiden almost felt bad for the older woman curled up on the dirty cot in the damp, moldy cell.

Almost.

Even if she hadn't been the one to force his hand, Donna was still part of the reason that Cora was lying traumatized in a bed upstairs, thinking about all the ways she despised him for turning her.

No, he didn't feel bad for this frail human with her quiet coughs and tiny groans of pain while she struggled to find a comfortable position. They let her into their home. Paid her generously. And she betrayed them. There was no forgiveness.

Sliding from the shadows where he'd been observing her, Saiden allowed his steps to be heard, alerting Donna to his presence.

Even as a vampire he found the dungeons to be a bit overkill. It wasn't necessary for them to look like they came straight out of the Catacombs of Paris, and he'd often championed for them to be cleaned up. He was always voted down in the end because the truth was atmosphere could be an extremely powerful influence when it came to intimidating a confession out of someone.

"Donna," he greeted bitterly, prowling closer to the thick metal bars.

Inside the cell, their once jovial housekeeper remained hunched up against the wall with her back to him. "Saiden," she replied just as bitterly, and he had to search for any semblance of the kind woman he'd known for decades.

"Look at me," he demanded. He wanted to see her eyes when she explained herself. Wanted to see if there was any hint of remorse for the damage she'd done.

"I'd rather not," she said quietly, her words swallowed up by the darkness of the dungeons. "And you don't have much to threaten me with now, do you? I made my peace with death the moment I came back to this place."

His fists clenched at his sides. Yanking her still beating heart from her chest really wouldn't get him the answers he needed. As tempting as it sounded.

"You think you have nothing to lose except your life?" Saiden let out a perfectly constructed evil laugh that was designed to make even the most hardened of killers a little uneasy. "You think we don't know everything about you? About your family? We know all about your daughter, Lindsey, and the job she took teaching first grade in Sioux Falls. We know all about your three grandkids, Josh, Micah, and Becca. I believe Josh just got accepted into Harvard, and I'm sure your generous salary is helping to pay for that. It would be a shame if he didn't live to see orientation. It would be a shame if none of them lived past tonight."

It had taken Baylin less than five minutes to hunt down Donna's family, and while he had no intentions of ever harming the innocents, the shaking human in front of him didn't know that. She must hate them more than he ever realized if she legitimately believed he was capable of such a thing.

"You wouldn't," Donna protested, finally rolling over.

"Your quivering voice tells me that you believe otherwise. That's smart."

His eyes scanned over her in the darkness. A few scrapes on her legs and the hint of a black eye but nothing too serious. Just a deep rumble in her empty stomach that he would have been able to hear even if he wasn't supernatural.

*Carrot or stick,* Saiden mused. *Carrot or stick.*

It was one of the most important skills he possessed that more than made up for his weak compulsion. The ability to determine if a prisoner would respond better to pleasure or pain was pivotal, especially when he only had one shot. The longer an interrogation went without his subject breaking, the less chance he had of ever cracking them open like a coconut to get the juicy information he needed.

Donna had shown her hand too soon, though. Revealed too much. He wouldn't waste his time offering her comfort, food, or empty promises that they could still recover from this. No. If she truly believed his family to be monsters, then no amount of bribing would convince her otherwise.

Pain it was.

"There are two directions this conversation can take," Saiden commented, casually leaning against the bars. "Well, three I suppose, but I truly don't think you'll start telling me everything I want to know, so that just leaves us with the first two. Option A, I torture you. Option B, I torture your family."

Damn, humans were so easy to read. A little twitch here, a slight widening of the eyes there.

"I see we're choosing Option B," he said, since that was the one that spiked her pulse exponentially. "That wouldn't have been my first choice, but to each their own. Personally, I believe people should be held accountable for their own actions."

Saiden dragged a finger along one of the metal bars, taking a second to let the woman soak in her own fear.

"Since I am in a bit of a time crunch here, I'll cut right to the chase," he said when he felt the tension was sufficiently built. "I'm going to ask a question. Answer truthfully, and nothing bad happens. Lie or refuse to answer, and Baylin gets to have fun with your family. He's already plotting out the most creative ways to destroy them. I don't think your daughter will get to keep her teaching job when her background report suddenly shows seven charges of drug possession and five charges of prostitution."

The disgust on Donna's face pained him, but he didn't let it show. He never enjoyed embracing the stereotype of the evil vampire, and seeing in her eyes how effortlessly he had pulled it off stung a little.

"You would destroy an innocent person?" she breathed out.

The cell bars groaned, and they started to bend under his grip. "I would burn this country to the ground and use the ashes to fertilize my front lawn if it got me what I wanted. And right now I want revenge for my mate. So, let's start easy. Why?"

Donna shrugged.

The fucking human just *shrugged*. As if his mate's death meant less than that of a housefly.

"When I was in town shopping," she began, "I was approached by a young girl who asked me how I really felt about my employers. I'm not sure why I told her the truth, but I did. I told her that you're all monsters. That I've spent decades at your beck and call, watching you live the high life, young and beautiful forever. You get whatever you want, but you know what I get? I get old. I get arthritis. I get my dreams ripped from my grasp. And any one of you could have changed it. Could have changed me. You hoard your power and watch us pathetic humans wither and die while you drink martinis and flit around the world to any exotic place you desire. You don't deserve the gift you've been given. So yes, I told her how I felt, and she offered to help me get even. All I had to do was distract security for thirty seconds while she scaled the outer wall, and she would take care of the rest."

A muscle feathered in Saiden's jaw. It was nothing he hadn't heard before. Humans begging to be turned so they didn't have to age and die. He was just surprised that they never suspected Donna of harboring those wishes.

"Did you know?" he asked, death riding shotgun alongside his question.

"Know what?"

"Did you know what Bianca was going to do?" His hold on the bars tightened, each of his fingers leaving elongated grooves in the metal.

"She said she wanted to get revenge for the death of her children. Beyond that..." Donna shrugged once more, and Saiden wanted to tear her arms from her body so he never had to see that casual lifting of her shoulders ever again.

"She murdered a human! She murdered my mate!" Rage exploded from him like a thunderstorm, rocking the tiny cell. "For all your scheming, the only person to die last night was a human. One of your kind!"

"But she wasn't going to stay that way, was she?" Donna shot back. "I heard Tressa and Raven talking. You were going to turn her. You brought her into this house and waved her under my nose. The human who would get what I always wanted. Sorry if I don't mourn for the collateral damage needed to destroy you."

The more Donna spoke, the less he recognized her. Deep-set bitterness twisted the wrinkles of her face into something grotesque and vicious. How long had it eaten away at her? That resentment. Writhing and boiling, getting worse the longer she had to keep it hidden.

Everyone showed their true face in the end, though, and there was nothing left to be saved in Donna.

"Last question. And believe me when I say that if you lie, I will hunt and drain every single living relative that you have all the way down to Jerry Fitzsimmons, your third cousin twice removed."

Donna gulped, and that tiny movement was all he needed to see.

She believed him.

"So ask," she replied weakly, all traces of defiance gone.

Saiden grinned. They were in the endgame now. He would have his revenge if it was the last thing he did. And it likely would be.

"Tell me where to find Bianca Holmgren."

# *Chapter Forty-Two*

## Cora

*They're actually kind of cute,* Cora thought, staring at her new baby fangs in the mirror. In and out they slipped, like tiny mouth daggers. She barely even felt the pinch when they emerged.

She scanned her face, noting the zit on her chin was gone and the space on her forehead where wrinkles had started to develop was now just a smooth expanse of perfect skin. Running a hand through her hair, she marveled at how much more lustrous and shiny it was. She'd thought Tressa and Raven just used exorbitantly expensive hair products, but nope. All it took was a little Essence of Undead.

To her immense relief, the myth about vampires and mirrors had turned out to be false. She could barely make herself look presentable even when she could see her reflection. Though, if the subtle glow to her cheeks and vibrancy of her eyes planned to stick around, she may never use makeup again.

It had taken at least an hour or two for her to calm down enough for Tressa and Raven to help her acclimate to her new senses. Everything was still a touch too bright, and she didn't like hearing people moving around down the hall, but the earplugs and sunglasses they gave her did help quite a bit. The girls said she would get used to everything relatively soon since vampires were nothing if not adaptable. You probably had to be when you lived forever.

Forever.

There was a concept she'd put on the backburner in her brain, deciding it would be best if she waited until later to dive into that can of worms.

But the worms had escaped and were now wriggling around in her mind, demanding she address them. How do you even face the concept of eternal life?

Would she need an alias when she got too old to match her driver's license?

Would that tiny 'REDRUM' tattoo on the back of her neck ever fade?

Should she invest in stocks or something?

Should she tell her father? Did she even want to tell her father?

Could she tell Jinx?

Could she still make movies?

So many questions bouncing around in her mind that remained unanswered. Granted, Tressa and Raven had spent *some* time going over what it meant to be a vampire. Yes, she needed blood but no, she didn't need to bite anyone because something called the Ruling Coalition controlled enough blood banks to keep them stocked up. She could determine when she needed to feed by the beating of her heart. If it was strong, her organs were getting all the necessary nutrients. Once it started to slow, she needed a top off. Like a car low on oil. It had been the best analogy they could come up with, apparently. As long as she kept all her parts lubricated and undamaged, she would run forever.

And no illness could ever touch her again.

She was still struggling with that more than anything. How the Huntington's—the thing that had defined her for so long despite her best efforts to the contrary—was just gone. Vanished without a trace as if it never happened. Only the painful memory remained, like a really bad one-night stand.

She should be ecstatic. She recognized that anybody else in her shoes would be shouting their joy from the rooftops, but she wasn't anybody else. It had taken her so long to come to terms with her impending demise, so many nights holding a razor and wondering if she should just get it over with, that it felt wrong to live forever now. Like she was cheating death.

It was ultimately what had driven her and her father apart. He wanted her to try every experimental treatment he could find, regardless of side effects or how it would destroy her quality of life. He would have seen her confined to a bed and hooked up to a feeding tube if it gave her an extra six months.

Cora didn't want any part of that, though, and it drove them apart in the end. It made her sad when she thought about him, but not enough to pick up the phone. He would only try to press his agenda on her again, and she wasn't interested in whatever new cutting-edge treatment he just discovered. All she cared about was the quality of her remaining years.

Life only mattered because you died. Knowing that the end was out there forced you to live your life while you could. Forced you to chase your dreams and find your happiness. Horror movies kept you glued to your seat because you knew the characters were in danger. Their story mattered because it could end at any second. The plot wasn't interesting if there were no stakes involved.

Her die had been cast, her fate accepted, only now the entire game board had been dumped on the floor. It just felt... wrong.

Her mind drifted off to Saiden while she continued to poke at the sharp little teeth that appeared and disappeared with only a thought, as effortless as sticking out her tongue.

She had said some pretty awful things after she found out what he did. She remembered screaming at him that she would rather claw out her eyes than continue to look at him, and she would rather stab her eardrums with knives than listen to anything else he had to say. And those had been the kindest words.

Horror directors could be viciously creative when pissed off.

A hand rapped softly against her door, but she didn't bother getting up. The vamps here would do whatever they wanted, regardless of her wishes.

She didn't even need to turn around to know that it was Raven who entered, the British vamp's scent acting as an identifier. It was strange because none of them wore perfume or any kind of artificial fragrance, and yet they all smelled different. Tressa, unsurprisingly, smelled like bubblegum. Raven, however, smelled like moist dirt and dying flowers, reminding Cora of a graveyard after it rained.

"Why do you smell like death?" Cora asked before she could stop herself. Good to know even as a vampire she was still socially awkward.

Raven sat on the edge of the bed and folded her hands as she carefully regarded Cora. "All humans have a unique scent that only other vampires can detect," she began tentatively as if afraid to set Cora off on another spiral. "Once they become a vampire, that scent is amplified. Unmated vampires usually smell like something bright or hopeful. Sunshine or ocean breezes, things like that. Saiden smells like fresh bread or pastries if you hadn't noticed yet."

Cora had definitely noticed. It was like she had only been catching faint hints of Saiden's vampire scent buried under his masculine smell before, but when she woke up in his bed a vampire, she'd briefly wondered if his family had just opened a bakery in their home. It had been the furthest thing on her mind to ask about at the time, though.

"Once a vampire meets their mate," Raven continued, "their smell starts to change. Blends with that of their beloved. All mates have complementary scents, you see. I used to smell like roses and my mate smelled of open grassy fields. When he died, so too did my scent. I've been told I now smell like an abandoned greenhouse."

That was considerably more polite than what Cora had been thinking.

"I'm so sorry that happened," she said, sinking down next to Raven on the bed. "Saiden told me how important they are. It must have been awful to lose yours."

Raven's eyes pinched shut for a moment. "It was. I would do anything to have him back. Anything, Cora. It's the reason all of us understand why Saiden did what he did. We hate him for throwing his life away, but we also understand."

Cora scoffed. "I'm sorry, but you think *he* threw *his* life away? I'm the one who freaking died."

Raven shifted to face her and raised one perfectly sculpted eyebrow. "Did Saiden not tell you all the rules of our kind? Turning a human against their will is punishable by death. The Ruling Coalition is coming for Saiden."

"What?" Cora squawked, jumping to her feet so she could pace around the room. She didn't like the feeling in the pit of her stomach. Not one bit. She despised Saiden for what he'd done, but she didn't want to see him die. Not for her.

"Then why the hell did he turn me?" she demanded. "I thought a vampire was supposed to hold out for their mate?"

"They are," Raven replied, far too calm for the situation.

"Then why?" Cora argued. "Why would he sign his own death

warrant for me? He should have waited for his mate."

"He did," Raven stated patiently, and Cora halted her pacing as everything suddenly clicked into place.

How Saiden couldn't compel her. How he reacted to finding out she was dying. How he tried so hard to take her on a perfect date. Even the pie he offered her at the diner. His favorite pie. Strawberry. The very scent she could now smell embedded in her own skin, mixing with the sweet pastry smell of Saiden's sheets.

It never once occurred to her when he was talking about mates by the waterfall that he had a reason for saying all that.

"What are you telling me?" Cora asked, her voice shaking more than when she'd asked Saiden if she was a vampire. That had only been her life on the line. This was her heart.

"I mean, Cora Lee, *you* are his mate."

# Chapter Forty-Three

## Saiden

*The Aston Martin would have been better,* Saiden thought, racing down Highway 299. Not only was it faster, but the sports car's convertible top would have allowed him to better hear any upcoming dangers on the road. When you were doing 135 mph, every millisecond counted. Even with his threat awareness he could still end up in a wreck at these speeds.

Since Bianca stole the optimal vehicle, though, he would just have to make do with the Porsche 911 Carrera. It wasn't a bad second choice, especially given the number of weapons he'd loaded into the more spacious trunk.

Regardless of what car got him there, it would still take an agonizing three and a half hours to reach Sacramento and even longer to establish a plan once he reached the warehouse and did recon.

*"She rests in the indomitable city with the many headed monster."*

It was all Donna gave him. All she'd been compelled to give him, more likely.

It had become clear to Saiden that Bianca had never intended to kill him at the compound. She only wanted Cora. Then she escaped back into hiding so they could play out the final scene in her lair. The whole setup felt just like one of his mate's beloved horror films, and for the first time ever, Saiden wished he'd paid attention to them.

Bianca's trap was laid bare, just waiting for him to walk right in.

Not that he cared about whatever twisted scenario she'd devised. He wasn't living past Sunday morning anyway. So long as he took Bianca down with him, that was all that mattered.

And he would take Bianca down. She could throw anything at him, and it wouldn't make a difference. One way or another, Bianca was dying a permanent death in that warehouse.

His only regret was not saying goodbye to Cora. He'd snuck by her room only to see her crying on the floor with Raven trying to comfort her. It killed him to see his love like that. To see his mate in so much pain yet unable to help. He would endure any level of creative and painful torture she could think up if it just meant he could take her suffering away.

But he had nothing to offer her except revenge. Violence, pain, and death were all he could ever offer anyone. He'd been a fool to think otherwise, to imagine a life filled with love and laughter with Cora at his side. A naïve dream for someone like him. Someone who had taken so many lives. Unstable and violent rogues every one of them, but it was murder all the same.

He was a reaper, a monster, and there would be no happily ever after.

Pushing the pedal down even further, Saiden coaxed the car up to 140 mph.

He should have died with the rest of his kin a long time ago. Fate had saved him back then, but it was always going to end this way. He'd known that fate would come back for him eventually.

You couldn't dance with death on a daily basis and not get your toes stepped on sooner or later.

It was the right ending for him. The kind Cora would have written. The monster goes up in flames. Inevitable, really.

He watched the speedometer tick up to 145 mph.

Best not to keep fate waiting.

# Chapter Forty-Four

## Cora

"How dare you?" Cora shouted, stomping into Baylin's room with Tressa and Raven at her back.

She'd spent nearly an hour on the floor of the guestroom, crying mostly and cursing Saiden's name for not telling her the truth, but now it was time to get her mate back.

Mate.

Saiden was her mate.

She'd gone through more emotions than a daytime soap opera when Raven had told her. Shock and confusion had quickly bled into anger that Saiden kept that little factoid from her, but after talking with the other vamp for a few minutes, the flames of her anger were quickly washed away by a tidal wave of sorrow.

It was all too much. Cora had only just begun to accept her future as a vampire, but to add the whole concept of a mate on top of that? They should all be thankful she wasn't catatonic.

Mate.

It was just a word. Just four little letters strung together to form one syllable that had seared itself into her brain. She'd just met Saiden, and yet she couldn't deny the attraction between them. The spark. Not to mention the fact that she slept like a baby kitten in his presence, and having sex with him felt like a spiritual awakening.

She couldn't change the fact that she was a vampire now, and she'd long ago learned to accept that her life would never be normal. She could, however, do something about the fact that she was staring down the barrel of an eternity spent alone.

Which is why when Tressa had burst in to inform them of Saiden's insane plan, the first thing Cora did was ask where to find this Baylin who called himself Saiden's brother.

"How dare you?" she demanded again, her vision tinged blood red.

The tired-looking male slumped in the computer chair didn't look like a vampire to Cora. He looked like an alcoholic with his flushed face and bottle of Jack Daniels clenched tightly in one hand. She spied two more empties behind him as well. Exactly how drunk was he?

"You two really are mates," the inebriated vampire muttered with a thick Irish brogue before taking another swig. "Neither one of you eejits knows how to knock."

Cora's jaw dropped. Was he really sassing her? Now?

"How could you let him go?" she growled. "You're supposed to be his brother, and you let him run off to get killed. Alone."

A tear tried to squeeze itself out, but she shoved it back where it belonged. She was done crying. If she was forced to live forever, she was damn well doing it with Saiden at her side. She couldn't deny that she was still pissed at him, mate or not, but he wasn't getting off that easy. He had some serious making-up to do. A lifetime's worth, in fact. Maybe more than one.

"I din't let him do anythin', cailín. He went off all doolally with that nutter plan on his own."

Cora blinked. Was he speaking English under that accent?

"You want to try that again for those of us raised on this side of the pond?" she barked, her patience long since frayed to a handful of very fine threads.

Baylin spun around in his chair and glared at her. Or at least that's what she thought he was doing. With as much alcohol as he'd imbibed, it came off more constipated moose than menacing.

"I said, Saiden is captaining his own vessel now. He doesn't want a first mate, he doesn't want a crew, he just wants to sail into the storm and go down with the feckin' ship."

Okay, that was better. She at least got the overall gist of what he was saying.

"And you're telling me that with all the fancy gadgets in here you had no way to stop him? Bullshit!"

While Raven had been comforting her after learning about Saiden's death sentence, he had apparently been telling the rest of the family about his revenge plan. And not a damn one of them stopped him. Baylin even helped.

Stomping over to his chair, Cora grabbed the whiskey bottle and slammed it down behind her. The glass shattered on the floor, and she enjoyed how loud it sounded to her. She wanted to break more things. If her world was going to fall apart, then it deserved the right soundtrack.

"You could have prevented all of this," she lashed out. "You're the one who solved Bianca's clue for him. You're the one who told him where to go so he could walk right into her trap. He would still be here if it weren't for you."

"No, he wouldn't be!" Baylin shouted, jumping to his feet and forcing her to take a step back. "Saiden ain't no gobshite, Cora. He's smart. Wicked smart. If I hadn't given him the answer, he would have sussed it out before he reached the front gate. It wasn't exactly complicated to figure out that it was the Hydra Warehouse."

She neglected to inform him that she wouldn't have gotten it save for Tressa filling her in. But in reality, how many people knew what Sacramento's slogan was? Not to mention knowing that a many-headed monster was called a hydra. Cora made monster movies but not, you know, *monster* movies.

"It doesn't matter," she gritted out. "You could have stalled him. Given him the wrong address."

"That's a gas," Baylin scoffed. "Saiden's ancient, but he still knows how to use Google Maps."

"You could have done something!" she screamed in his face, cursing her new vamp senses when the whiskey smell wafting off him burned her nose like she just huffed straight from the bottle. "Instead you did nothing. You let him go off to die."

"Me?" Baylin asked quietly, a low rage simmering in his eyes. "What about you? Do you know why he ran off to sacrifice himself for re-venge? Because of you! He loved you, and you rejected him. It broke his heart when you said that you wanted nothing to do with him. So you can shut yer gob with that judgey shite because all of this is just as much *your fault.*"

His words slapped Cora in the face so hard they probably left a mark. What hurt worse, though, was the fact that he wasn't wrong. The last thing she'd said to Saiden was that if he ever came near her again, she would shove a stake through her own heart.

At the time she didn't know the whole staking thing was cliché, and that vampires could die in most ways a human could provided the wound was sufficiently lethal. Vamp healing was great, but it couldn't save them from a well-placed bullet or a beheading. Regardless, the intent had been there. He'd seen the unfiltered hatred in her eyes and left.

Cora's legs gave out, and she hit the floor knees first in the pile of glass.

It should have hurt. She'd fallen so many times from her muscles spasming that she was intimately familiar with pain. Slamming her joints into Baylin's marble floor *should* have sent a bolt of lightning through her, and yet there was barely a hint of mild discomfort.

Because she was a vampire she would never again have to feel all the aches and pains of a frail human body. Would never have her muscles betray her at the worst time. Would never be scared to have dinner in public because she might choke and cause a scene. And most importantly, she would never die a slow and painful death confined to a bed while her illness stole her life away. Saiden had done that. He had saved her from that fate.

And by way of thanks, she told him to go to hell.

It really was all her fault.

"He didn't give me any time," she whispered, mostly to herself. "I was just so upset at first and... he didn't give me any time."

"He didn't have any to give," Raven corrected gently, kneeling at Cora's right side while Tressa took the left. "From the very beginning, time has never been on your side. For either of you."

"And now he's gone," Baylin said, reaching in a drawer to pull out a fourth bottle of Jack. "Even if we wanted to save him, and even if there was a chance we could appeal to the Coalition, we'd never get to Sacramento before my thick brother did somethin' stupid."

"Damn," came a smooth, velvety voice from the doorway. "Do I have timing, or do I have timing?"

Cora whipped around to see who felt the need to make light of a terrible situation. She didn't recognize the handsome blond man leaning against the doorframe, grinning like a Cheshire cat, but he looked like he just walked off the set for a GQ photoshoot. Fashion wasn't her forte, but she was pretty sure his shoes alone could have paid the rent on her apartment for at least a couple months.

"Who the hell are you?" she growled. The last thing she needed right now was some smarmy asshat inserting himself into the worst moment of her life. She'd thought nothing could beat the day of her Huntington's diagnosis in terms of heart-wrenching agony. She'd been wrong.

"Derrick, when did you get back?" Tressa asked, rising to her feet.

"Just now," the cover model replied. "Eliana called me yesterday and said I should cut my vacay short. Looks like I made it just in time. So," he said, rubbing his hands together. "Shall we go save our wayward cousin?"

Cora frowned. "And how exactly do you propose we do that? Saiden drives like a cracked-out Formula One racer when he's not in a rush. I don't care how fast your car is, we'll never catch him."

The son of a bitch winked at her. Fucking *winked*.

"Who said anything about a car?"

# Chapter Forty-Five

## Saiden

Sunrise was just starting to peek over the horizon when Saiden pulled the Porsche up to the curb a few blocks away from his destination. Reaching below his seat, he tapped a hidden switch, and an all too familiar click sounded from the trunk. Conditioned by hundreds of missions, a cold kind of confidence washed through his chest. Neither soothing nor calming, it was the guarantee of violence, and as sure as the moon rises each night, death would soon follow.

Exiting the Porsche, Saiden went to the trunk, knocked a few skeins of yarn aside, and removed the unlocked false bottom to reveal rows of weapons that glinted in the morning light. Saiden slipped on a tactical vest with the kind of smooth grace only attained with years of repetition, then began loading the pockets with his assortment of throwing daggers, mace, and flash-bang grenades, snatching up each new item before the previous had finished settling into place. There was nothing Bianca could throw at him that he wasn't prepared for.

Lastly, he pulled out one final surprise that he nestled into the elastic webbing across his chest then yanked on his leather jacket.

Saiden eased the lid of the trunk shut and took in the dingy warehouse district around him. The golden light of the new day cast the city in a sepia tone that didn't feel right for what he was about to do. Revenge was something best saved for the dark of night when the shadows ruled and you could hide all your dirty deeds.

But he didn't exactly have the luxury of time to wait for nightfall. If by some miracle he survived, then he needed to be back at the compound when the Coalition arrived in just over twenty-four hours. They would tag him as a rogue if he didn't show up, and his family would be punished for harboring him. Nobody else was going to suffer because of him.

Nobody except Bianca.

He would just have to take the unhinged vampire out in the light of early morning. And fast, before any commuters started filling the streets and ended up as collateral damage.

Saiden approached on foot from the west, slipping past the rows of boxy brown warehouses that filled the streets in this part of town. He paused occasionally, ducking behind semi-trucks or vans to focus his hearing. Mixed amongst wrapped pallets, trucks, and shipping equipment, multiple sets of booted feet moved with the smooth care and gentle step of someone sneaking through the dark on the hunt for hidden prey.

Well, those wearing the boots thought they were stealthy. Against Saiden's hearing they may as well have been running around in honking clown shoes. These had to be freshly made rogues or possibly human thralls under Bianca's spell.

He took a deep inhale to scent the wind for further intel. Buried under Bianca's sickeningly sweet smell that made him want to gag, he confirmed three humans among the standard odors of the warehouse district. Oil and manufacturing chemicals mostly. A faint whiff of something fruity and familiar danced by on the breeze, but it was gone before he could identify it.

Bianca was considerably younger than Saiden, but a century or two made little difference after a certain point. If he made the slightest sound, she would hear him coming. His only option was to silently neutralize the human thralls before they could raise an alarm. A minor challenge for someone like Saiden. He wasn't the West Coast enforcer because he had the stealth of a hippo. No one saw or heard *him* coming.

Saiden forced himself to hold still while he analyzed the movements of the thralls. One was headed closer to his position, so he blurred forward and dropped into a baseball slide beneath a parked semi-trailer. Emerging on the other side, his extended foot slammed into the back of the human's ankle. Saiden caught the falling man and rolled to muffle the impact while he snaked an arm around their throat.

Thirty seconds later they were unconscious, hands zip-tied and mouth gagged with their own sock, and Saiden tucked them deep into the shadows under the semi.

Leaping straight up, his feet gently alighted on the roof of the trailer. Three quick skipping jumps took him from semi, to forklift, to stack of wooden pallets, then finally dropping down atop his next target. Saiden winced at the soft cracking of bone as he unintentionally snapped the human's clavicle, but it wasn't anything six weeks of rest and PT couldn't fix. Though Saiden quickly clamped a hand over the thrall's mouth when they fell, his knockout shot to the temple didn't land before a muffled cry of pain escaped out into the once silent morning.

*Shit! Sloppy, Saiden. Sloppy as hell.*

He trussed up the second thrall while he cursed his lack of control. *I'm better than this*, he thought, gently lowering the man into a nearby dumpster.

A dozen tingling daggers of ice suddenly plunged into his lower back.

In a flash, Saiden leapt up, kicking off the lip of the dumpster to flip backward through the air. His hands snapped out as he tumbled end over end, snatching a Mossberg pump action shotgun from the hands of the shocked human who had the weapon poised to fire.

Gripping the barrel with one hand, Saiden slammed the butt of the gun into the base of the man's skull and grabbed their collar with his free hand, quickly easing them to the ground.

The three pawns were off the board which meant Saiden could hunt the queen bitch next.

If he was smart, he wouldn't even confront Bianca. He'd take her out from a distance before she even had a chance to run. But this wasn't a cold, calculated execution. This was personal. Bianca stole his mate's mortal life and sentenced him to death. He was going to look her in the eyes when he killed her, and if that meant he burned too, then so be it.

Climbing atop a two-trailer semi, Saiden leapt from the massive truck onto the roof of the Hydra Warehouse. With all the agility of a ninja-trained jungle cat, he landed in a soundless crouch.

Holding his position, he switched his focus and allowed the noises inside the warehouse to filter up from below.

*Well, shit.*

Bianca wasn't even trying to be quiet. In fact, she was singing.

Saiden felt the enchantment in her song reaching for him, whispering sweet promises, but he slapped the side of his face, and the siren call slid right off him. He knew then just how easily she could have gotten to Donna. Bianca's voice was so powerful that most vampires aside from the oldest would fall at her feet, slaves to her bidding.

It didn't forgive anything Donna had done, though. The bitterness he'd heard in the older woman was all her own. Bianca just took advantage of it.

He let his ears focus on the words of the gentle lullaby she was currently crooning. The lyrics sent a chill down his spine.

He clearly hadn't been as stealthy as he had hoped. Bianca knew he was there.

> *Twinkle, twinkle, little bat,*
> *How I wonder where you're at.*
> *Up above the roof so high,*
> *Like a demon in the sky.*

Saiden let the song fade from his focus while he revised his next steps. He'd been aiming for the element of surprise, but that plan went out the window along with his patience. If Bianca wanted to get this over with, fine by him.

Saiden checked the small failsafe that was secured to his chest, then zipped up the leather jacket. All pretense of stealth was abandoned when he strolled over to the nearest skylight and shattered it with one well-placed kick. As the glass rained down into the open warehouse below, Saiden tossed in a flash grenade along with it, allowing the falling shards to mask the incoming explosion.

Crouching on the roof, hands clamped tight to the side of his head, he braced himself for the deafening sound.

As soon as the ringing in his ears faded enough for his heightened senses to return, Saiden dropped into the warehouse. Landing on the concrete floor, the broken bits of glass fanned out around him. His eyes swept the darkened space but registered no movement. The place was completely vacant save for an office door at the back, rows of empty shelves, and a dust-covered conveyor belt. Nowhere for him to hide, but nowhere for Bianca to hide either.

He maintained his position, assessing any tactical advantage to making a move. She was here somewhere. In his current position, she would have to reveal herself to attack.

"Come out, come out, and play," he whispered, hoping to appeal to her unhinged side that saw all this as a fun little game.

He closed his eyes, directing his energy to searching the silence for any hint of her location.

It was so tiny, that little sound, and he wondered if she even knew one of her nails had scratched against metal.

He let out a low chuckle. "Really, Bianca? This is so cliché that I'm almost embarrassed for you." Then he looked up, straight into the eyes of the blonde vamp hanging from the ceiling like the bat she'd just accused him of being.

Bianca hissed at him like something out of a Bram Stoker novel and dropped to the floor, her yellow sundress floating around her like a curtain of sunflowers as she fell. She landed gracefully on black slippers with only a slight bend of the knees to absorb the impact. He watched her plump her curls and smooth her dress since she obviously believed that appearances mattered in a fight to the death.

"You know, Saiden, despite the pain in my ears I'm still glad to see you made it," she cooed. Her voice held no sway for him and she knew it, but it was like she couldn't turn it off. Like years of enthralling everyone around her had warped her sense of reality until all she saw were puppets just waiting for their strings to be pulled.

"Yeah, I got your invitation. Really classy, by the way, compelling a bunch of humans. But I guess if that's the only way you could beat me..." He let his words linger for a second then added, "No wonder you couldn't protect your children."

He saw the moment his verbal arrow hit its mark. Bianca bared her teeth, and a low growl slipped out.

"I'm sorry," he mocked. "Is that a sensitive subject? How I murdered your progeny? How others like me have done the same for over a century?" He watched Bianca's face grow more and more red. Her actions might be unpredictable, but her emotions could be played like a fiddle. "You're a disease, Bianca. A virus. And you keep spreading corruption to innocent people."

Her eyes narrowed on him. "I'm a disease? Try again, Saiden. You and your bullshit Coalition have murdered their own kind for centuries. You have carte blanche to kill anyone who disagrees with you, but I'm the problem here?"

He hated the way she reduced his job to little more than butchery, but unlike her he could keep his emotions in check. He let his eyes appear to wander over the desolate space, as if she wasn't even worth his attention. "I keep our kind safe. Secret," he remarked casually. "You would have us killing humans in the streets like animals. Practically begging them to seek out and destroy us all."

Bianca let out a melodic laugh that was equal parts adorable child and insane hellspawn. "Is that what you believe I want? Oh, Saiden. You really don't even know how to think for yourself, do you? You're just the Coalition's rabid dog. Do you even know why I started growing my family?"

He shrugged. "Don't know, don't care. You murdered your sire and lost your marbles. It's not my job to help you find them."

Bianca prowled around the edge of the glass shards as if they formed some kind of invisible barrier, when in reality she probably didn't want to ruin her cute little shoes. "Witty, witty, Saiden," she purred. "I wonder what clever retort you will have after I rip out the throat of your freshly turned mate?"

And now he was done entertaining this bitch.

"You'll never get the chance," Saiden threatened, unzipping his jacket to reveal his ace in the hole. His guarantee that no threat Bianca made would ever come to pass. The off-white brick of putty strapped to his chest looked like nothing of consequence, but it was more than enough to accomplish his goal. If he couldn't kill Bianca in a fair fight, then he would take her out with a cheap low blow. Any means necessary to keep Cora safe.

Bianca assessed the slab of C-4 for a second then laughed. "Come now, Saiden. We're vampires, not humans. I'm insulted here. We don't fight with guns or bombs."

Saiden let out a mirthless laugh. "And that's why you'll lose. Why you'll die here, Bianca. You think we're still living in the 1800's where you could get away with killing as you pleased. Things don't work that way anymore, and sooner or later you'll expose us all. You're a liability, and I can't let you leave this warehouse."

"Is that so?" she mused, picking at a bit of dirt under her dagger-sharp nail. "I don't know, Saiden. Things didn't work out so well for you last time we were in a standoff, or have you already forgotten?"

A growl rumbled through Saiden's chest at the reminder. "You don't have Cora as leverage this time."

Bianca grinned. An evil, sadistic grin that made his blood run cold. "Don't I?"

# Chapter Forty-Six

## Cora

*Guess I really do care about him,* Cora thought as she gripped her seat tight enough to dent the metal. If she thought flying commercial was bad, nothing could have prepared her for flying in a Cessna 172. She felt everything in the tiny four-seater. Every bit of turbulence, every little burp and growl the engine made. She hadn't been this nervous since she was eighteen, terrified that she and Jinx wouldn't get into film school.

Cora clenched her eyes shut as they passed over a mountain range that really shouldn't be so close to them.

"Not a fan of flying, little vamp?" Derrick asked over the headset, and she had to stop herself from cussing him out. The quippy Casanova had been poking her buttons ever since they first reached the airfield in Fall River Mills and she had seen the plane that turned her whiter than an emaciated movie vampire.

"It could be worse," he offered. "We could have taken the Gulfstream G650. Those have a much higher crash rate."

*Don't do it,* she told herself. *Do. Not. Do. It.* If she and Saiden were going to have a chance, she couldn't start their relationship off by murdering his cousin.

The plane hit a patch of turbulence that dropped her stomach off the highest part of a rollercoaster, and Derrick let out a gleeful whoop of joy.

On the other hand, Saiden might understand. Anybody who spent five minutes with this jackass would understand.

"Derrick," Tressa's calming voice came over the headset. "You do realize that if you traumatize his mate, Saiden will turn your head into a birdhouse and hang it outside his room."

"Yeah, yeah, big scary Saiden," Derrick grumbled, but there must have been some real concern in there because he kept his trap shut after that.

"It'll be okay," Tressa said, reaching over to pat Cora's arm.

Truthfully, Tressa didn't even need to be there. They'd quickly concocted a plan to save Saiden before heading to the airfield, and it all rested on Cora's shoulders. Both because of her human skill and her newly acquired Lilith's Gift, something the other vamps were seriously jealous of once they'd figured it out.

She didn't think she would survive the flight with Derrick alone, though, so Tressa volunteered to be a buffer. Cora really did miss the calming influence she used to get from the perky vampire, even if she had declared it was never to be used on her again. She'd been a bit peeved when she realized Tressa had been soothing her anxiety, but was starting to debate whether she should ask for another hit or not. Nothing waiting for her in Sacramento could even come close to the terror coursing through her veins as they bobbled their way south.

Pain.

Suffering.

Torture.

That's what always waited for her at the end of a flight.

*Not this time*, she reminded herself, steeling her nerves. She wasn't sick Cora anymore. She was badass vamp Cora, and no plane ride was keeping her from saving Saiden.

Still, it was probably a good thing that there was nothing left inside her to throw up.

The sun hadn't quite crested the horizon when they arrived at the tiny airfield just outside Sacramento, so there was still a faint hint of darkness to the city. Not that it meant anything to Cora. Not anymore. Her vampire sight cut through the shadows like a flashlight, revealing everything the night normally hid from mortals.

Which wasn't a particularly comforting benefit when Derrick landed the plane, and she had to watch the ground rush up to meet them in ultra high-def.

A town car waited for them at the edge of the landing strip, and Cora spent the entire trip to the warehouse trying to calm her thundering heart. She'd survived the hard part. Now all she needed to do was save Saiden from a psycho barbie doll with fangs.

Was it weird that she would prefer taking on an unhinged vampire over getting back in that bucket of bolts excuse for an airplane?

Derrick didn't have Saiden's death wish driving skills, but he still had a vampire's reaction time that let him push the car to dangerous speeds. It was only a few minutes before he slid to a stop, two blocks east of the warehouse.

Tressa turned around from the front seat and reached back to cup

Cora's face with her soft hands. "You can do this. You're one of us now, Cora. Do you hear me? You're family. You are stronger than you realize."

Cora gulped. She really wished they were coming with her, but Bianca would smell them in a second. She was on her own, and that would have to be enough. She'd nearly died once and had no intentions of doing that again. Nor would she watch Saiden die to save her. He might be the enforcer you saw coming, but Cora would be the assassin who snuck through the back door and stabbed you in the kidney. Metaphorically, anyway. In reality, she had the stealth of a hippo, but luckily stealth wasn't needed for her plan.

Tressa pressed a small blade into the palm of Cora's hand. "Go bring our boy home, okay?"

Derrick twisted in his seat to grin at her. "And tell him he owes me a new pair of pants while you're at it."

With those words of encouragement, Cora slid out of the car and started toward the brown building with the Hydra Warehouse sign. Glancing down at her watch, she knew Saiden had to be in the city already, if not closing in on the industrial district.

She took off at a jog toward the door on the side of the building. Her plan only worked if she could beat Saiden to Bianca.

*Please,* she begged anyone who would listen as she quickly ate up the distance with her vamp speed.

*Please don't let me be too late.*

# Chapter Forty-Seven

## Saiden

Blood no longer pumped through Saiden's veins. The only thing inside him was pure ice. Or at least that's how it felt when Bianca waved a hand, and he whipped around in time to see Cora emerge from the office at the back of the warehouse.

No. Not her. It wasn't possible. His mate was safe at the compound, protected by nearly his entire cadre, all of whom would do anything to keep her from harm.

It had to be a nightmare. He crashed the Porsche and was currently lying half dead and hallucinating on the side of I-5 somewhere.

That was the only logical scenario because it simply couldn't be the love of his life walking hesitantly toward him. He'd scanned the warehouse. There's no way he wouldn't have heard her heart beating. Or smelled her delicious strawberry scent. A scent that now mingled with his own fresh bread aroma, reminding him of their first and only date and the strawberry pie they never got to share.

If the circumstances had been different, he would have spent an hour just drinking her in. She'd been beautiful as a human, but as a vampire she was radiant. Glowing with a self-assurance and vibrancy that made her seem so alive that nobody would ever believe she was undead.

She was incredible, and perfect, and definitely *not* supposed to be here.

"Cora?" he croaked out.

"I'm sorry, Saiden," his mate whispered when she moved past him to gaze at Bianca. "I thought I could help."

A crack splintered through his heart. "But how? Why didn't I smell you?"

Bianca's smile stretched so wide that she looked like a demented doll with her inhuman grin. "Oh, didn't I tell you why I picked this place? The previous owner hated that his office was right next to the assembly lines, so he soundproofed it and installed an isolated air system. That combined with all the security cameras made this a perfect home. It's a shame I'm going to have to burn it down soon to hide your bodies, but we all have to make sacrifices."

Cora kept her blank eyes glued to Bianca's face, and it broke Saiden's heart to see her so submissive.

"Cora, love," Bianca sang out and wiggled her fingers as if encouraging an errant child to return home. "Come closer."

Saiden watched Cora move like a puppet, drawn by the lure of Bianca's voice. Something broke inside him, and the growl that escaped was nothing short of feral.

He took a step forward to pounce on Bianca, but halted when the blonde vamp said, "Cora, dear, won't you protect me?"

It made him sick to see his mate step in front of Bianca, shielding her from attack.

He stared at the back of Cora's head, and his brain cycled through his options at top speed. He was faster than either of them. He could draw the knife from his belt and sink it into Bianca's flesh before they could stop him. Problem was he had to get the heart. Stabbing her neck or anywhere else would do little more than piss her off, giving her a chance to escape and heal. It had to be a killing blow. Had to be the heart. The only problem was that a far more important heart was currently standing in front of Bianca's.

"You know I won't let you leave here with her," he snarled when Bianca slid one hand around Cora's waist, pulling his mate tighter to her chest in what looked like a lovers embrace.

"Of course you will. Sure, you could blow us all up, but then your precious Cora would die too. No, I think you'll do exactly what I want because there's always a chance that Cora lives this way. A chance that someday she escapes me, or one of your cadre swoops in to save her. Hope, Saiden. That's your downfall. You have hope."

Still holding Cora in a death grip with one hand, Bianca slid the long fingers of her other hand into Cora's hair. She twisted and toyed with the strands, like a cat playing with a bit of string. "My hope died the day that my sire told me his little secret. How he had lied to me. See, I only agreed to let him turn me because I'd spent my mortal life alone, and he promised me a big family. Told me how we could travel the world, finding others who wanted to become vampires. They would become our new family. My children. Eight years he strung me along until finally he was forced to confess. There would be no big family for us. I could choose one person to turn, and that was it."

Bianca released Cora's hair and slid her hand down the side of Cora's cheek.

Saiden wanted to leap forward and snap every one of Bianca's fingers off for daring to touch his mate. But those sharp nails were too close to Cora's jugular, and he wasn't going to have a repeat of the other night.

He would wait for his moment.

"Needless to say," Bianca continued, her evil villain monologue starting to bore him. "I might have reacted a bit irrationally when I stripped all the skin from his body and roasted him over the hearth. But you know what they say, hell hath no fury like a vampire scorned. And since I was already doomed by your precious Coalition because of that little mistake, I figured that meant I was free. Free to turn whoever I wanted. Free to surround myself with the love of my own devoted family."

Her voice turned cold then, and the look she gave Saiden over Cora's shoulder would have been terrifying if her face wasn't framed with the cutest blond curls. He wondered how many enforcers she'd killed because they underestimated her.

"I kept things reasonable for almost a century," Bianca droned on. "I only turned one or two a year at most. Then I met someone who opened my eyes. Showed me that I didn't need to bow to the Coalition's unnecessary rules. Perhaps I increased a bit in recent years due to their tutelage, but I have never been unreasonable. The trouble is, people like you just won't leave me in peace. I let my children kill no more than a couple of humans a month and always in a larger city. But every time I start to build my family, one of you has to show up and ruin everything. Now does that sound fair? What do you think, Cora?"

"No, Bianca," Cora responded as if on a dreamy autopilot.

Her hypnotized voice hit him harder than when she kneed him in the balls, and he ached to grab her, to scream at her to turn around. Just once before he died he wanted to look into her gorgeous golden eyes. He wanted her to see how sorry he was that he'd gotten her into this mess.

"What do you want, Bianca?" he gritted out, despising her inane rambling yet needing to keep her talking until he could figure out how to save Cora. His options were getting slimmer by the second, and he was about to start praying to Lilith for a miracle.

"Now you care about what I want? So fickle, Saiden." She clucked her tongue at him. "At first I just wanted to kill your girl in front of you so you'd suffer a bit before I ended your miserable existence, but now..." Bianca leaned down and sniffed Cora's hair. "I think I'll keep this one. She's just too pretty to pass up. Don't worry, I'll take excellent care of her. She'll never miss you for a second, will you, Cora?"

"No, Bianca," his mate replied in that dazed robotic voice.

"Delightful. Now how about a little kiss. Let Saiden see how little you'll care when he's gone."

Saiden's stomach dropped out when Cora started to move on command. She shifted forward, pressing her chest up against the evil vampire and tilting her head back.

Keeping nearly black eyes locked on Saiden, Bianca leaned down to press her lips against Cora's.

It made him want to vomit, the sight of his mate in the grip of that damned harpy.

"Mmmm," Bianca sighed, pulling back a second later. "I see why you like her, Saiden. She is absolutely—"

There was no mistaking the squelching sound that filled the air. A dagger sinking into flesh, sliding past bone to bury itself into a heart.

Bianca's heart.

The deranged vampire's eyes grew wide, and she released Cora to step back, staring down at the jeweled hilt sticking out of her. A crimson stain quickly spread out from the wound like a deadly rose blooming among the cheery sunflower pattern of her dress.

Cora straightened and smoothed down the front of the black dress that had to be one of Raven's. Turning, she grinned at him. "You know, I think I could get used to long flowy skirts with pockets. Easy to hide things in the folds."

Saiden opened his mouth to say something—he had no idea what he might say since he was still in shock—but Bianca beat him to the punch.

Leaping forward, she crashed to the ground on top of Cora and pummeled his mate's face repeatedly before yanking the knife from her own heart and plunging it into Cora's stomach. "You will pay for that," she hissed. "If I die, you die."

Saiden jolted forward, prepared to tackle Bianca and potentially set off the bomb early if she killed Cora.

Before he could make the call, Cora held up a hand, and it stopped him in his tracks. It took less than a heartbeat to see the determination in her eyes. His mate wanted to claim the kill, and if anyone deserved revenge, it was her.

Cora wrenched the knife from her own stomach as if it hurt no more than plucking a speck of lint off her shirt and slammed the dagger into the side of Bianca's head.

The blonde vamp collapsed to the ground, blood pooling around her adorable curls as her life seeped out all over the concrete floor.

"But... you were mine," Bianca wheezed, and Saiden could hear her ruptured heart slowing down as it pulsed out its final beats. "You were m-mine."

"No, Bianca. I wasn't," Cora replied, standing up and pulling out a pair of long black earplugs. Definitely not the thin orange ones Eliana had given her earlier. "I was never under your spell." Cora glanced back to Saiden and added, "Who knew I could ever be such a good actor? Maybe I've been wasting my time with directing."

Saiden couldn't believe it. His mate, his perfect mate, had fooled them both. And now she was cracking jokes seconds after stabbing someone when she should be doubled over in pain from her own wounds.

He truly did not deserve her.

Blood burbled up out of Bianca's mouth. "You think this ends with me?" the dying vampire choked out. "She might overlook you killing her rabid children, but she'll never let my death go unpunished. You think all the new rogues are just coincidence? You have no idea what's coming for you now."

Saiden was tempted to try to save Bianca. Stabilize her just enough to take her prisoner and find out what she knew. But the fading thumps in her chest told him it was too late for that. They would have to deal with any other threats when the time came.

If it ever came.

Awkwardly nudging a piece of glass aside, Saiden resisted the urge to run to Cora, wrap her up in his arms, and never let her go.

She had come for him. She saved him. Did that mean...?

He was too afraid to say anything, so they both silently watched as Bianca succumbed to her wounds. It was only after he could no longer discern even the faintest of heartbeats that he turned to face his mate. His future. However short it may be.

Cora stepped over to him shyly, her small feet crunching in the glass that still coated much of the warehouse floor.

She looked up at him, and he would have given anything to be able to read her mind. To know what she was thinking. Did his family force her to come? Did she want to be here? How did she pull it all off? Did her showing up mean that things had...?

"Did you really threaten her with a bomb for me?"

Well that was the last thing he expected her to ask.

Saiden glanced down at the C-4 still strapped to his chest. "For you? I'd threaten her with a nuke if I had one."

Shaking her head admonishingly, Cora made a tsk tsk noise. "That's not very vampiric of you."

"Yeah, yeah, so she told me."

Cora glanced around at the warehouse, then her eyes slid back to his, a mischievous glint sparkling in their depths. "Kinda seems like a shame to waste it at this point."

"Why Cora, you little firebug." He stepped forward, testing her limits. When she didn't move away, he risked it all to run a hand gently over her messy hair. Cora leaned into his touch, and he almost lost it with that subtle but tender movement. He felt like he was the one who had a knife in his heart, and she'd pulled it free.

"Just saying," she murmured as she stepped closer to him, less than a few inches away now. "I always wanted to have the budget to put a big explosion scene in a movie."

"And I would deny you nothing," he said, closing the distance and sweeping her up into his arms. He waited to see if she would push him away.

She didn't. Instead, she wrapped her arms around his neck. "You would deny me nothing, huh?" she asked coyly. "Does that mean I can still get that third question? Because your family told me the truth and there's one thing I'd like to know about this whole mate situation."

Saiden tensed, and his heart started beating faster than Cora's had on their first drive together. "Ask me anything."

She licked her lips nervously, and it took all his willpower not to lean forward and trace his own tongue along the same spot. When she met his gaze, the uncertainty in her eyes nearly destroyed him. "Do you actually want it?" she asked quietly. "Do you want *me*? Or is it just because fate chose you for me?"

He knew what Bianca must have felt before she died because Cora's words sank into him like the sharpest of daggers, his heart shredding itself beat by thundering beat against the blade he could almost feel in his chest. The fact that she even thought for one second that she mattered so little to him ate at his insides and tore his soul into confetti.

"Fuck fate," he growled, gripping her tighter. "I would choose you even if the stars tried to rip us apart. I love you, Cora. I love you for the incredible, beautiful person that you are, and it has nothing to do with Lilith or anyone else. I don't think mates are chosen for us. I think the universe saw how deeply I was going to fall in love with you and decided to give me the mating bond as a kick in the pants. You are it for me, Cora. Until death comes to claim me again, I am yours."

He waited for her to say something, but for possibly the first time ever, she had no words. Not that he needed words, because when she leaned forward and pressed her lips to his, the kiss gave him everything he had never allowed himself to dream about.

She kissed him with the kind of intensity that only came on the heels of avoiding death. She kissed him with the kind of passion that only came from finding the person who owned every part of your soul. And she kissed him with the kind of love he had only ever dreamt of—the kind he could carry with him into the next life.

He let it all sink into him as his tongue found a perfect synchronicity with hers. Pulling her to his chest tightly, he didn't know where he ended and she began. They were together, and that was all that mattered. For as long as he had.

It was the faint click-beep followed by a ticking that forced them to end the kiss sooner than he would have liked. Hell, a hundred years could pass, and he still wouldn't want to stop kissing her.

But that would have to wait since they both glanced down and saw the timer on the bomb counting down from thirty.

"There goes my cinematic ending," Cora said with a playful smack on his arm.

"Don't worry, we have plenty more at home," he assured her, unhooking the C-4 and setting it on the floor next to Bianca's body.

He scooped Cora up and dashed out of the warehouse, pushing his vampiric speed to the limit.

They'd just gotten out the door and across the parking lot when the warehouse went up in flames. Arms wrapped around each other, they watched the building burn. It wasn't the revenge he wanted, but he would take it. He had Cora by his side, and that was all he cared about.

He turned to her, the glow of the burning building dancing across her porcelain face. "Now that we're safe are you going to tell me how you pulled that off in there?"

Cora grinned a little mischievously. "I just pretended to be under her influence. When Jinx lost her hearing in a childhood accident, she struggled with feeling different from everyone else, so I learned how to read lips alongside her. It's never completely accurately, but it allowed me to understand enough to respond to Bianca's commands. Combined with the special ear plugs I got from Baylin that blocked her ability, I figured I could fake it long enough to get within stabbing distance."

Saiden nodded, and his hand drifted down to the blood stain on Cora's abdomen. He blinked at the smear of red over an otherwise smooth patch of skin visible through the tear in her dress. There wasn't even a trace of evidence that a dagger had been sticking out of her moments before.

"How?" he murmured.

"My Gift," Cora replied. "I don't feel pain anymore, and I heal faster than even Eliana or Marquin." She swallowed roughly and stared up at him with so much love in her eyes that it almost hurt Saiden to know he wouldn't get to spend a hundred lifetimes with her looking at him just like that.

"I'll never be sick or injured again, Saiden," she whispered. "It might be called Lilith's Gift, but it was you who gave me that."

With no other thought in his head beyond claiming his mate, Saiden crushed his lips against hers, wanting to savor every last second they had together. Cora pulled back before he had the chance to fully enjoy her taste, though.

"I'm not saying I'm okay with the fact that you hid things from me and turned me against my will, but..." She reached up and tucked a stray bit of hair behind his ear. "I understand why you did it. Why you couldn't let me go if I was your mate."

The smile dropped from his face, and he searched her eyes for any reservation. "You know how I feel, but are *you* okay with that? With being my mate?"

It wouldn't matter in the long run—the sand in his hourglass was almost up—but he hoped he might get to experience at least a brief moment of complete and utter happiness.

She bit her lip, absently chewing at the soft pink flesh. "It's a lot to process since we just met a few days ago, but yeah, I think I want it. You slipped inside my heart when I wasn't looking, and now I don't want you to leave. When they told me I might never see you again... I love you, Saiden. I didn't expect to fall so hard, but I did. Eternity is a long time to ask of someone, but I don't know anyone else I would choose to have by my side."

It was everything he wanted to hear, yet at the same time her words crushed him, denying him the joy he thought he would feel. Anguish twisted his stomach into knots as he rubbed his thumb over her abused lower lip. "Oh, Cora. I think this might be easier if you hated me. As much as I want forever with you, I don't exactly have much time left."

She nodded slowly, her expression betraying nothing of her thoughts about his statement. "That's right," she replied softly. "Your family told me about the Coalition."

He would have thought she might be a bit more upset for him, but he really had no right to ask for her tears. Instead, he forced a tiny grin even though there was nothing remotely amusing about the situation. Better to laugh than cry. "At least you won't have to worry about being stuck with me forever."

Cupping the back of his neck, Cora pulled him lower and pressed her forehead to his.

"About that..."

# Chapter Forty-Eight

## Cora

**Six Months Later**

Cora's cheeks hurt from smiling so much as she watched the credits roll in the darkened theater. It was a good thing she and Saiden were seated in the back row. If anybody noticed her grinning like a madwoman at the end of an impressively bloody vampire movie, they might have thought something was wrong with her.

Except nothing was wrong with her. Not anymore.

After the fight with Bianca, she spent the entire day with Saiden. They drove back to the compound together and discussed anything and everything they could think of. Cora had a plan on how to deal with the Coalition, and Saiden had an idea for how she could still make movies.

But just in case things didn't pan out, they spent the entire night and well into the morning locked in his bedroom, testing out just how much her new vampiric body could endure. Turns out there were a lot of new possibilities now that she was less breakable. Possibilities that still made her blush as she thought about them.

She still hadn't fully forgiven him, though. That would come eventually but not quite yet. There were still moments when she got lost in the sadness that her old life was gone. When that happened, Saiden would just hold her while she cried, understanding that some things simply took time to accept.

Time they finally had after she'd successfully convinced the Coalition that her being turned against her will was all just a huge misunderstanding. See, what happened was that Saiden brought her to the compound to introduce his mate to his cadre, and when she lay bleeding and dying after the attack, she had asked him to turn her. Yes, it was sooner than they planned, but ultimately it was their end game all along. Whoever sent that anonymous tip must have been trying to stir up trouble. Probably that rogue vampire, Bianca, who'd been after them. Not to worry though, she wouldn't be giving anybody trouble ever again.

As much as they looked like they wanted to argue, the Coalition had no basis to condemn Saiden because only he and Cora knew for certain what was said that night. Since Saiden had also taken care of a rogue that had eluded them for years, they had no choice but to let it go. So the three Praetorians—cranky, ancient vampires with zero sense of humor—left the compound twenty minutes after they arrived, and Cora hoped she would never have to see them again.

Once that was resolved, she and Saiden locked themselves back in his room for another two days, celebrating the fact they finally had time to see what life together might bring.

She hadn't even minded letting him take credit for her kill.

As the lights in the theater rose, Cora pulled the brim of her hat down a bit further since nobody was supposed to know she was there. Not that she would have missed it for the world.

Saiden's plan had been genius. She would tell Jinx that she made up with her father, and that he helped her get accepted into a non-invasive experimental program for Huntington's patients. Saiden was trying to convince her to actually speak with her dad, but Cora wasn't quite ready to take that step just yet. Maybe someday.

The lie served her purposes, though. Jinx never noticed the subtle changes to Cora's appearance over the fuzzy video connection they used to communicate.

And with Saiden chipping in more money than she would have dreamed of, they'd even been able to hire a decent actor to play the villain, as well as drastically infuse the FX budget.

They finished the movie with Cora directing things from the compound, and six months later she was sitting in a small theater off Hollywood and Vine, watching her best friend make her way onto the stage for the Q & A. It was everything Cora ever dreamed of, but she wasn't bothered in the slightest that Jinx got to be the face of the movie. Her pseudo sister more than deserved a chance in the spotlight.

Jinx hadn't even blinked an eye when Cora asked to be credited with an alias since they were both used to eccentric Hollywood types. Carmilla De Beaufort was the director mentioned in Fangoria's rave review, and Cora was perfectly content with that.

The only thing Marquin refused to budge on was the reason Saiden had come to see her in the first place. There were a few things he allowed her to keep, like vampires being able to spend small amounts of time in the sun, but there was one small plot point that was a little too accurate.

Cora had nearly died a second time from laughing when Saiden told her what it was. Of all the things she'd written, she never thought her half-assed, last-minute addition would cause so much trouble. Garlic was just so overrated, and she'd wanted to try something new.

"Why oregano?" came a voice from the front row, and Cora felt Saiden shake with suppressed laughter beside her.

"That," Jinx answered excitedly after the ASL interpreter finished translating, "was all the work of our incredible writer and director Ms. De Beaufort. We thought vampires needed an update in terms of their vulnerabilities. The various mythologies believed vamps didn't like garlic because it has antibiotic properties since vampirism was thought to be a disease originally. Oregano, on the other hand, has antimicrobial, antifungal, *and* antiviral properties. Way more effective in our minds."

The crowd murmured their agreement, and Jinx went on to answer another question about their casting choices.

"You know," Cora commented, keeping her voice lower than any human could register. "You're lucky the oregano swap worked out. You could have told me before I was turned that vampires are allergic to apples. No more apple pie. No more apple fritters. Might as well put a stake in me right now."

Saiden chuckled, fully aware that her threat was harmless. "Next time you're dying in my arms I'll be sure to go over the list of food restrictions first."

It still boggled her mind that apples were deathly poisonous to vampires. Saiden told her it had something to do with Lilith and the origins of the vampiric species, but all she heard was that her Halloween tradition of making caramel apples needed to be replaced with something a little less lethal.

If it wasn"t for her originally choosing that innocuous red fruit, though, then she never would have met Saiden, Cora realized as they slipped quietly from the theater. She couldn't even remember why she put apples in the first version of her script to begin with, so maybe there was something to this whole nudged by fate idea.

She opened the door to the McLaren that she was starting to become rather fond of and slid into the passenger seat, promptly locking the door. Of course the action would become second nature after she no longer needed it.

Saiden settled into the driver's side and turned to face her. "Where to now, my beautiful mate?"

Cora smiled. She would never get tired of hearing those words. Would never get tired of him. Sure, they fought at times as all couples do. He could be unreasonably protective, and she could be obstinate. She didn't like him risking his life by being an enforcer, and he didn't exactly love her skating the edge of discovery by continuing to make horror films. Eventually, they compromised. She promised to stay away from vampire-themed movies, and he agreed to share the workload when it came to his hunting.

Even so, things weren't always sunshine and daisies. Sometimes they were gray clouds and wilting roses. But in the end, all that mattered was the fact that they loved each other—flaws and all—and the turbulent moments meant nothing when compared to everything she'd gained.

A mate.

A family.

A future.

And most importantly, the time to enjoy it all.

# About the author

T. M. Kirk writes paranormal rom-coms and romantasy books filled with heart, humor, and heat. Originally from Alaska, she is a rolling stone, eternally searching for that perfect place to call home. Currently residing in California with her partner and two fur babies, her days are spent riding her motorcycle, traveling to new places, and creating fantasy and paranormal worlds as a much needed escape from reality.